SPY BOY

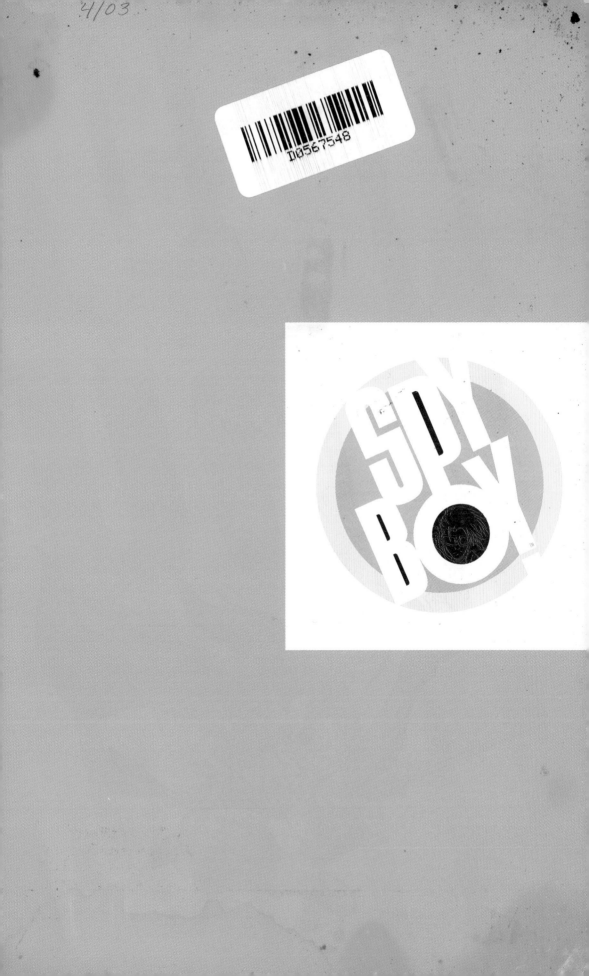

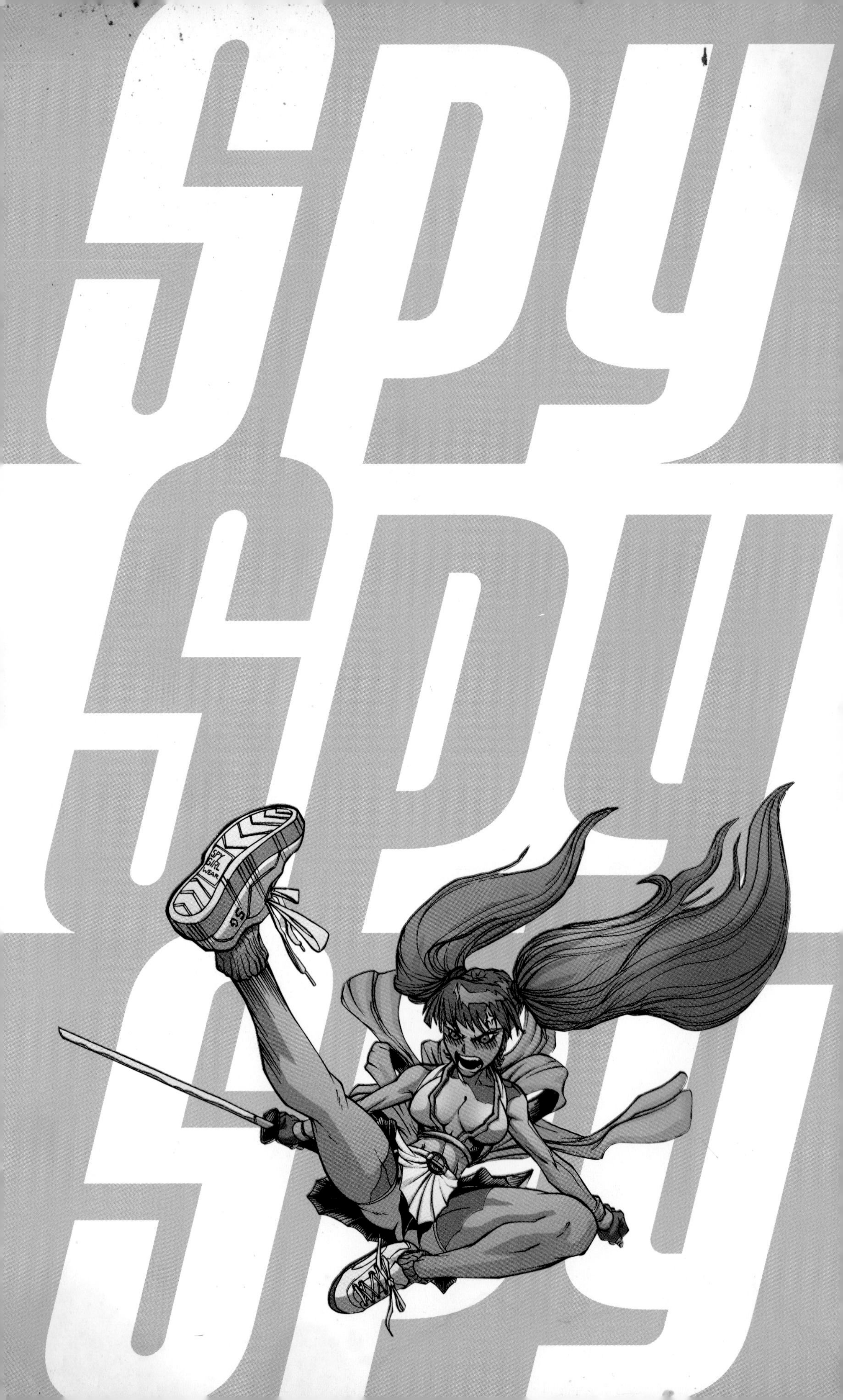
SPY
SPY
SPY
SPY GIRL WEAR
SG

BOY BOY BOY

SpyBoy

in

Undercover, Underwear!

Story
Peter David

Pencils
Pop Mhan
and
Sunny Lee

Inks
Norman Lee

Lettering
Clem Robins

Colors
Guy Major

Dark Horse Comics

PUBLISHER
Mike Richardson

ASSISTANT EDITOR
Philip Simon

EDITOR
Phil Amara

BOOK DESIGN
Mark Cox & David Nestelle

SPYBOY™: UNDERCOVER, UNDERWEAR!

This volume collects issues #10-12 of the Dark Horse comic-book series, *SpyBoy*.

Published by
Dark Horse Comics, Inc.
10956 S.E. Main Street
Milwaukie, OR 97222

www.darkhorse.com

To find a comics shop in your area, call the Comic Shop Locator Service toll-free at 1-888-266-4226.

First edition: January 2002
ISBN: 1-56971-664-1

10 9 8 7 6 5 4 3 2 1
Printed in Singapore

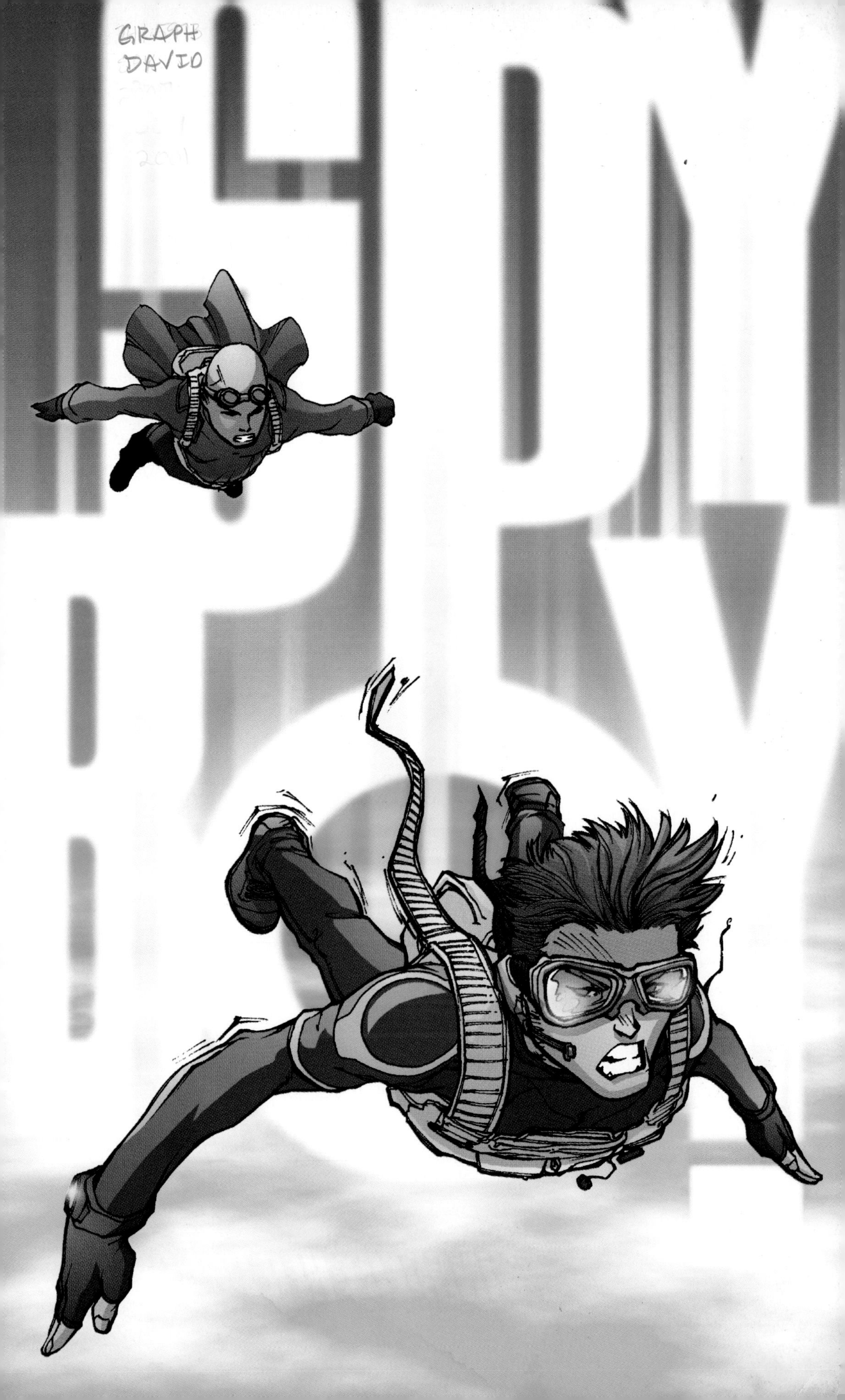

INFOMERCIAL

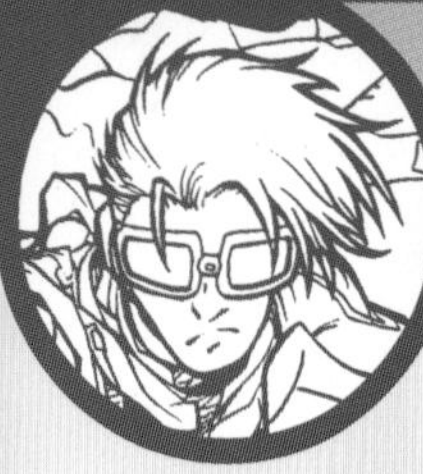

SPYBOY SAYS,

"FOR YOUR PEEPERS ONLY!"

Gadget: **The Glider Keeper**
Designed by: **Nik Havert**

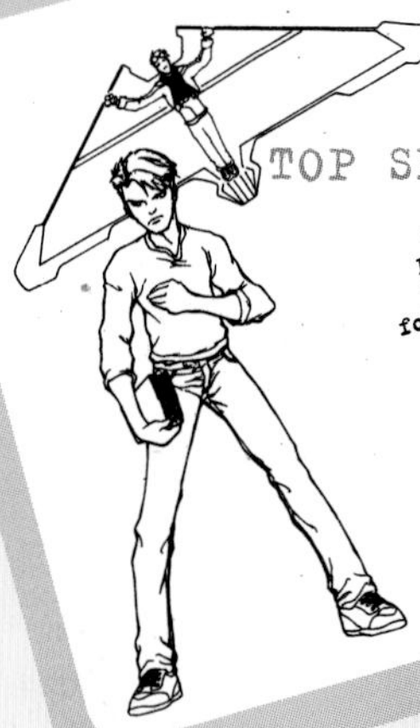

TOP SECRET

The Glider Keeper is a binder that folds out into a personal hang glider for quick escape.

Gadget: **O.D.D. Ball**
Designed by: **Roderick Edwards**

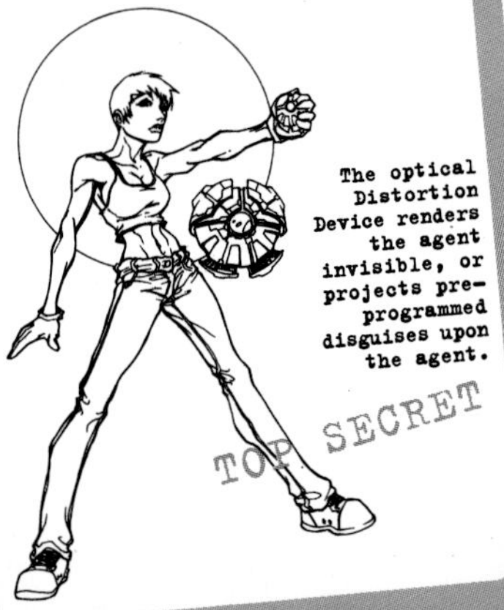

The optical Distortion Device renders the agent invisible, or projects pre-programmed disguises upon the agent.

TOP SECRET

Gadget: **Spyders**
Designed by: **David Yager**

TOP SECRET

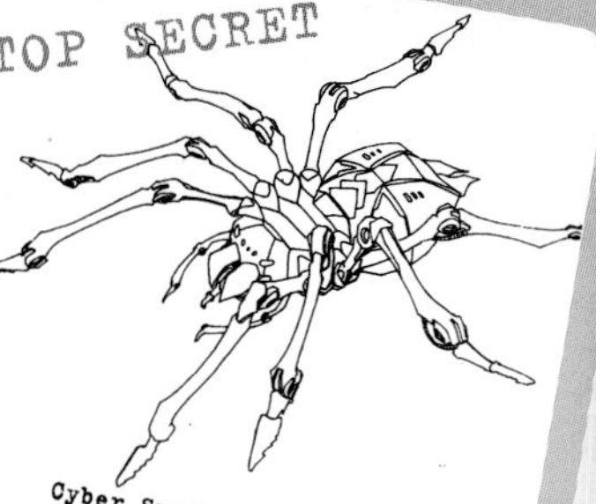

Cyber Spyders are the ultimate surveillance devices, with the ability to extract audio and video from nearby locations, monitor fiber optics, and tap into computer systems, yet still look like little spiders.

If you want to stay on top in the world of high adventure, you will need the latest in hi-tech help!

Not available in any stores!

SPYBOY'S SPY★TOYS

CREATED EXCLUSIVELY FOR **S.H.I.R.T.S.** BY H·E·Y INDUSTRIES Havert, Edwards, and Yager INDUSTRIES "Tech too cool to keep secret!"

1 "INSPECT HER GADGET!"

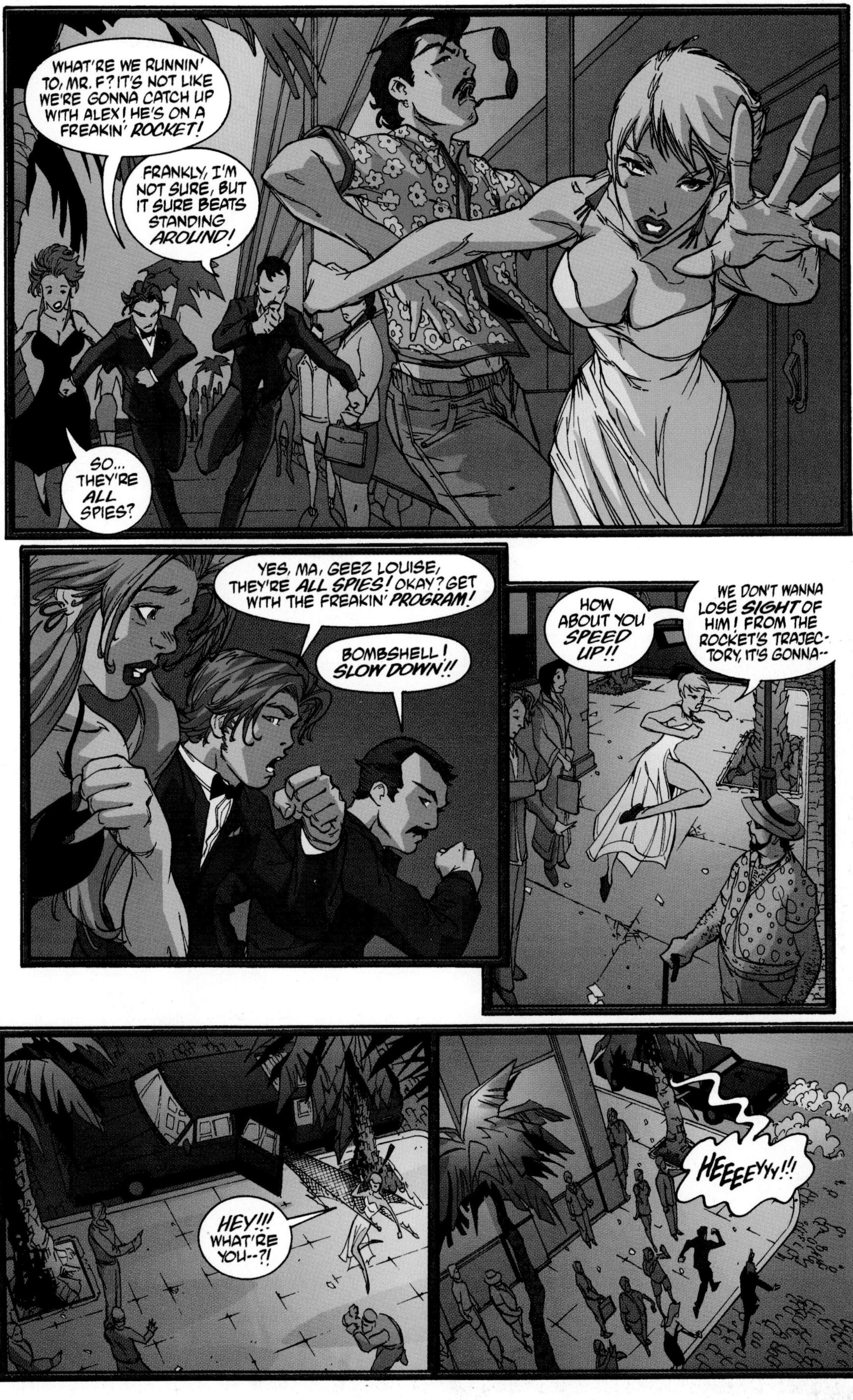
WHAT'RE WE RUNNIN' TO, MR. F? IT'S NOT LIKE WE'RE GONNA CATCH UP WITH ALEX! HE'S ON A FREAKIN' ROCKET!
FRANKLY, I'M NOT SURE, BUT IT SURE BEATS STANDING AROUND!
SO... THEY'RE ALL SPIES?
YES, MA, GEEZ LOUISE, THEY'RE ALL SPIES! OKAY? GET WITH THE FREAKIN' PROGRAM!
BOMBSHELL! SLOW DOWN!!
HOW ABOUT YOU SPEED UP!!
WE DON'T WANNA LOSE SIGHT OF HIM! FROM THE ROCKET'S TRAJEC-TORY, IT'S GONNA--
HEY!!! WHAT'RE YOU--?!
HEEEEYYY!!!

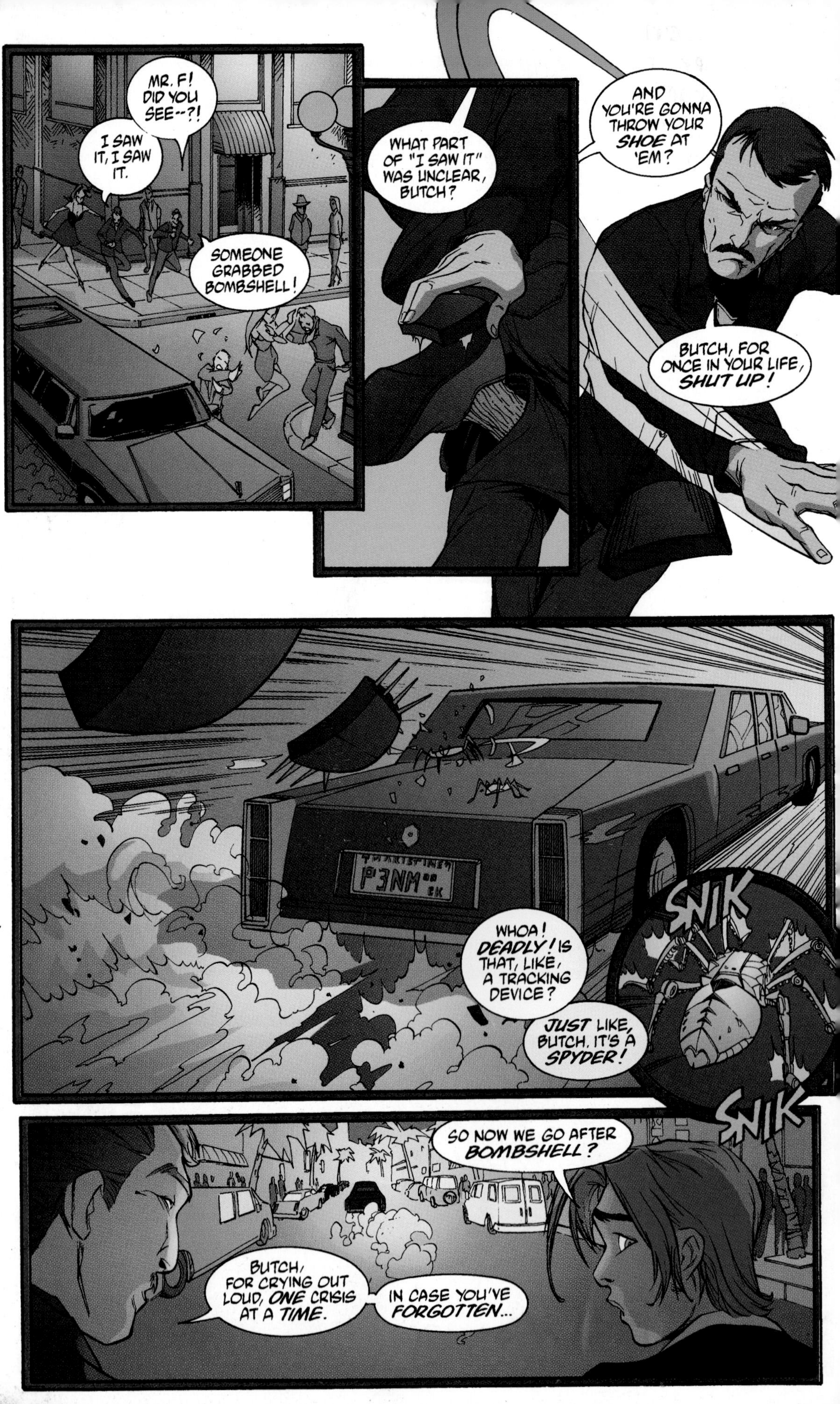
MR. F! DID YOU SEE--?!
I SAW IT, I SAW IT.
SOMEONE GRABBED BOMBSHELL!
WHAT PART OF "I SAW IT" WAS UNCLEAR, BUTCH?
AND YOU'RE GONNA THROW YOUR SHOE AT 'EM?
BUTCH, FOR ONCE IN YOUR LIFE, SHUT UP!
P3NM
WHOA! DEADLY! IS THAT, LIKE, A TRACKING DEVICE?
JUST LIKE, BUTCH. IT'S A SPYDER!
SNIK
SNIK
SO NOW WE GO AFTER BOMBSHELL?
BUTCH, FOR CRYING OUT LOUD, ONE CRISIS AT A TIME.
IN CASE YOU'VE FORGOTTEN...

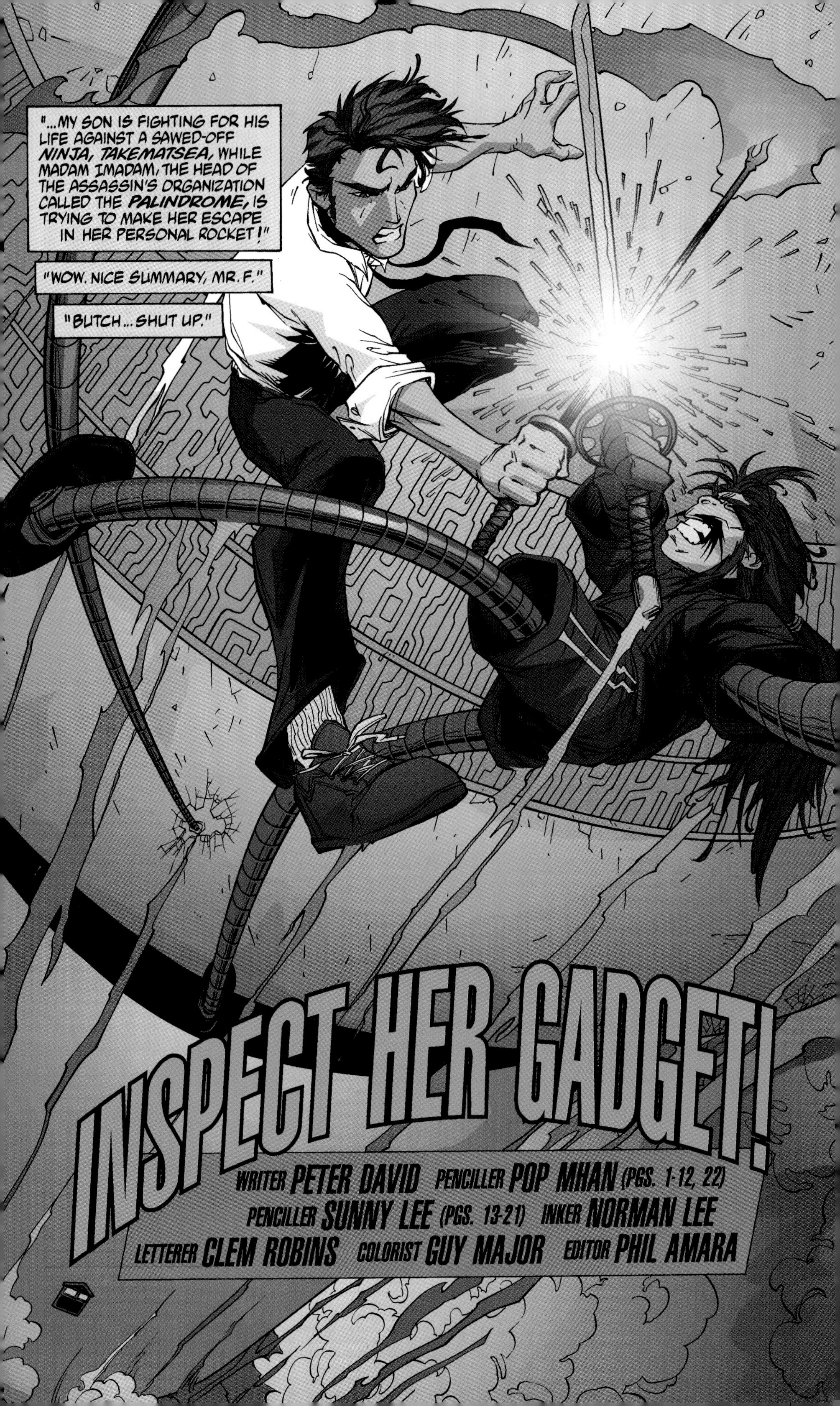
"...MY SON IS FIGHTING FOR HIS LIFE AGAINST A SAWED-OFF NINJA, TAKEMATSEA, WHILE MADAM IMADAM, THE HEAD OF THE ASSASSIN'S ORGANIZATION CALLED THE PALINDROME, IS TRYING TO MAKE HER ESCAPE IN HER PERSONAL ROCKET!"
"WOW. NICE SUMMARY, MR. F."
"BUTCH... SHUT UP."
INSPECT HER GADGET!
WRITER PETER DAVID PENCILLER POP MHAN (PGS. 1-12, 22)
PENCILLER SUNNY LEE (PGS. 13-21) INKER NORMAN LEE
LETTERER CLEM ROBINS COLORIST GUY MAJOR EDITOR PHIL AMARA

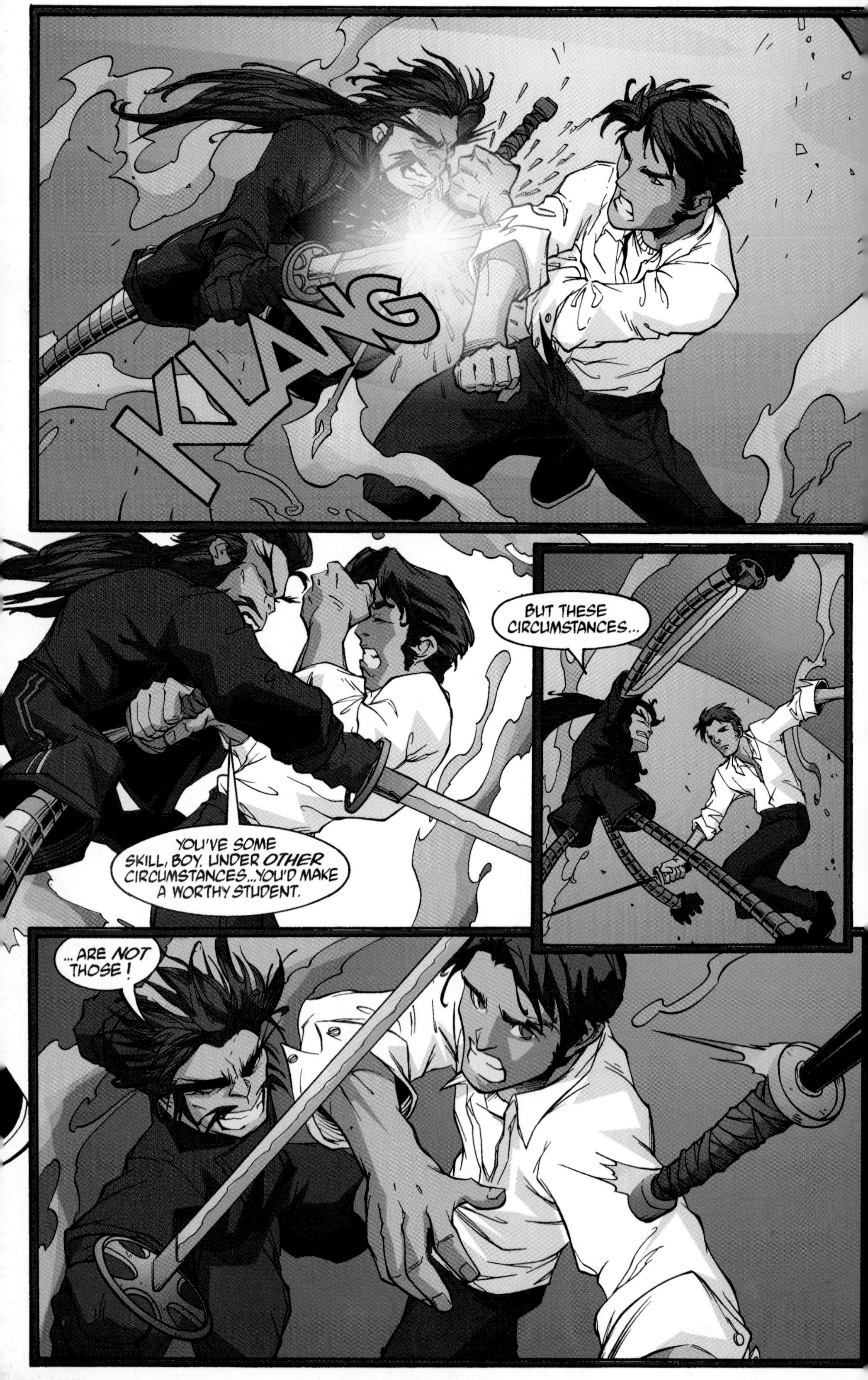
KLANG
YOU'VE SOME SKILL, BOY. UNDER *OTHER* CIRCUMSTANCES...YOU'D MAKE A WORTHY STUDENT.
BUT THESE CIRCUMSTANCES...
...ARE *NOT* THOSE!

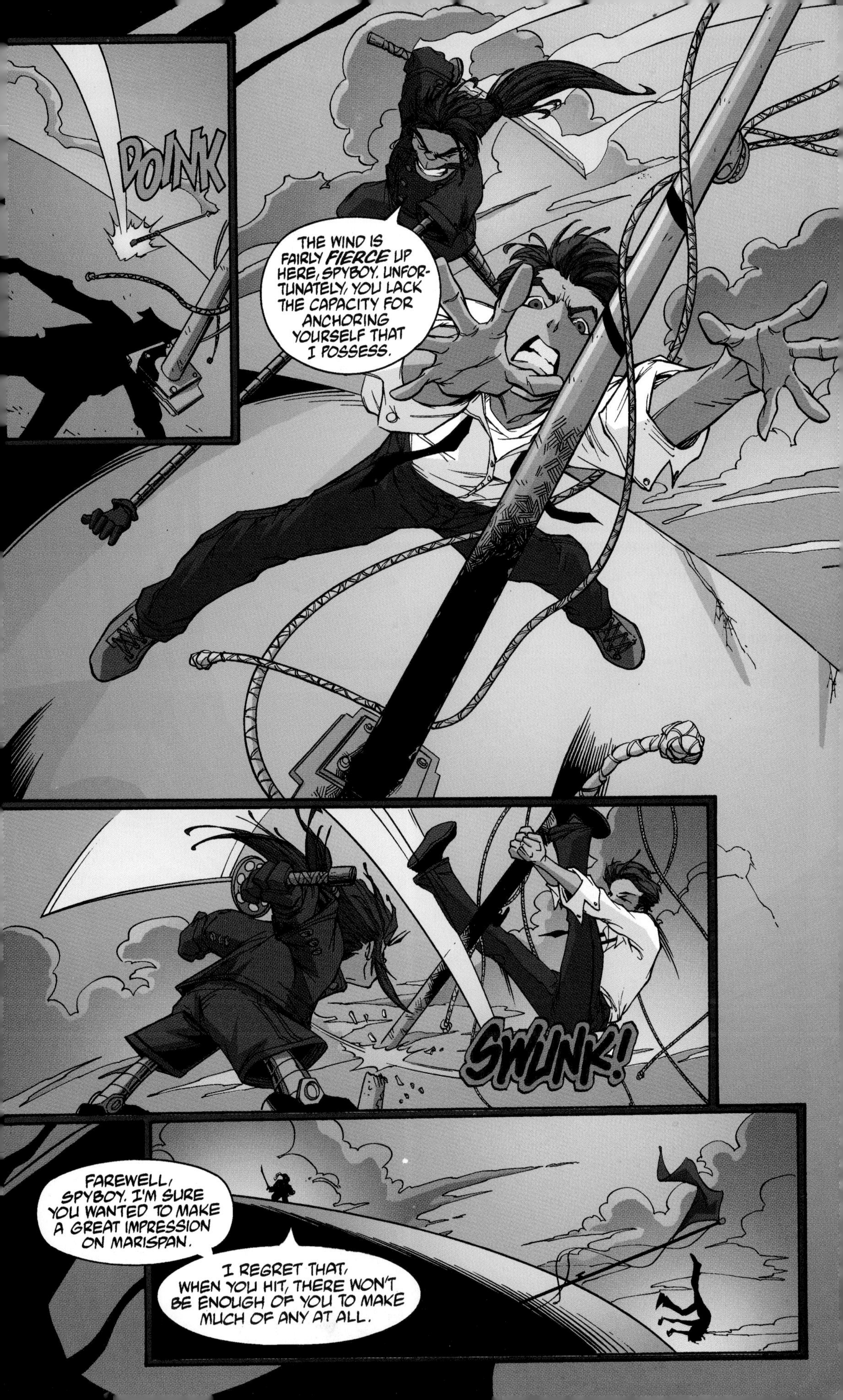
DOINK
THE WIND IS FAIRLY FIERCE UP HERE, SPYBOY. UNFORTUNATELY, YOU LACK THE CAPACITY FOR ANCHORING YOURSELF THAT I POSSESS.
SWUNK!
FAREWELL, SPYBOY. I'M SURE YOU WANTED TO MAKE A GREAT IMPRESSION ON MARISPAN.
I REGRET THAT, WHEN YOU HIT, THERE WON'T BE ENOUGH OF YOU TO MAKE MUCH OF ANY AT ALL.

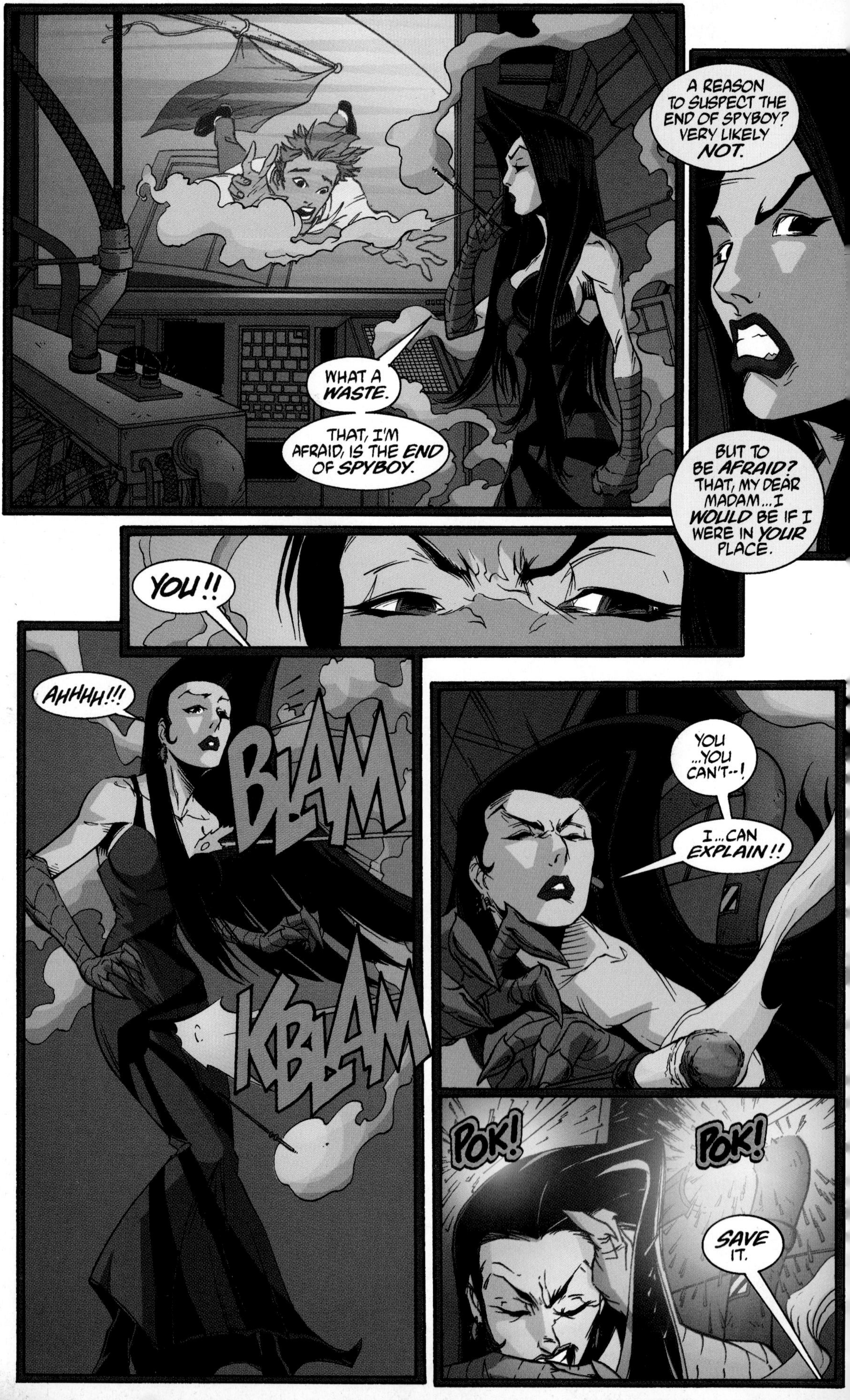
WHAT A WASTE.
THAT, I'M AFRAID, IS THE END OF SPYBOY.
A REASON TO SUSPECT THE END OF SPYBOY? VERY LIKELY NOT.
BUT TO BE AFRAID? THAT, MY DEAR MADAM... I WOULD BE IF I WERE IN YOUR PLACE.
YOU!!
AHHHH!!!
BLAM
KBLAM
YOU ...YOU CAN'T--!
I...CAN EXPLAIN!!
POK!
POK!
SAVE IT.

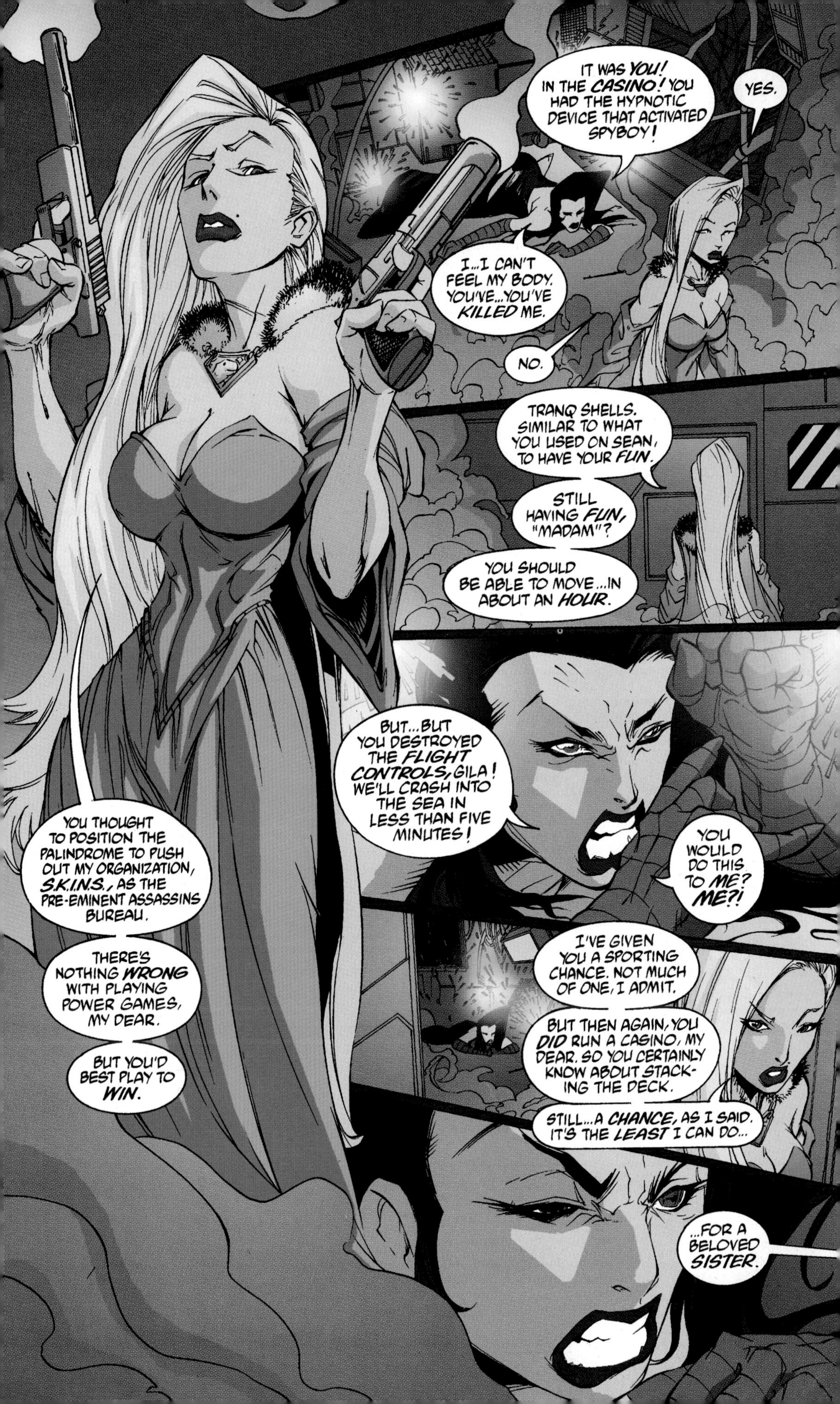
IT WAS YOU! IN THE CASINO! YOU HAD THE HYPNOTIC DEVICE THAT ACTIVATED SPYBOY!
YES.
I...I CAN'T FEEL MY BODY. YOU'VE...YOU'VE KILLED ME.
NO.
TRANQ SHELLS. SIMILAR TO WHAT YOU USED ON SEAN, TO HAVE YOUR FUN.
STILL HAVING FUN, "MADAM"?
YOU SHOULD BE ABLE TO MOVE...IN ABOUT AN HOUR.
YOU THOUGHT TO POSITION THE PALINDROME TO PUSH OUT MY ORGANIZATION, S.K.I.N.S., AS THE PRE-EMINENT ASSASSINS BUREAU.
THERE'S NOTHING WRONG WITH PLAYING POWER GAMES, MY DEAR.
BUT YOU'D BEST PLAY TO WIN.
BUT...BUT YOU DESTROYED THE FLIGHT CONTROLS, GILA! WE'LL CRASH INTO THE SEA IN LESS THAN FIVE MINUTES!
YOU WOULD DO THIS TO ME? ME?!
I'VE GIVEN YOU A SPORTING CHANCE. NOT MUCH OF ONE, I ADMIT.
BUT THEN AGAIN, YOU DID RUN A CASINO, MY DEAR. SO YOU CERTAINLY KNOW ABOUT STACKING THE DECK.
STILL...A CHANCE, AS I SAID. IT'S THE LEAST I CAN DO...
...FOR A BELOVED SISTER.

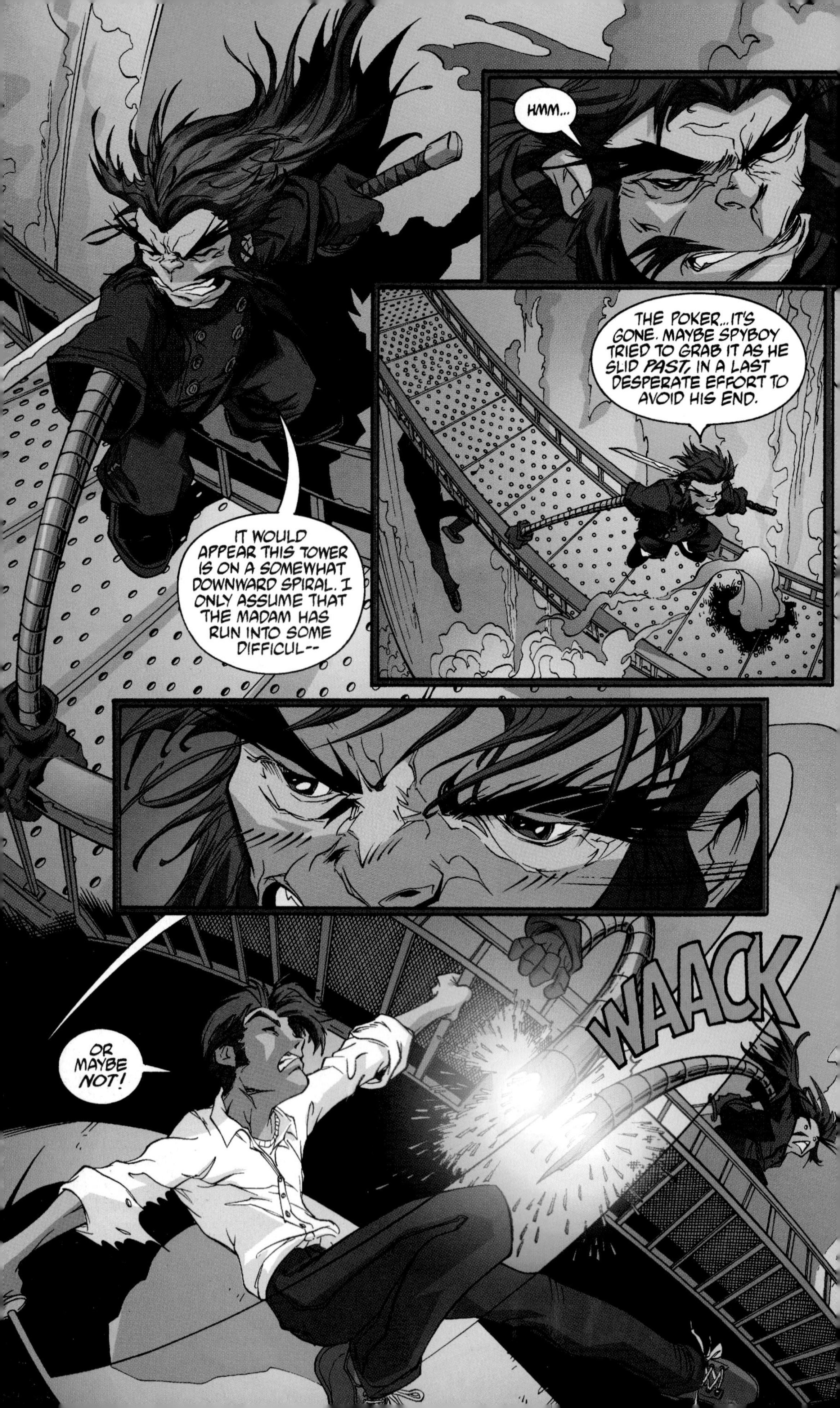
HMM...
IT WOULD APPEAR THIS TOWER IS ON A SOMEWHAT DOWNWARD SPIRAL. I ONLY ASSUME THAT THE MADAM HAS RUN INTO SOME DIFFICUL--
THE POKER... IT'S GONE. MAYBE SPYBOY TRIED TO GRAB IT AS HE SLID *PAST,* IN A LAST DESPERATE EFFORT TO AVOID HIS END.
OR MAYBE *NOT!*
WAACK

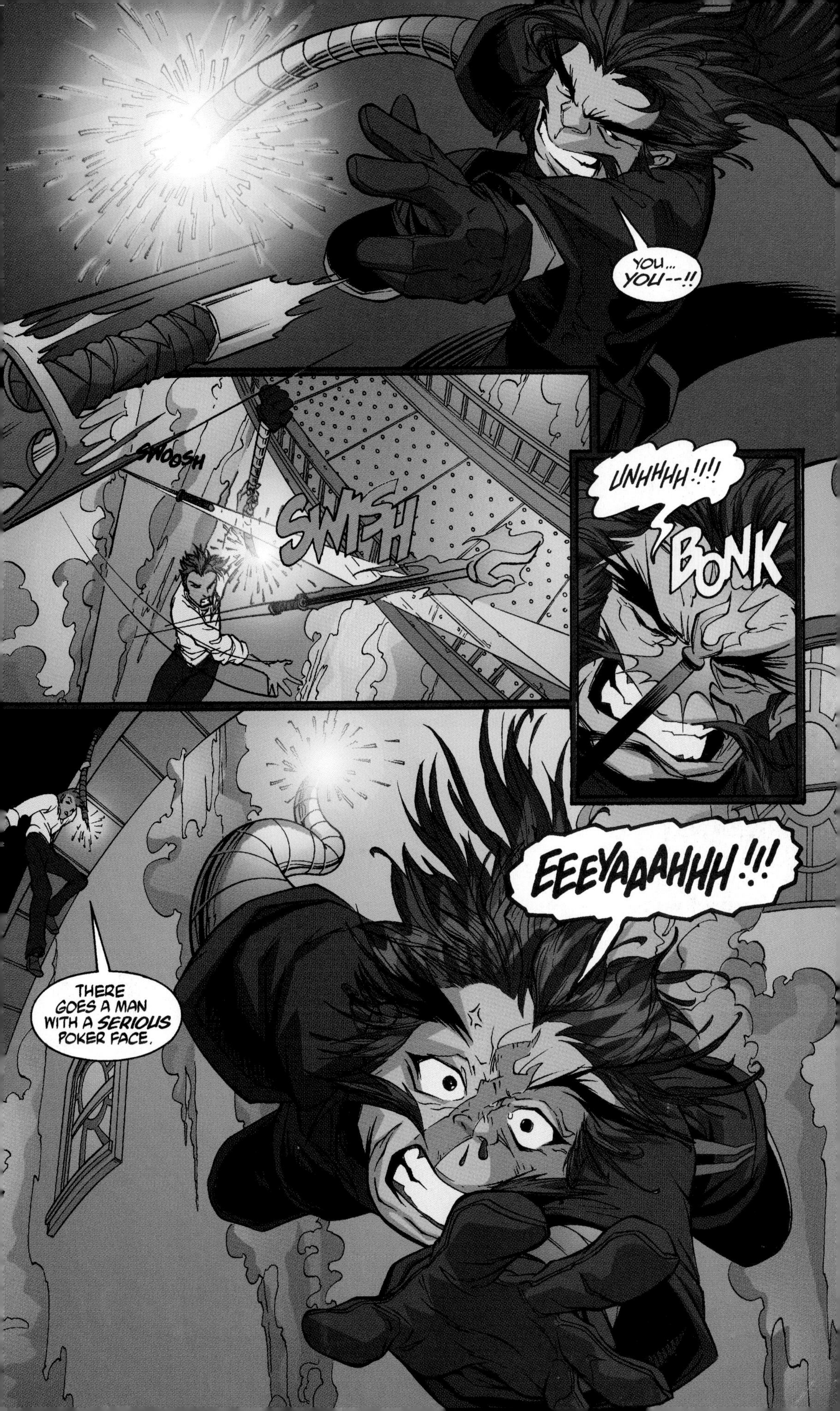
YOU... YOU--!!
SWOOSH
SWISH
UNHHHH!!!!
BONK
EEEYAAAHHH!!!
THERE GOES A MAN WITH A SERIOUS POKER FACE.

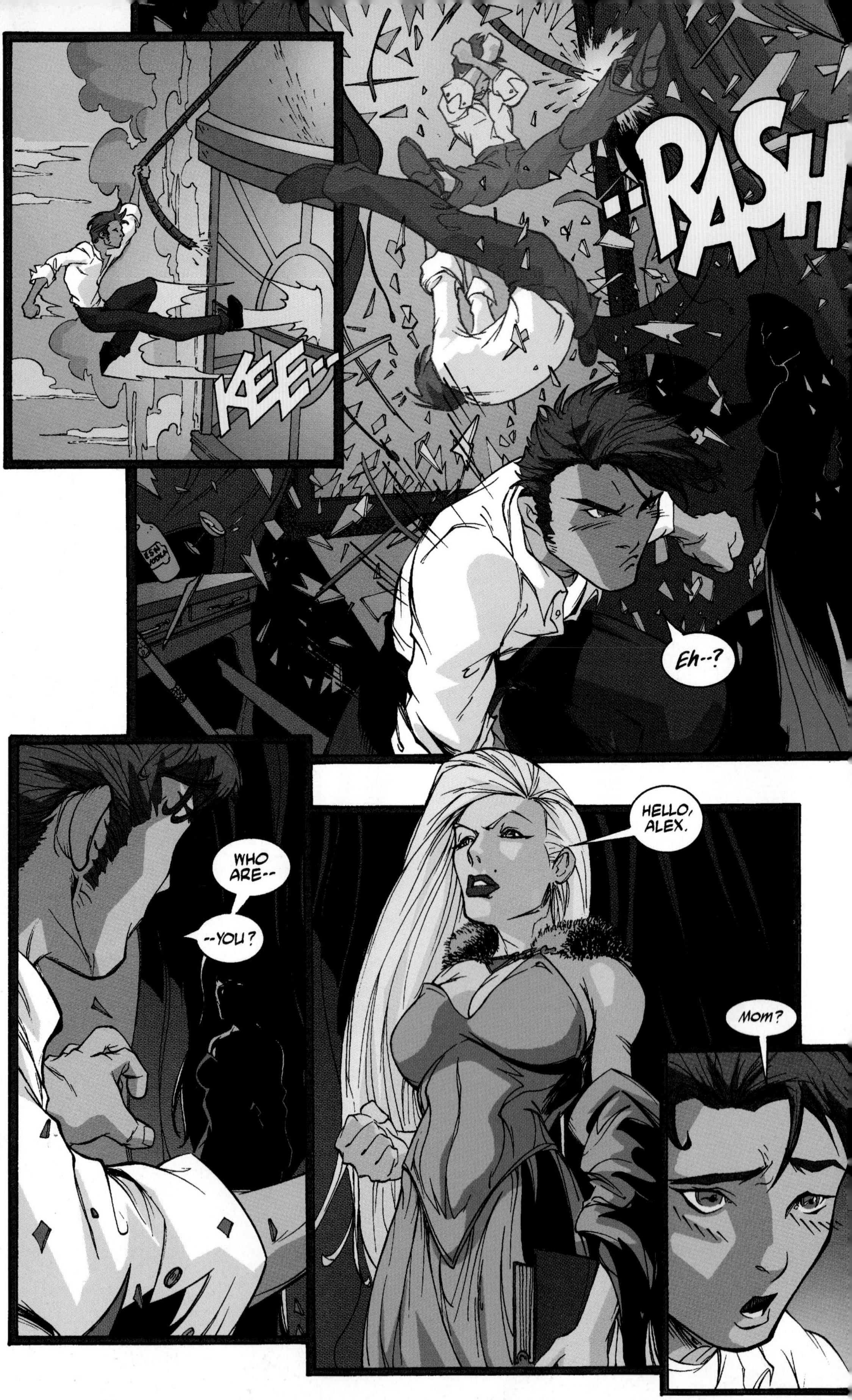

KEE--
--RASH
Eh--?
WHO ARE--
--YOU?
HELLO, ALEX.
Mom?

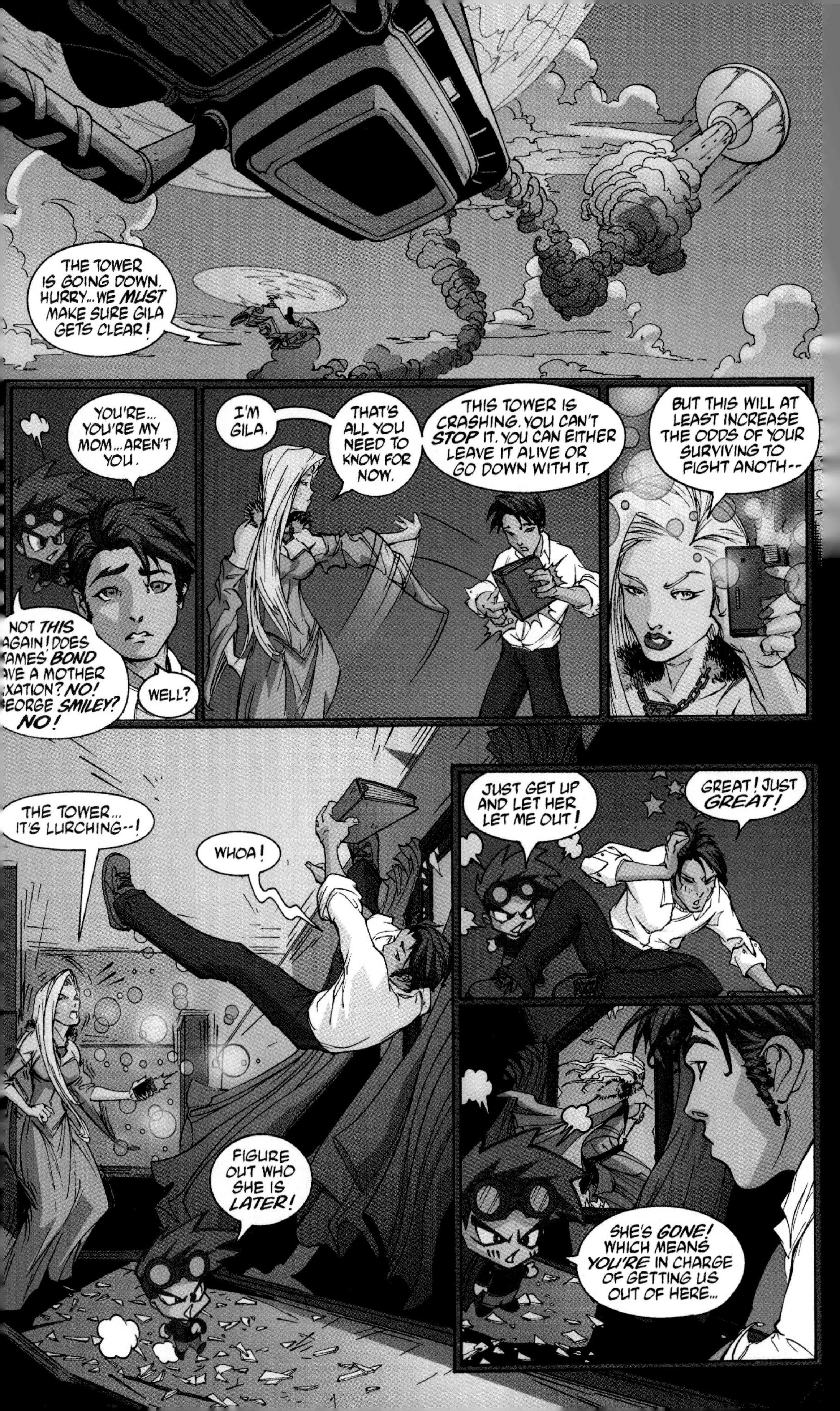

THE TOWER IS GOING DOWN. HURRY...WE MUST MAKE SURE GILA GETS CLEAR!
YOU'RE... YOU'RE MY MOM...AREN'T YOU.
NOT THIS AGAIN! DOES JAMES BOND HAVE A MOTHER FIXATION? NO! GEORGE SMILEY? NO!
WELL?
I'M GILA.
THAT'S ALL YOU NEED TO KNOW FOR NOW.
THIS TOWER IS CRASHING. YOU CAN'T STOP IT. YOU CAN EITHER LEAVE IT ALIVE OR GO DOWN WITH IT.
BUT THIS WILL AT LEAST INCREASE THE ODDS OF YOUR SURVIVING TO FIGHT ANOTH--
THE TOWER... IT'S LURCHING--!
WHOA!
FIGURE OUT WHO SHE IS LATER!
JUST GET UP AND LET HER LET ME OUT!
GREAT! JUST GREAT!
SHE'S GONE! WHICH MEANS YOU'RE IN CHARGE OF GETTING US OUT OF HERE...

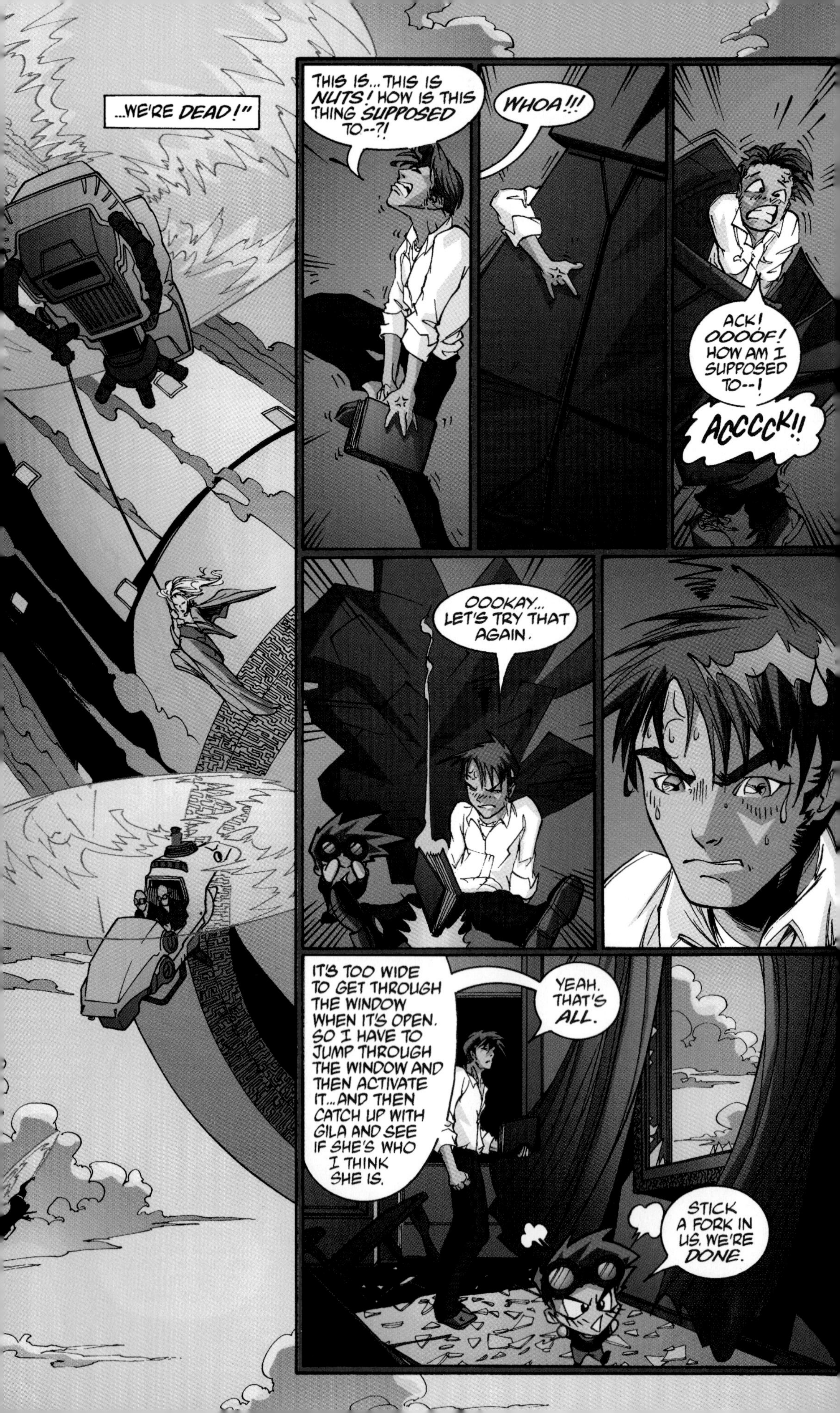
...WE'RE DEAD!"
THIS IS... THIS IS NUTS! HOW IS THIS THING SUPPOSED TO--?!
WHOA!!!
ACK! OOOOF! HOW AM I SUPPOSED TO--!
ACCCCK!!
OOOKAY... LET'S TRY THAT AGAIN.
IT'S TOO WIDE TO GET THROUGH THE WINDOW WHEN IT'S OPEN. SO I HAVE TO JUMP THROUGH THE WINDOW AND THEN ACTIVATE IT... AND THEN CATCH UP WITH GILA AND SEE IF SHE'S WHO I THINK SHE IS.
YEAH. THAT'S ALL.
STICK A FORK IN US. WE'RE DONE.

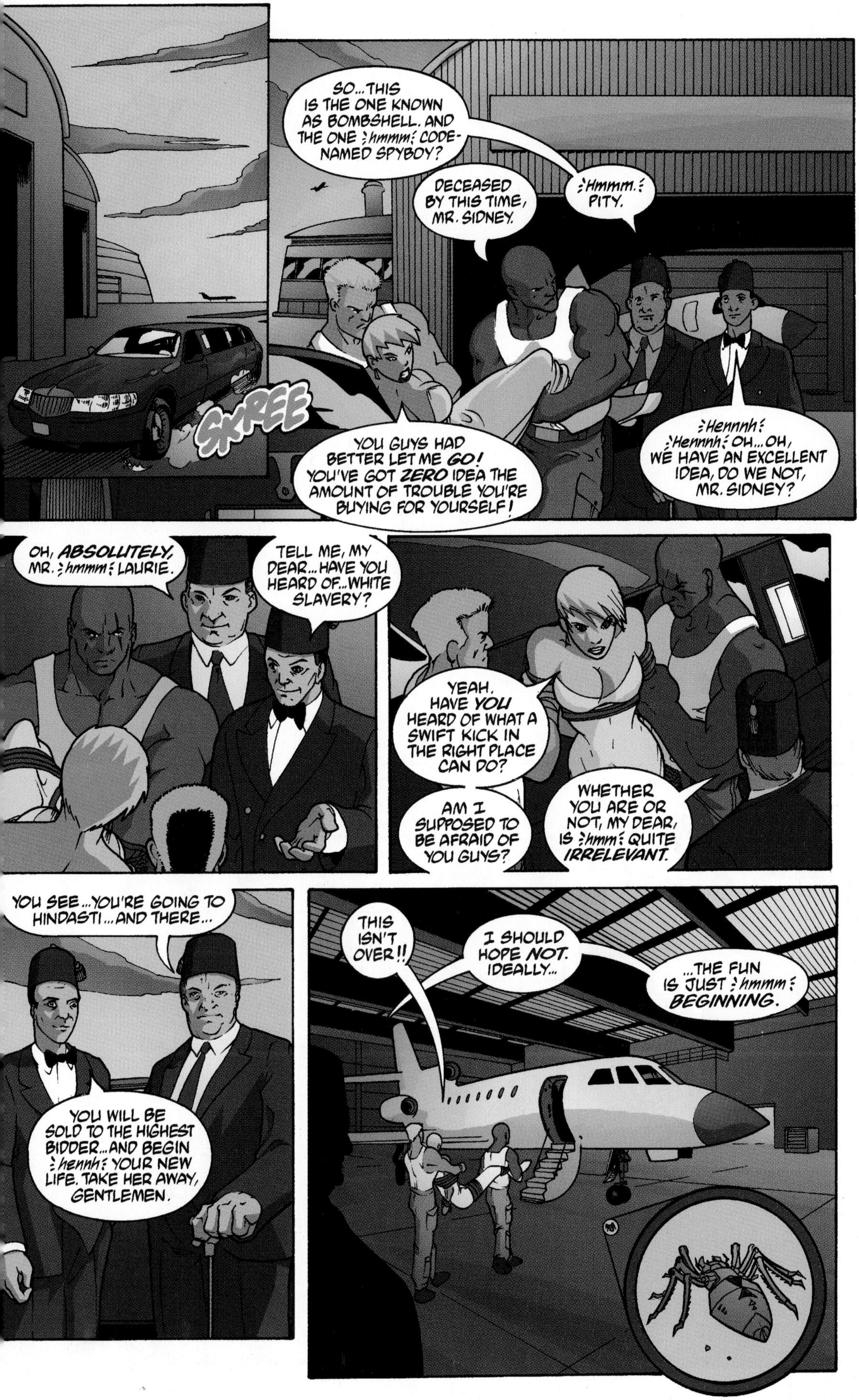
SO...THIS IS THE ONE KNOWN AS BOMBSHELL. AND THE ONE hmmm CODE-NAMED SPYBOY?
DECEASED BY THIS TIME, MR. SIDNEY.
Hmmm. PITY.
SKREE
YOU GUYS HAD BETTER LET ME GO! YOU'VE GOT ZERO IDEA THE AMOUNT OF TROUBLE YOU'RE BUYING FOR YOURSELF!
Hennnh Hennnh OH...OH, WE HAVE AN EXCELLENT IDEA, DO WE NOT, MR. SIDNEY?
OH, ABSOLUTELY, MR. hmmm LAURIE.
TELL ME, MY DEAR...HAVE YOU HEARD OF...WHITE SLAVERY?
YEAH. HAVE YOU HEARD OF WHAT A SWIFT KICK IN THE RIGHT PLACE CAN DO?
AM I SUPPOSED TO BE AFRAID OF YOU GUYS?
WHETHER YOU ARE OR NOT, MY DEAR, IS hmm QUITE IRRELEVANT.
YOU SEE...YOU'RE GOING TO HINDASTI...AND THERE...
YOU WILL BE SOLD TO THE HIGHEST BIDDER...AND BEGIN hennh YOUR NEW LIFE. TAKE HER AWAY, GENTLEMEN.
THIS ISN'T OVER!!
I SHOULD HOPE NOT. IDEALLY...
...THE FUN IS JUST hmmm BEGINNING.

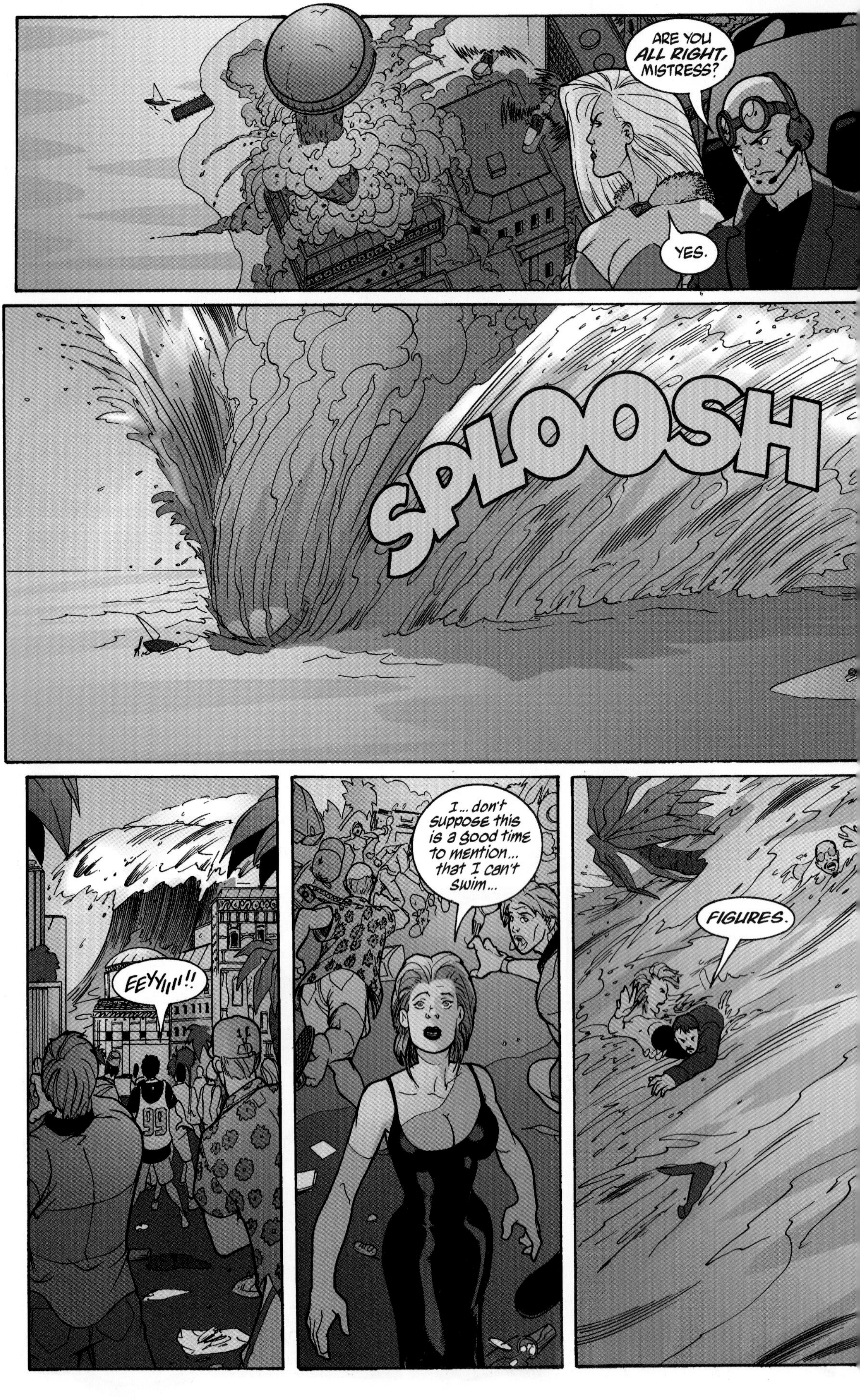
ARE YOU ALL RIGHT, MISTRESS?
YES.
SPLOOSH
EEYYIIII!!
I... don't suppose this is a good time to mention... that I can't swim...
FIGURES.

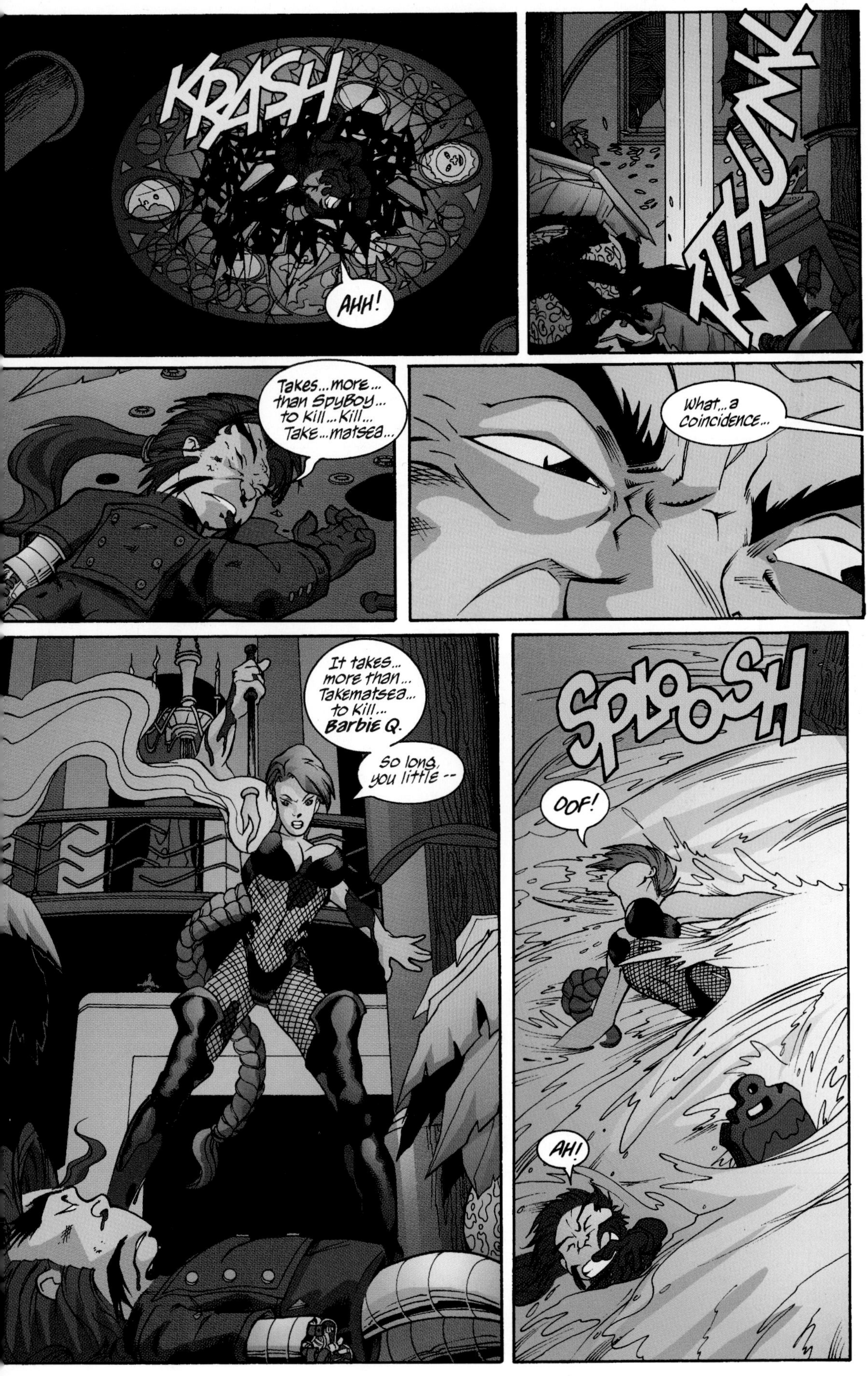
KRASH
AHH!
THUNK
Takes...more... than SpyBoy... to kill...Kill... Take...matsea...
What...a coincidence...
It takes... more than... Takematsea... to kill... Barbie Q.
So long, you little --
SPLOOSH
OOF!
AH!

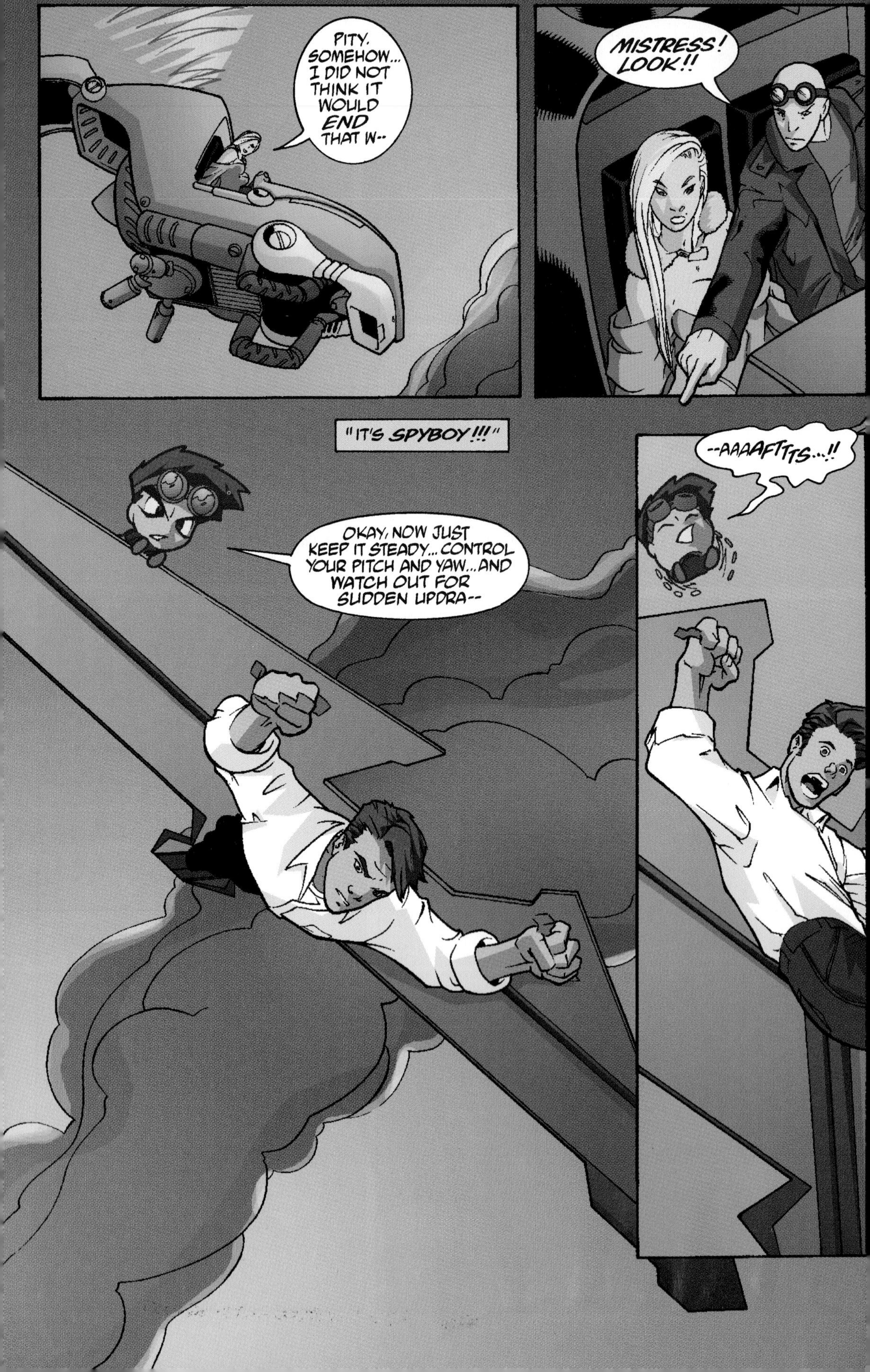
PITY. SOMEHOW... I DID NOT THINK IT WOULD END THAT W--
MISTRESS! LOOK!!
"IT'S SPYBOY!!!"
OKAY, NOW JUST KEEP IT STEADY... CONTROL YOUR PITCH AND YAW...AND WATCH OUT FOR SUDDEN UPDRA--
--AAAAFTTTS...!!

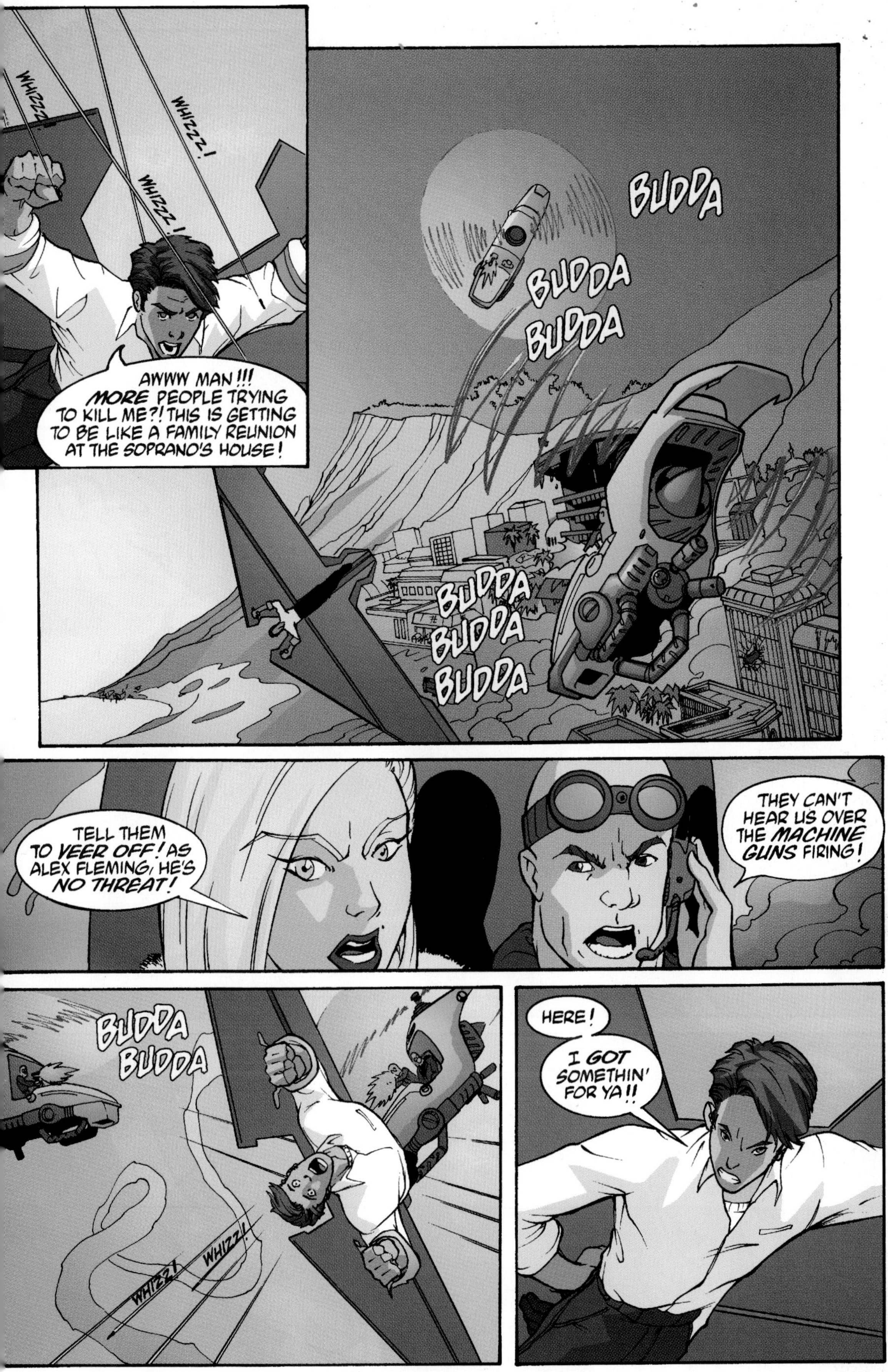
WHIZZZ
WHIZZZ!
WHIZZZ!
AWWW MAN!!! MORE PEOPLE TRYING TO KILL ME?! THIS IS GETTING TO BE LIKE A FAMILY REUNION AT THE SOPRANO'S HOUSE!
BUDDA
BUDDA BUDDA
BUDDA BUDDA BUDDA
TELL THEM TO VEER OFF! AS ALEX FLEMING, HE'S NO THREAT!
THEY CAN'T HEAR US OVER THE MACHINE GUNS FIRING!
BUDDA BUDDA
WHIZZ!
WHIZZ!
HERE!
I GOT SOMETHIN' FOR YA!!

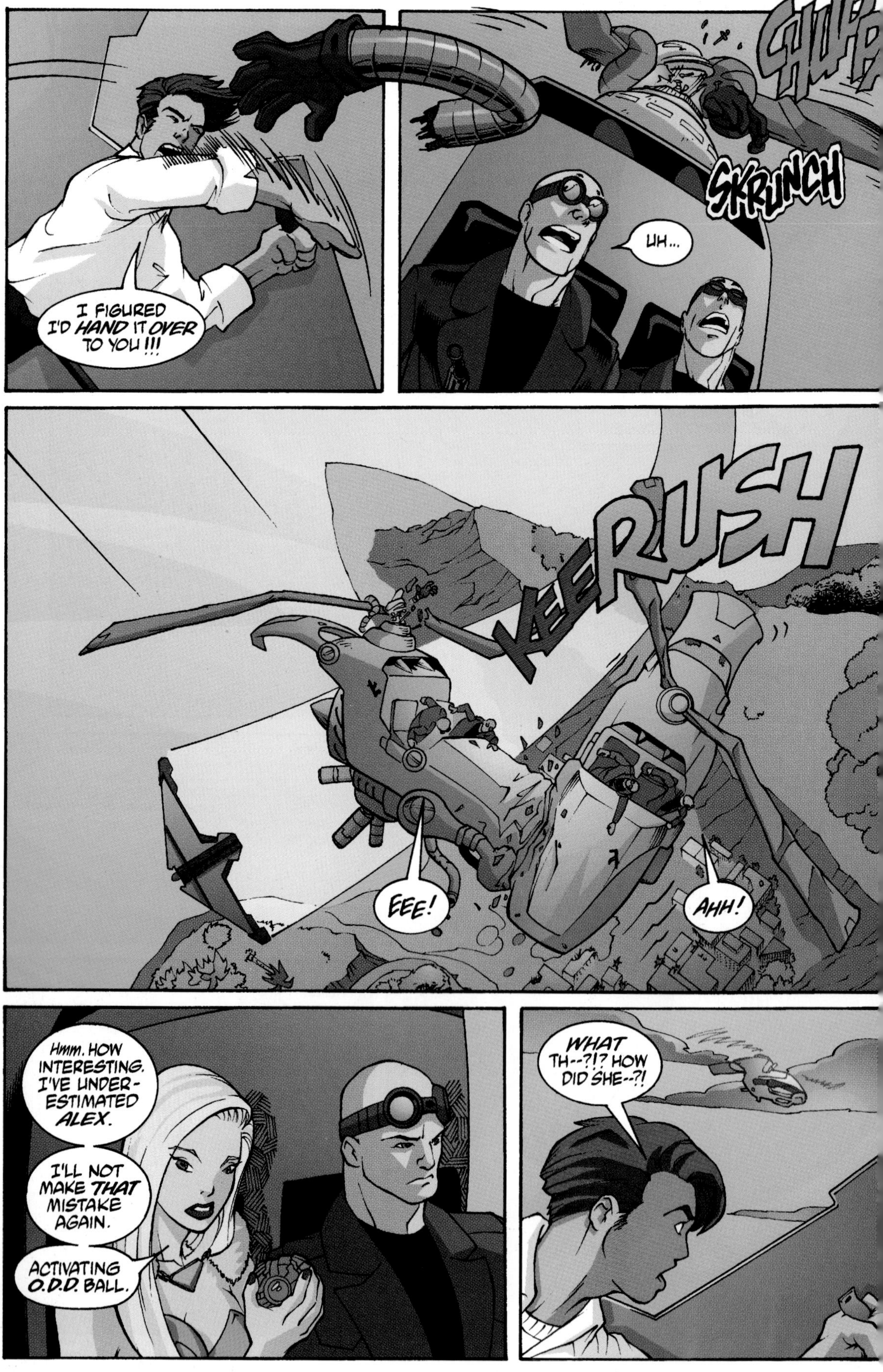
I FIGURED I'D HAND IT OVER TO YOU!!!
CHUP
SKRUNCH
UH...
KEERUSH
EEE!
AHH!
Hmm. HOW INTERESTING. I'VE UNDER-ESTIMATED ALEX.
I'LL NOT MAKE THAT MISTAKE AGAIN.
ACTIVATING O.D.D. BALL.
WHAT TH--?!? HOW DID SHE--?!

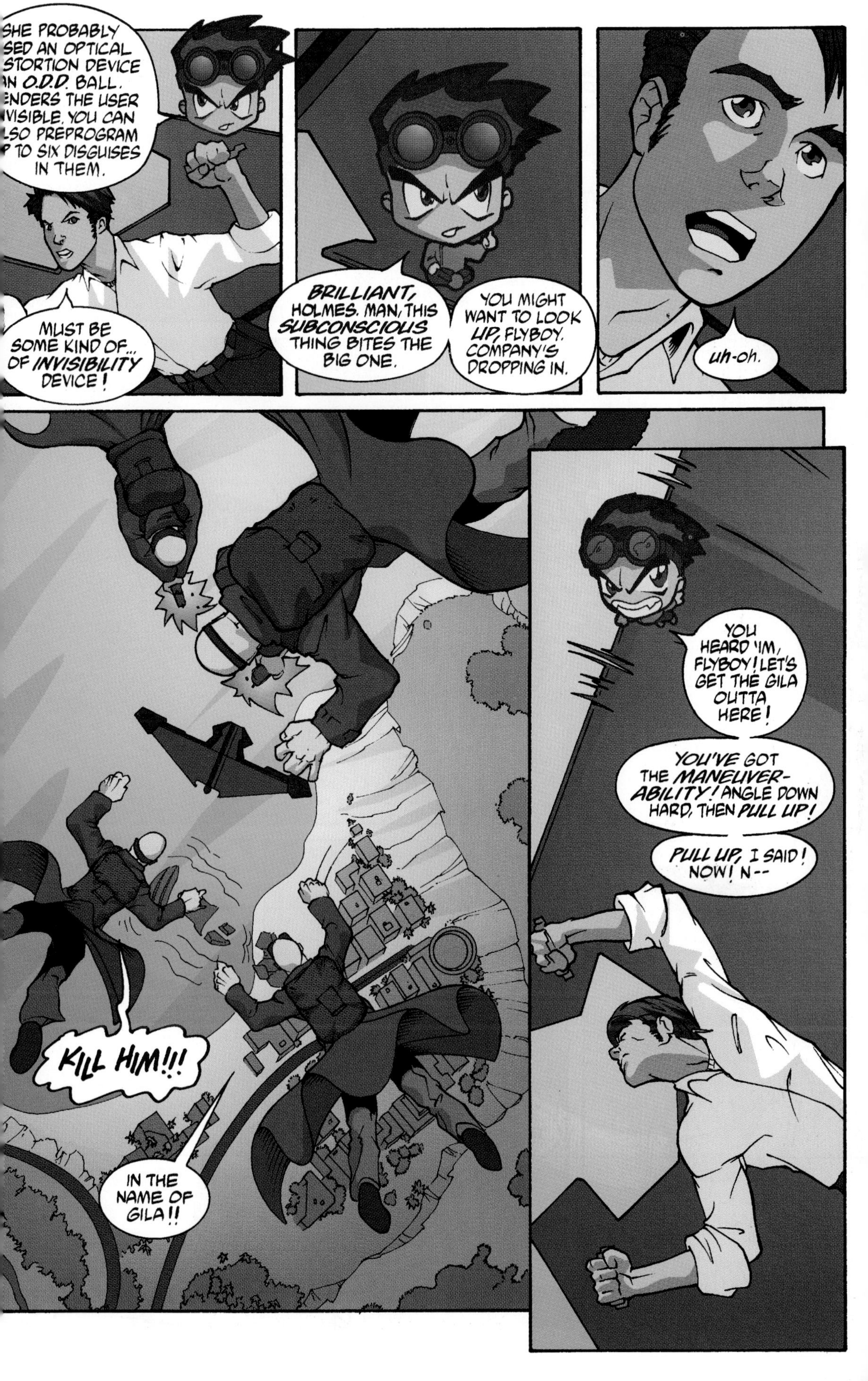

SHE PROBABLY SED AN OPTICAL STORTION DEVICE N O.D.D. BALL. ENDERS THE USER VISIBLE. YOU CAN LSO PREPROGRAM P TO SIX DISGUISES IN THEM.
MUST BE SOME KIND OF... OF INVISIBILITY DEVICE!
BRILLIANT, HOLMES. MAN, THIS SUBCONSCIOUS THING BITES THE BIG ONE.
YOU MIGHT WANT TO LOOK UP, FLYBOY. COMPANY'S DROPPING IN.
uh-oh.
KILL HIM!!!
IN THE NAME OF GILA!!
YOU HEARD 'IM, FLYBOY! LET'S GET THE GILA OUTTA HERE!
YOU'VE GOT THE MANEUVER-ABILITY! ANGLE DOWN HARD, THEN PULL UP!
PULL UP, I SAID! NOW! N--

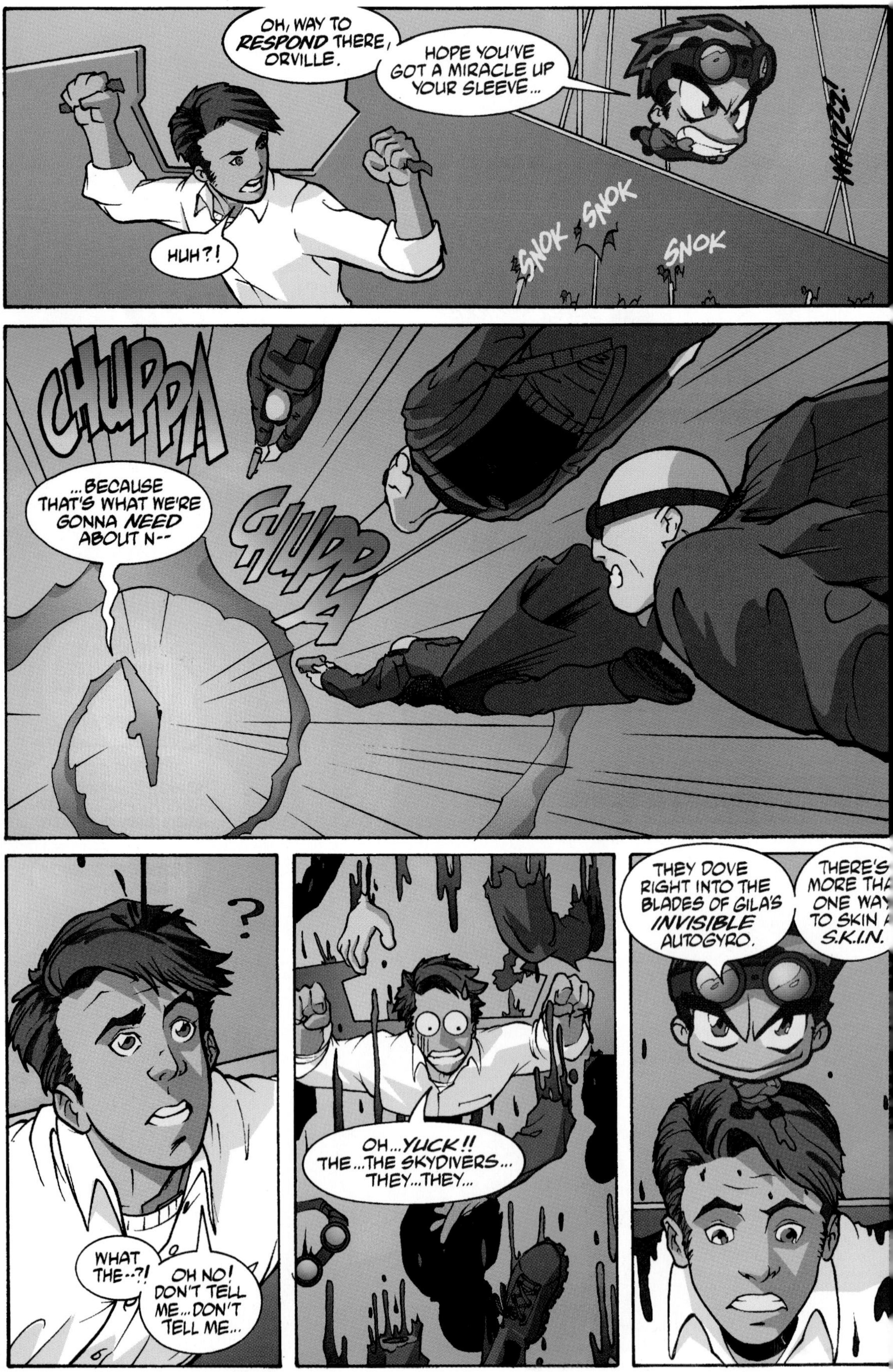
OH, WAY TO RESPOND THERE, ORVILLE.
HOPE YOU'VE GOT A MIRACLE UP YOUR SLEEVE...
WHIZZZ!
HUH?!
SNOK SNOK
SNOK
CHUPPA
...BECAUSE THAT'S WHAT WE'RE GONNA NEED ABOUT N--
CHUPPA
?
WHAT THE--?!
OH NO! DON'T TELL ME...DON'T TELL ME...
OH...YUCK!! THE...THE SKYDIVERS... THEY...THEY...
THEY DOVE RIGHT INTO THE BLADES OF GILA'S INVISIBLE AUTOGYRO.
THERE'S MORE THA ONE WAY TO SKIN A S.K.I.N.

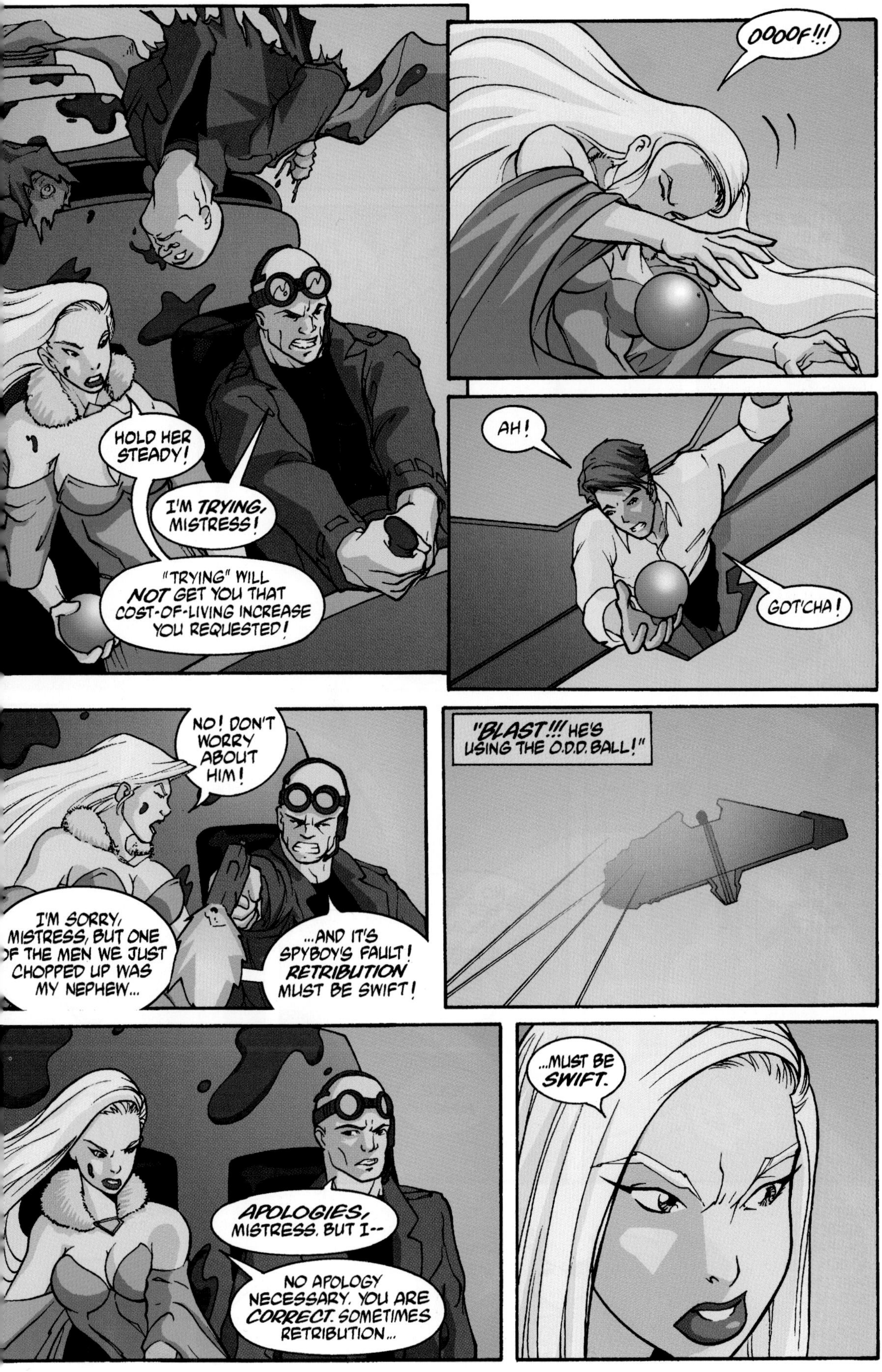
HOLD HER STEADY!
I'M TRYING, MISTRESS!
"TRYING" WILL NOT GET YOU THAT COST-OF-LIVING INCREASE YOU REQUESTED!
OOOOF!!!
AH!
GOT'CHA!
NO! DON'T WORRY ABOUT HIM!
I'M SORRY, MISTRESS, BUT ONE OF THE MEN WE JUST CHOPPED UP WAS MY NEPHEW...
...AND IT'S SPYBOY'S FAULT! RETRIBUTION MUST BE SWIFT!
"BLAST!!! HE'S USING THE O.D.D. BALL!"
APOLOGIES, MISTRESS. BUT I--
NO APOLOGY NECESSARY. YOU ARE CORRECT. SOMETIMES RETRIBUTION...
...MUST BE SWIFT.

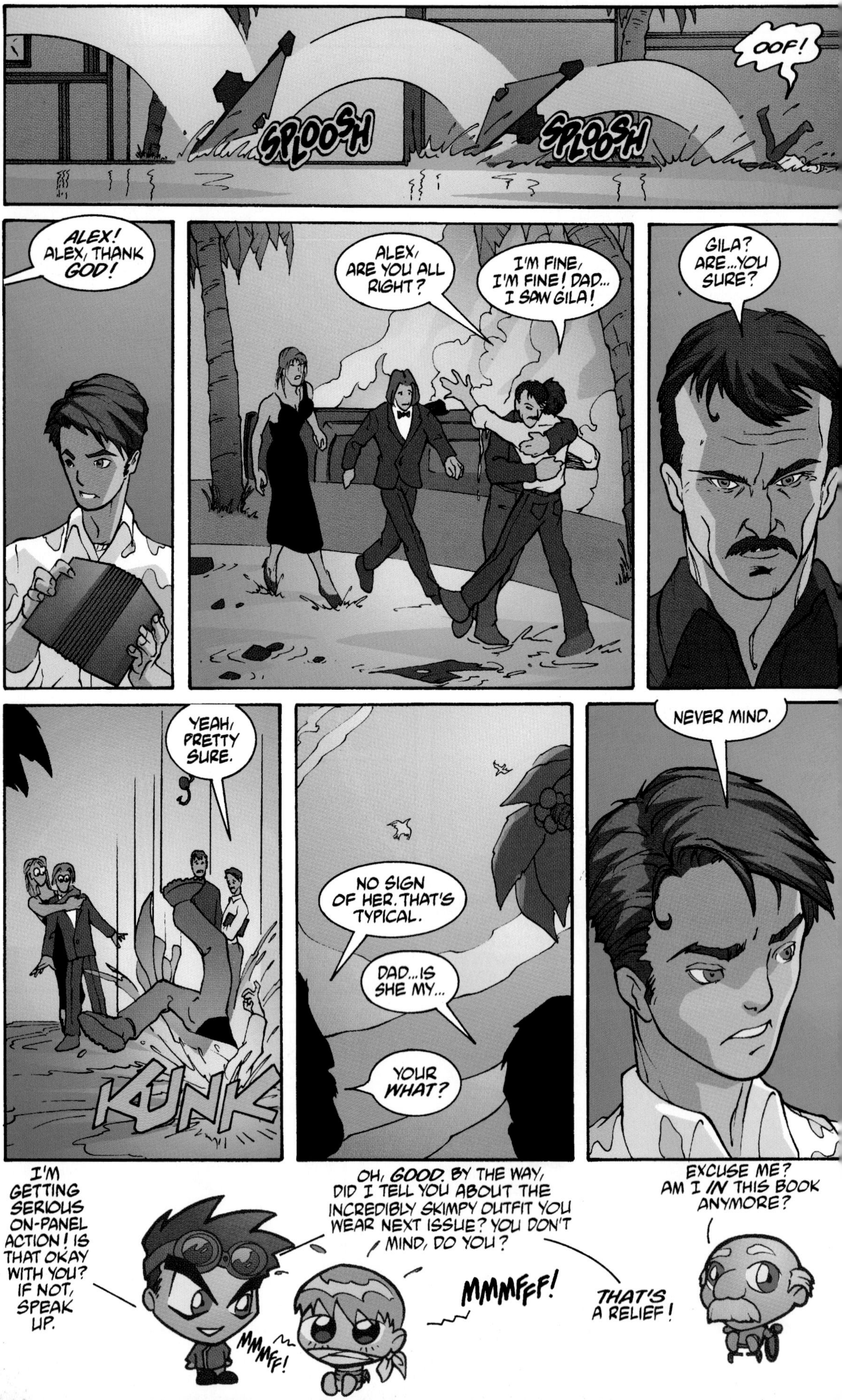

SPLOOSH
SPLOOSH
OOF!
ALEX! ALEX, THANK GOD!
ALEX, ARE YOU ALL RIGHT?
I'M FINE, I'M FINE! DAD... I SAW GILA!
GILA? ARE...YOU SURE?
YEAH, PRETTY SURE.
KUNK
NO SIGN OF HER. THAT'S TYPICAL.
DAD...IS SHE MY...
YOUR WHAT?
NEVER MIND.
I'M GETTING SERIOUS ON-PANEL ACTION! IS THAT OKAY WITH YOU? IF NOT, SPEAK UP.
MMMFF!
OH, GOOD. BY THE WAY, DID I TELL YOU ABOUT THE INCREDIBLY SKIMPY OUTFIT YOU WEAR NEXT ISSUE? YOU DON'T MIND, DO YOU?
MMMFFF!
THAT'S A RELIEF!
EXCUSE ME? AM I IN THIS BOOK ANYMORE?

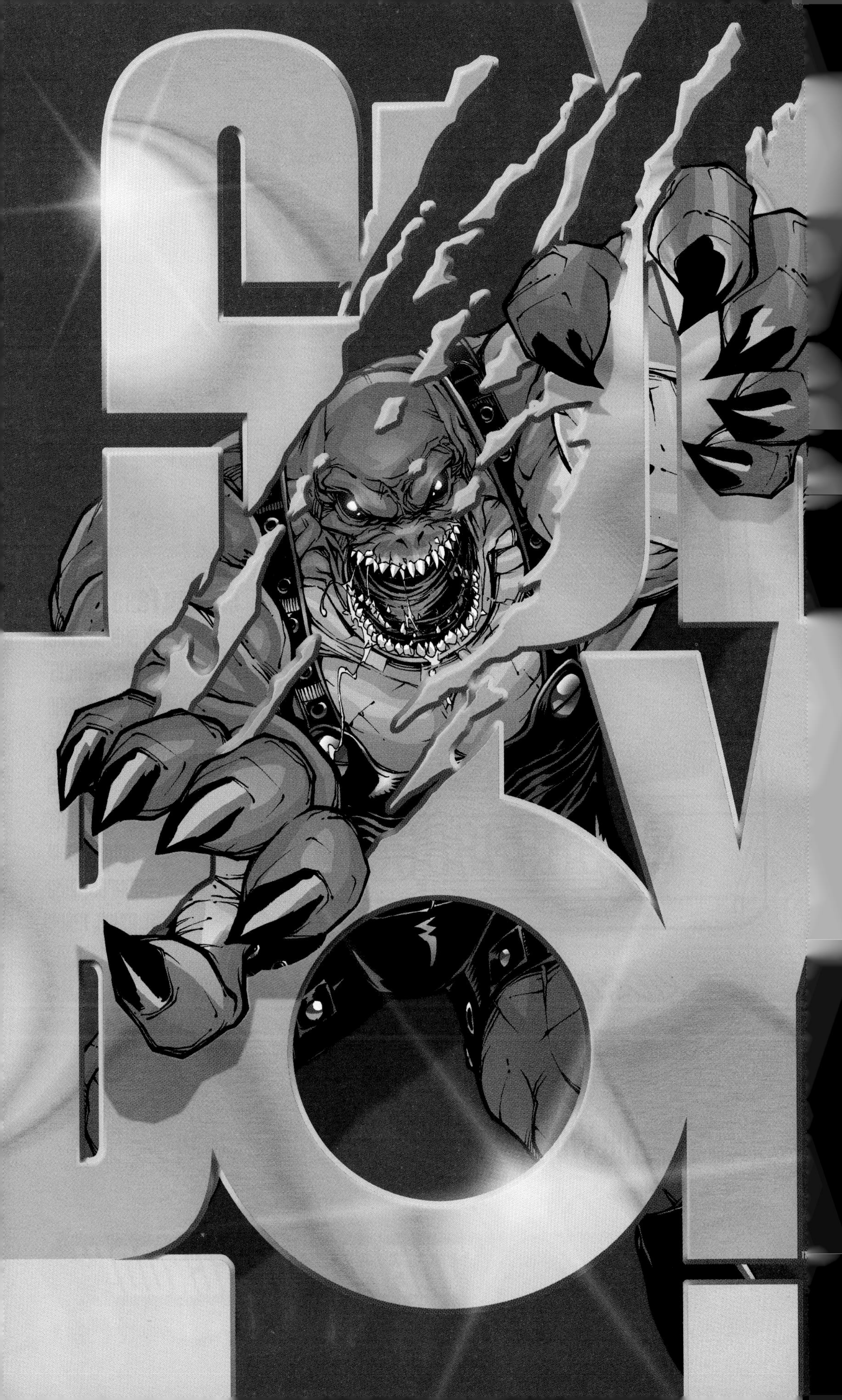

2 "THE FIST OF SCROD!"

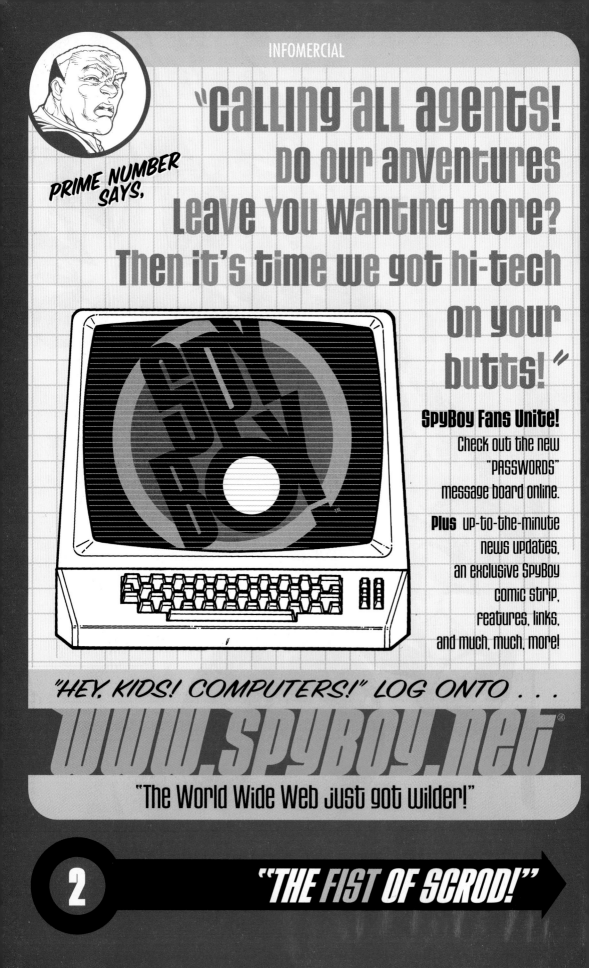

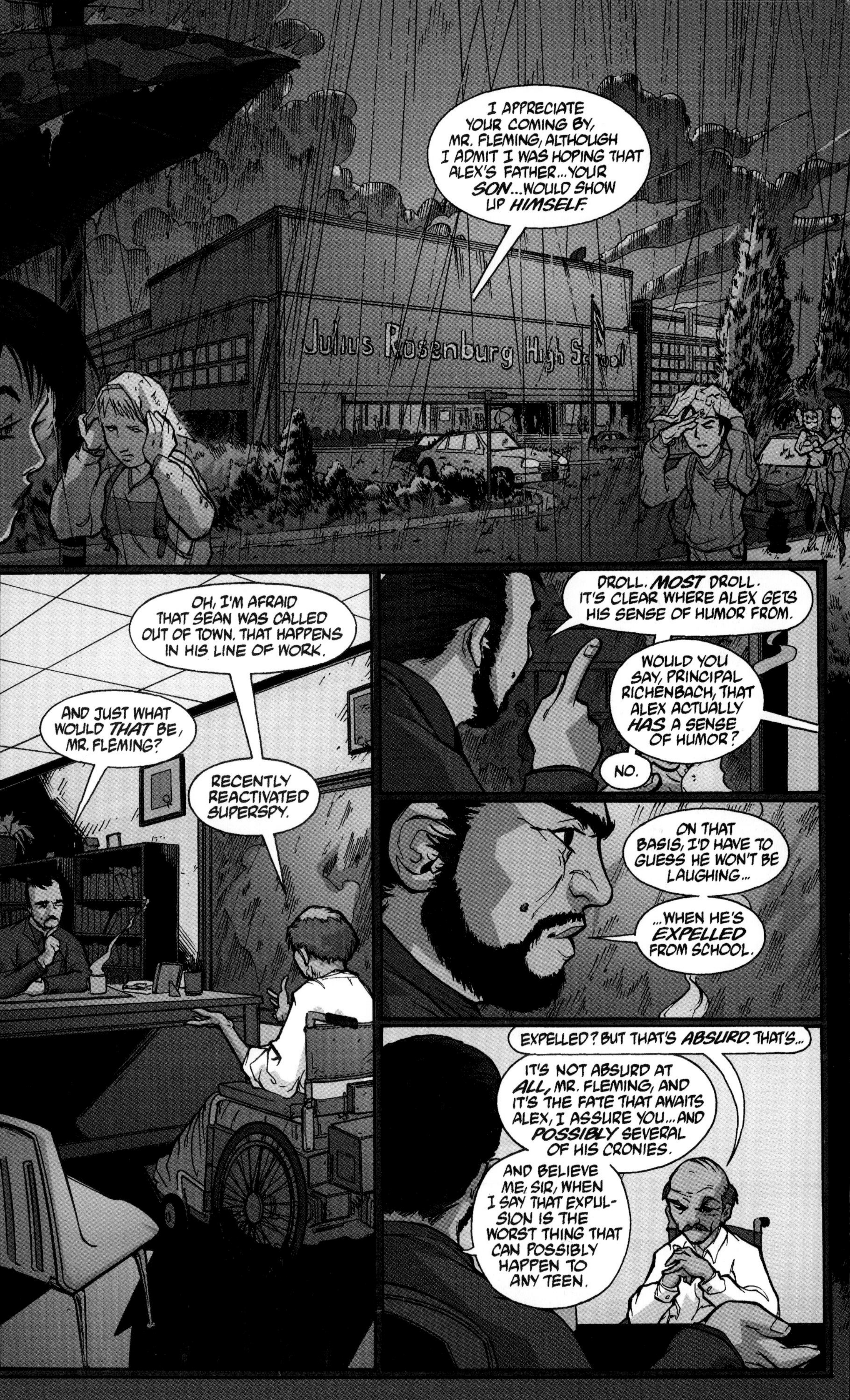
I APPRECIATE YOUR COMING BY, MR. FLEMING, ALTHOUGH I ADMIT I WAS HOPING THAT ALEX'S FATHER...YOUR SON...WOULD SHOW UP HIMSELF.
Julius Rosenburg High School
OH, I'M AFRAID THAT SEAN WAS CALLED OUT OF TOWN. THAT HAPPENS IN HIS LINE OF WORK.
AND JUST WHAT WOULD THAT BE, MR. FLEMING?
RECENTLY REACTIVATED SUPERSPY.
DROLL. MOST DROLL. IT'S CLEAR WHERE ALEX GETS HIS SENSE OF HUMOR FROM.
WOULD YOU SAY, PRINCIPAL RICHENBACH, THAT ALEX ACTUALLY HAS A SENSE OF HUMOR?
NO.
ON THAT BASIS, I'D HAVE TO GUESS HE WON'T BE LAUGHING...
...WHEN HE'S EXPELLED FROM SCHOOL.
EXPELLED? BUT THAT'S ABSURD. THAT'S...
IT'S NOT ABSURD AT ALL, MR. FLEMING, AND IT'S THE FATE THAT AWAITS ALEX, I ASSURE YOU...AND POSSIBLY SEVERAL OF HIS CRONIES.
AND BELIEVE ME, SIR, WHEN I SAY THAT EXPULSION IS THE WORST THING THAT CAN POSSIBLY HAPPEN TO ANY TEEN.

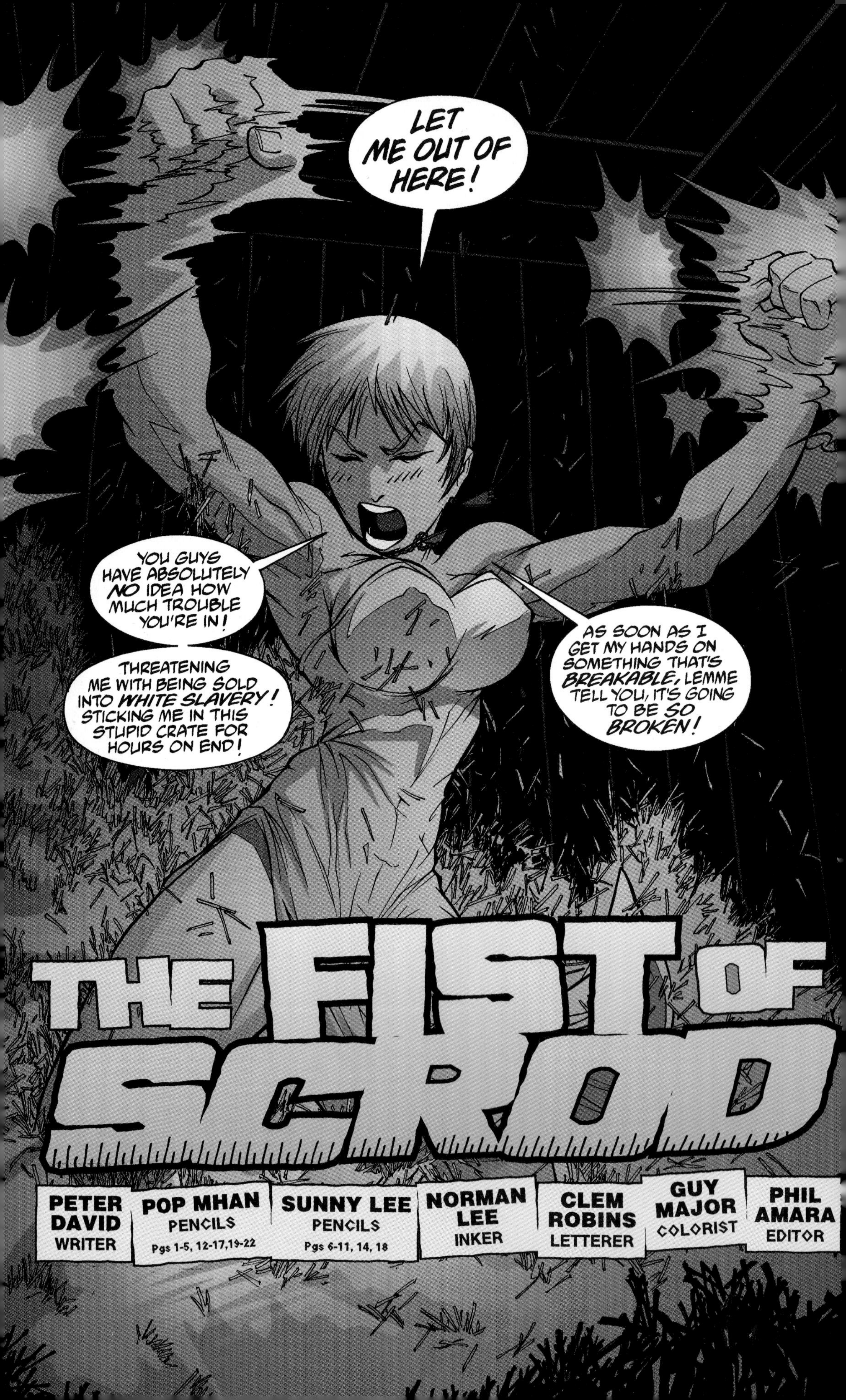

LET ME OUT OF HERE!
YOU GUYS HAVE ABSOLUTELY NO IDEA HOW MUCH TROUBLE YOU'RE IN!
THREATENING ME WITH BEING SOLD INTO WHITE SLAVERY! STICKING ME IN THIS STUPID CRATE FOR HOURS ON END!
AS SOON AS I GET MY HANDS ON SOMETHING THAT'S BREAKABLE, LEMME TELL YOU, IT'S GOING TO BE SO BROKEN!
THE FIST OF SCROD
PETER DAVID WRITER
POP MHAN PENCILS Pgs 1-5, 12-17, 19-22
SUNNY LEE PENCILS Pgs 6-11, 14, 18
NORMAN LEE INKER
CLEM ROBINS LETTERER
GUY MAJOR COLORIST
PHIL AMARA EDITOR

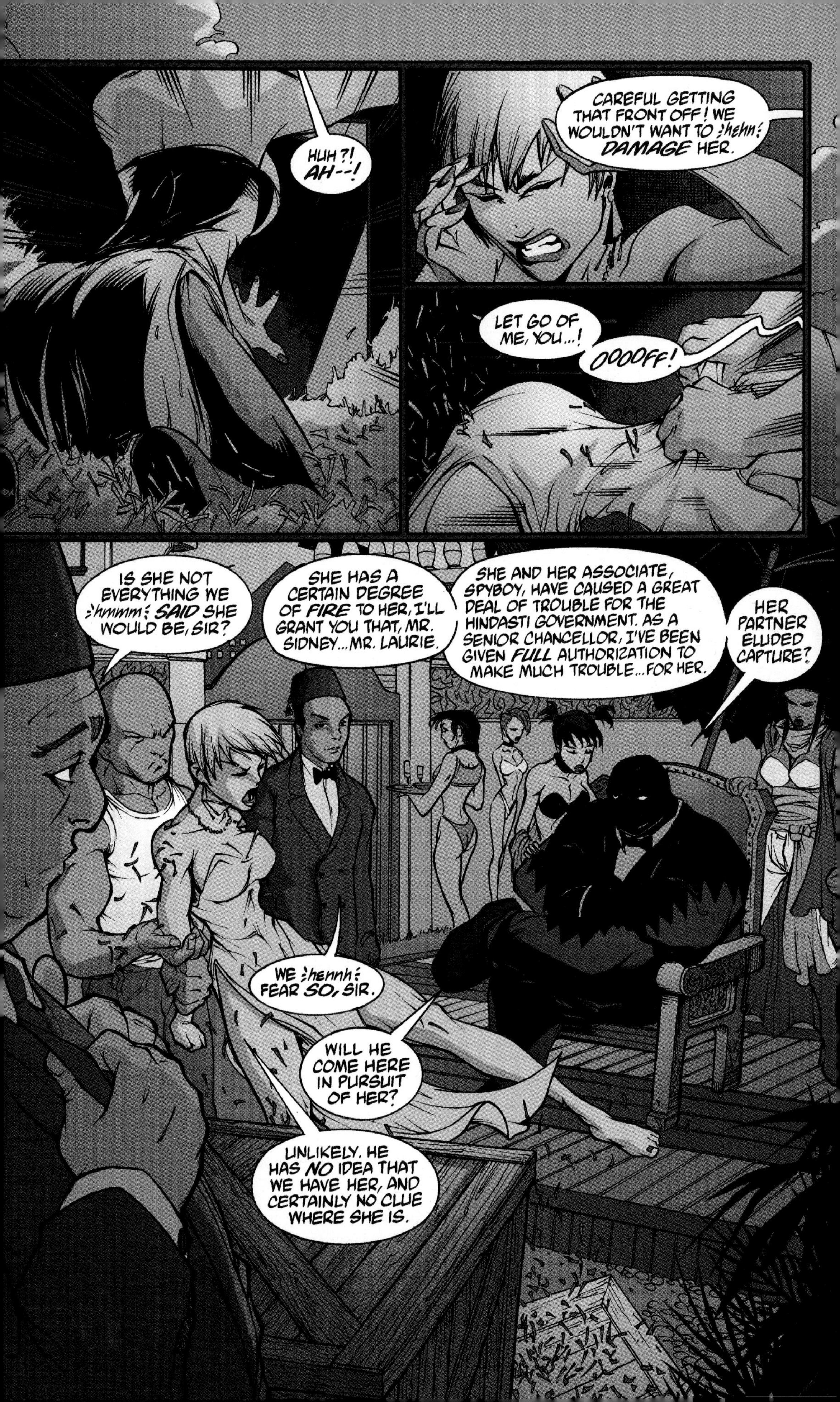
HUH?! AH--!
CAREFUL GETTING THAT FRONT OFF! WE WOULDN'T WANT TO ;hehn; DAMAGE HER.
LET GO OF ME, YOU...!
OOOOFF!
IS SHE NOT EVERYTHING WE ;hmmm; SAID SHE WOULD BE, SIR?
SHE HAS A CERTAIN DEGREE OF FIRE TO HER, I'LL GRANT YOU THAT, MR. SIDNEY...MR. LAURIE.
SHE AND HER ASSOCIATE, SPYBOY, HAVE CAUSED A GREAT DEAL OF TROUBLE FOR THE HINDASTI GOVERNMENT. AS A SENIOR CHANCELLOR, I'VE BEEN GIVEN FULL AUTHORIZATION TO MAKE MUCH TROUBLE...FOR HER.
HER PARTNER ELUDED CAPTURE?
WE ;hennh; FEAR SO, SIR.
WILL HE COME HERE IN PURSUIT OF HER?
UNLIKELY. HE HAS NO IDEA THAT WE HAVE HER, AND CERTAINLY NO CLUE WHERE SHE IS.

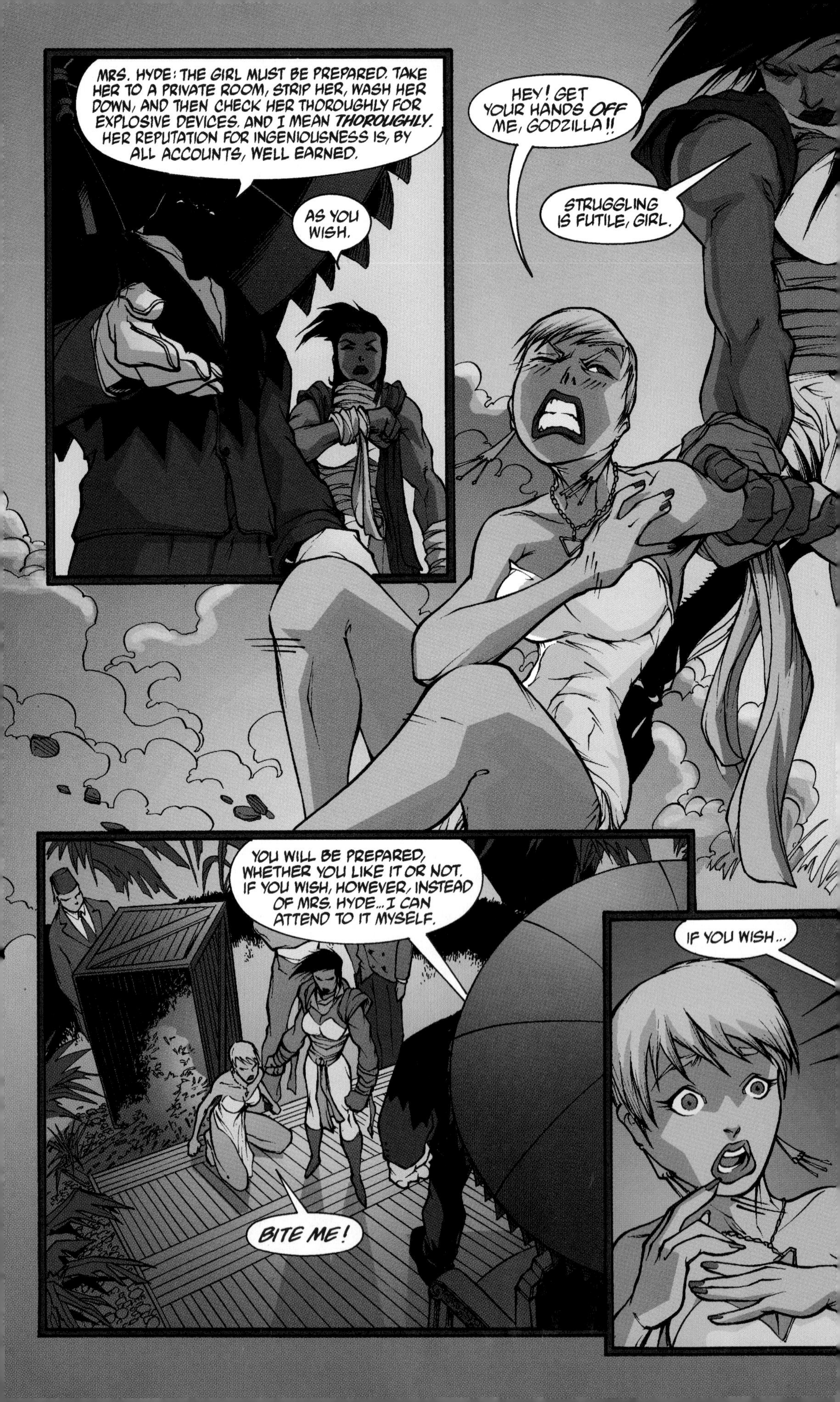
MRS. HYDE: THE GIRL MUST BE PREPARED. TAKE HER TO A PRIVATE ROOM, STRIP HER, WASH HER DOWN, AND THEN CHECK HER THOROUGHLY FOR EXPLOSIVE DEVICES. AND I MEAN THOROUGHLY. HER REPUTATION FOR INGENIOUSNESS IS, BY ALL ACCOUNTS, WELL EARNED.
AS YOU WISH.
HEY! GET YOUR HANDS OFF ME, GODZILLA!!
STRUGGLING IS FUTILE, GIRL.
YOU WILL BE PREPARED, WHETHER YOU LIKE IT OR NOT. IF YOU WISH, HOWEVER, INSTEAD OF MRS. HYDE... I CAN ATTEND TO IT MYSELF.
BITE ME!
IF YOU WISH...

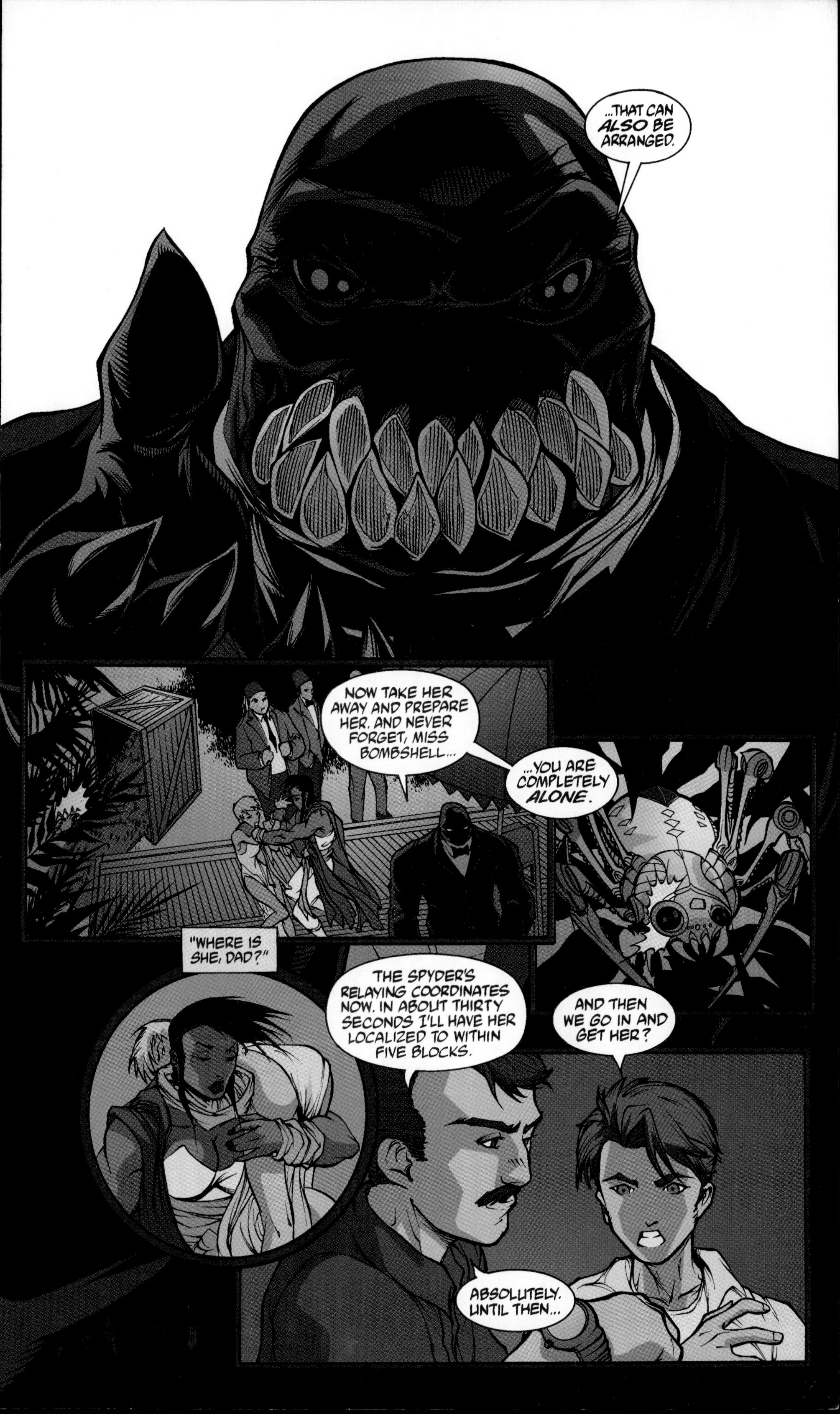
...THAT CAN ALSO BE ARRANGED.
NOW TAKE HER AWAY AND PREPARE HER. AND NEVER FORGET, MISS BOMBSHELL...
...YOU ARE COMPLETELY ALONE.
"WHERE IS SHE, DAD?"
THE SPYDER'S RELAYING COORDINATES NOW. IN ABOUT THIRTY SECONDS I'LL HAVE HER LOCALIZED TO WITHIN FIVE BLOCKS.
AND THEN WE GO IN AND GET HER?
ABSOLUTELY. UNTIL THEN...

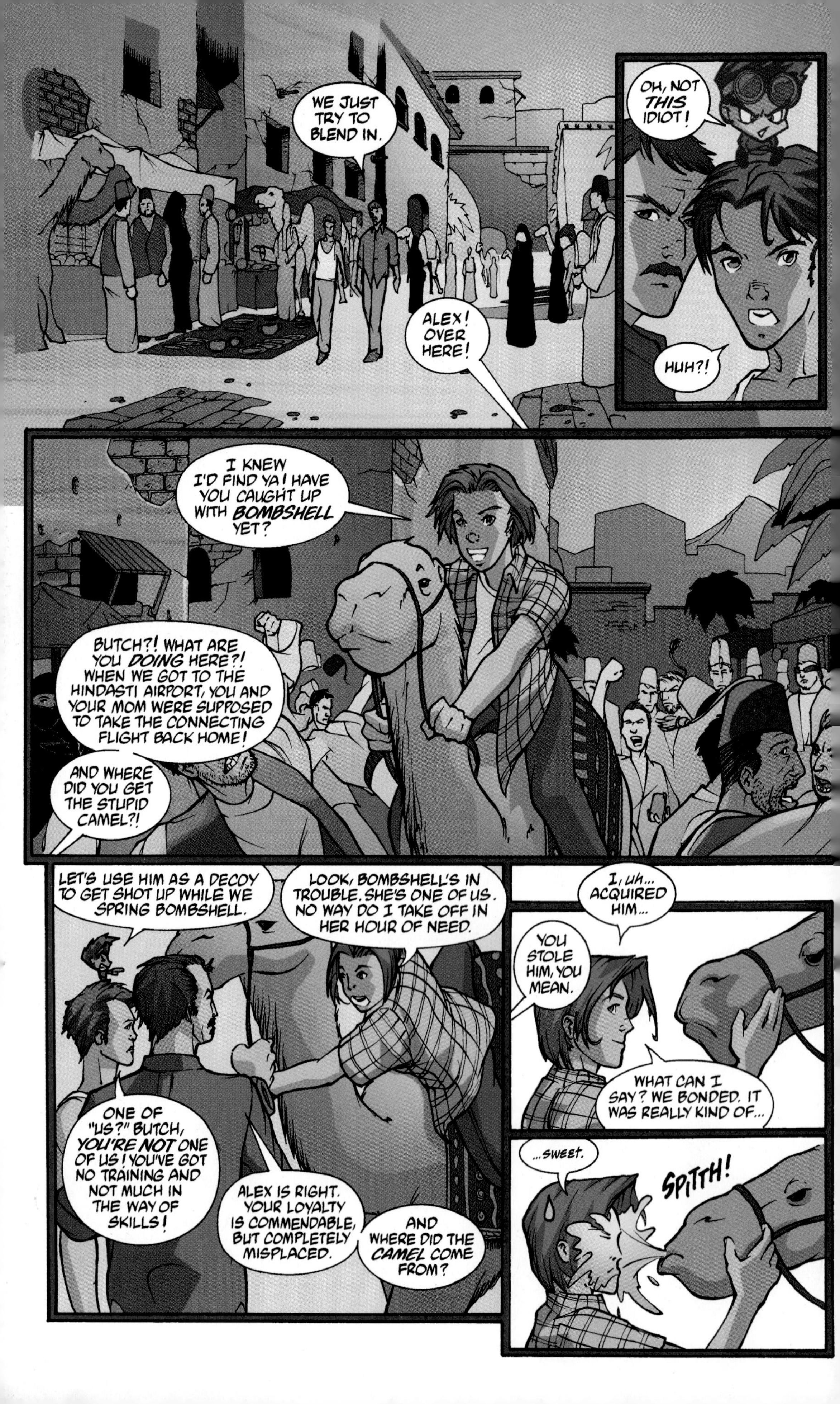

WE JUST TRY TO BLEND IN.
ALEX! OVER HERE!
OH, NOT THIS IDIOT!
HUH?!
I KNEW I'D FIND YA! HAVE YOU CAUGHT UP WITH BOMBSHELL YET?
BUTCH?! WHAT ARE YOU DOING HERE?! WHEN WE GOT TO THE HINDASTI AIRPORT, YOU AND YOUR MOM WERE SUPPOSED TO TAKE THE CONNECTING FLIGHT BACK HOME!
AND WHERE DID YOU GET THE STUPID CAMEL?!
LET'S USE HIM AS A DECOY TO GET SHOT UP WHILE WE SPRING BOMBSHELL.
LOOK, BOMBSHELL'S IN TROUBLE. SHE'S ONE OF US. NO WAY DO I TAKE OFF IN HER HOUR OF NEED.
ONE OF "US?" BUTCH, YOU'RE NOT ONE OF US! YOU'VE GOT NO TRAINING AND NOT MUCH IN THE WAY OF SKILLS!
ALEX IS RIGHT. YOUR LOYALTY IS COMMENDABLE, BUT COMPLETELY MISPLACED.
AND WHERE DID THE CAMEL COME FROM?
I, uh... ACQUIRED HIM...
YOU STOLE HIM, YOU MEAN.
WHAT CAN I SAY? WE BONDED. IT WAS REALLY KIND OF...
...sweet.
SPITTH!

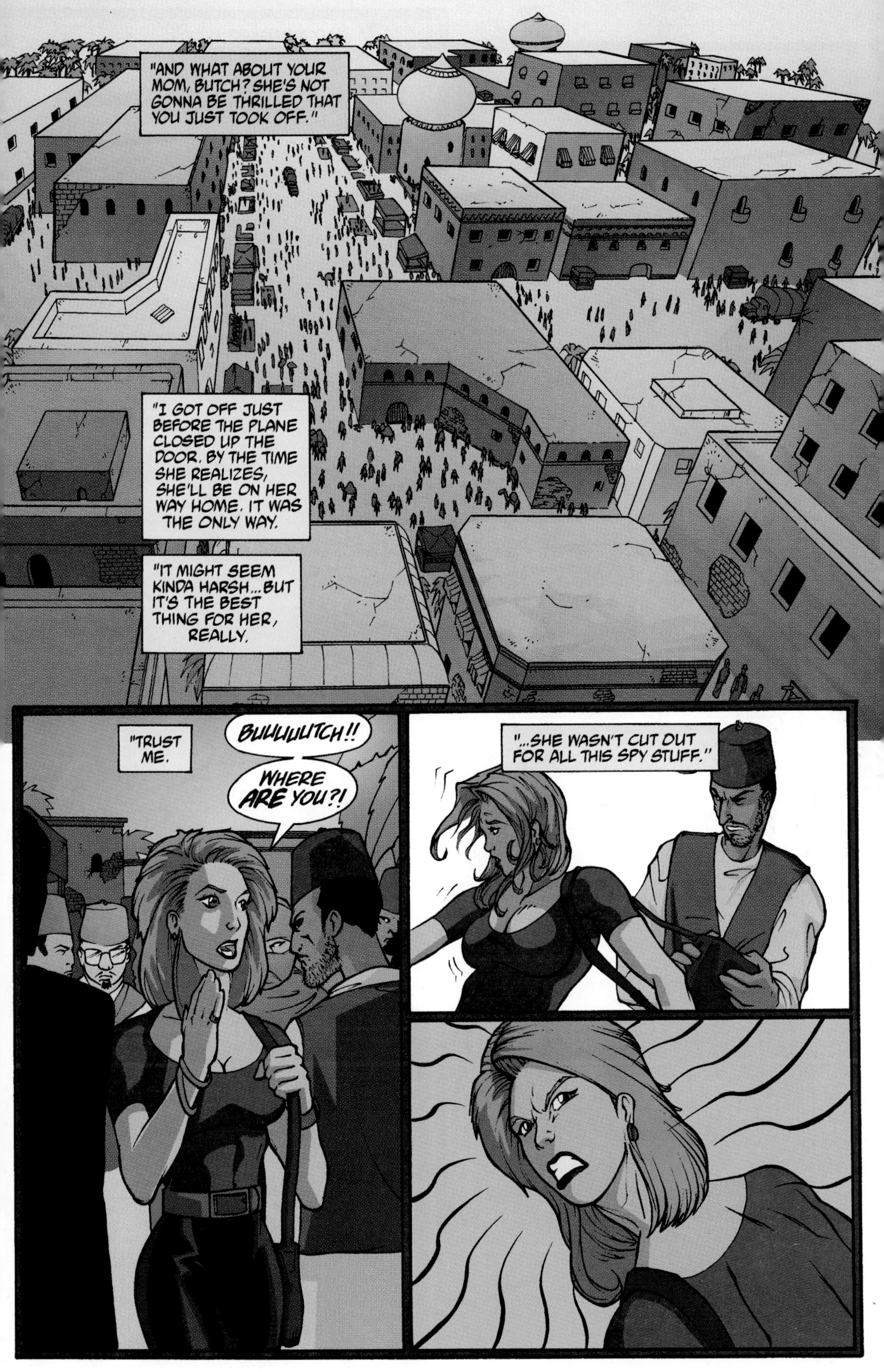
"AND WHAT ABOUT YOUR MOM, BUTCH? SHE'S NOT GONNA BE THRILLED THAT YOU JUST TOOK OFF."
"I GOT OFF JUST BEFORE THE PLANE CLOSED UP THE DOOR. BY THE TIME SHE REALIZES, SHE'LL BE ON HER WAY HOME. IT WAS THE ONLY WAY.
"IT MIGHT SEEM KINDA HARSH...BUT IT'S THE BEST THING FOR HER, REALLY.
"TRUST ME.
BUUUUUTCH!!
WHERE ARE YOU?!
"...SHE WASN'T CUT OUT FOR ALL THIS SPY STUFF."

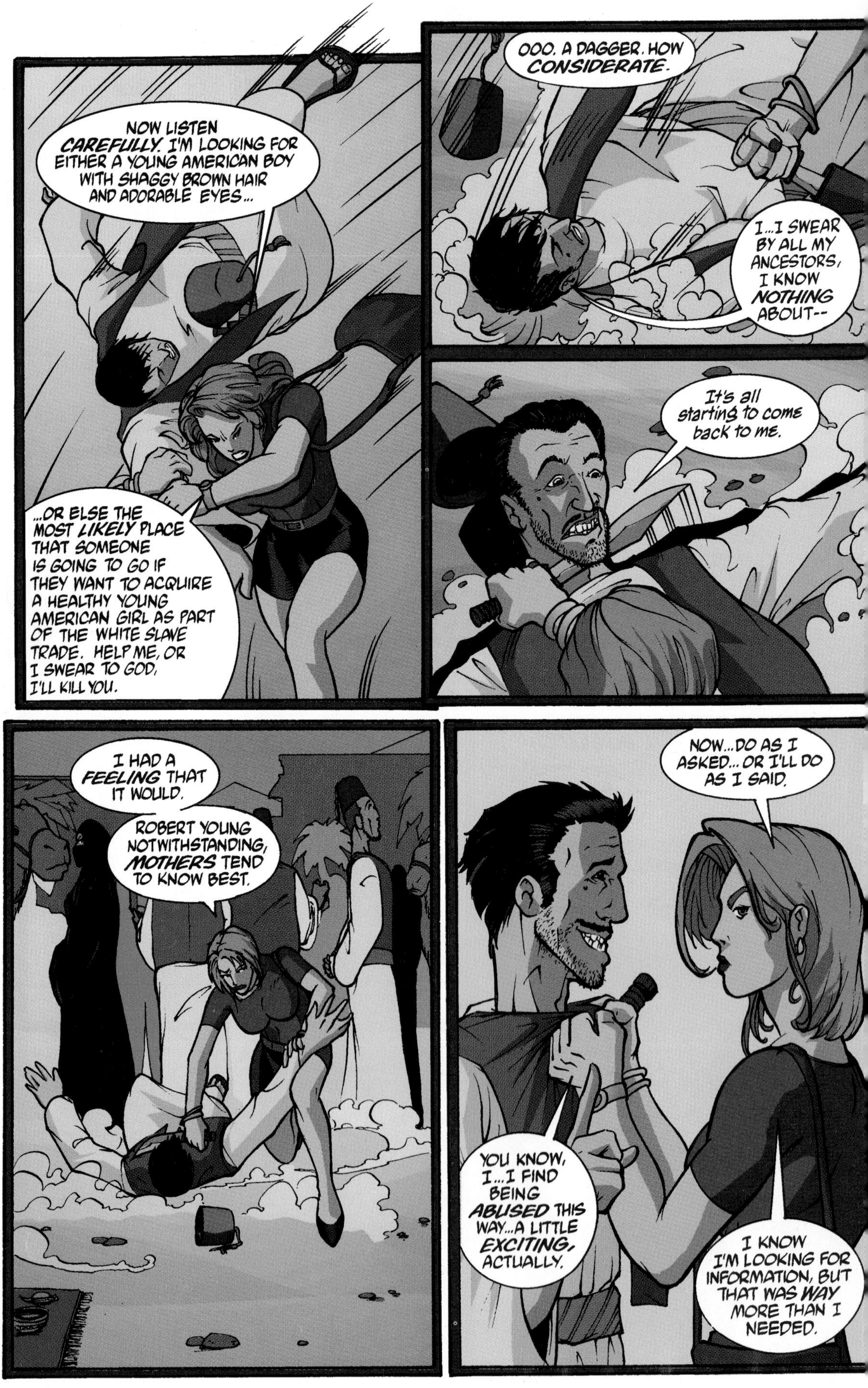
NOW LISTEN CAREFULLY. I'M LOOKING FOR EITHER A YOUNG AMERICAN BOY WITH SHAGGY BROWN HAIR AND ADORABLE EYES...
...OR ELSE THE MOST LIKELY PLACE THAT SOMEONE IS GOING TO GO IF THEY WANT TO ACQUIRE A HEALTHY YOUNG AMERICAN GIRL AS PART OF THE WHITE SLAVE TRADE. HELP ME, OR I SWEAR TO GOD, I'LL KILL YOU.
OOO. A DAGGER. HOW CONSIDERATE.
I...I SWEAR BY ALL MY ANCESTORS, I KNOW NOTHING ABOUT--
It's all starting to come back to me.
I HAD A FEELING THAT IT WOULD.
ROBERT YOUNG NOTWITHSTANDING, MOTHERS TEND TO KNOW BEST.
NOW...DO AS I ASKED...OR I'LL DO AS I SAID.
YOU KNOW, I...I FIND BEING ABUSED THIS WAY...A LITTLE EXCITING, ACTUALLY.
I KNOW I'M LOOKING FOR INFORMATION, BUT THAT WAS WAY MORE THAN I NEEDED.

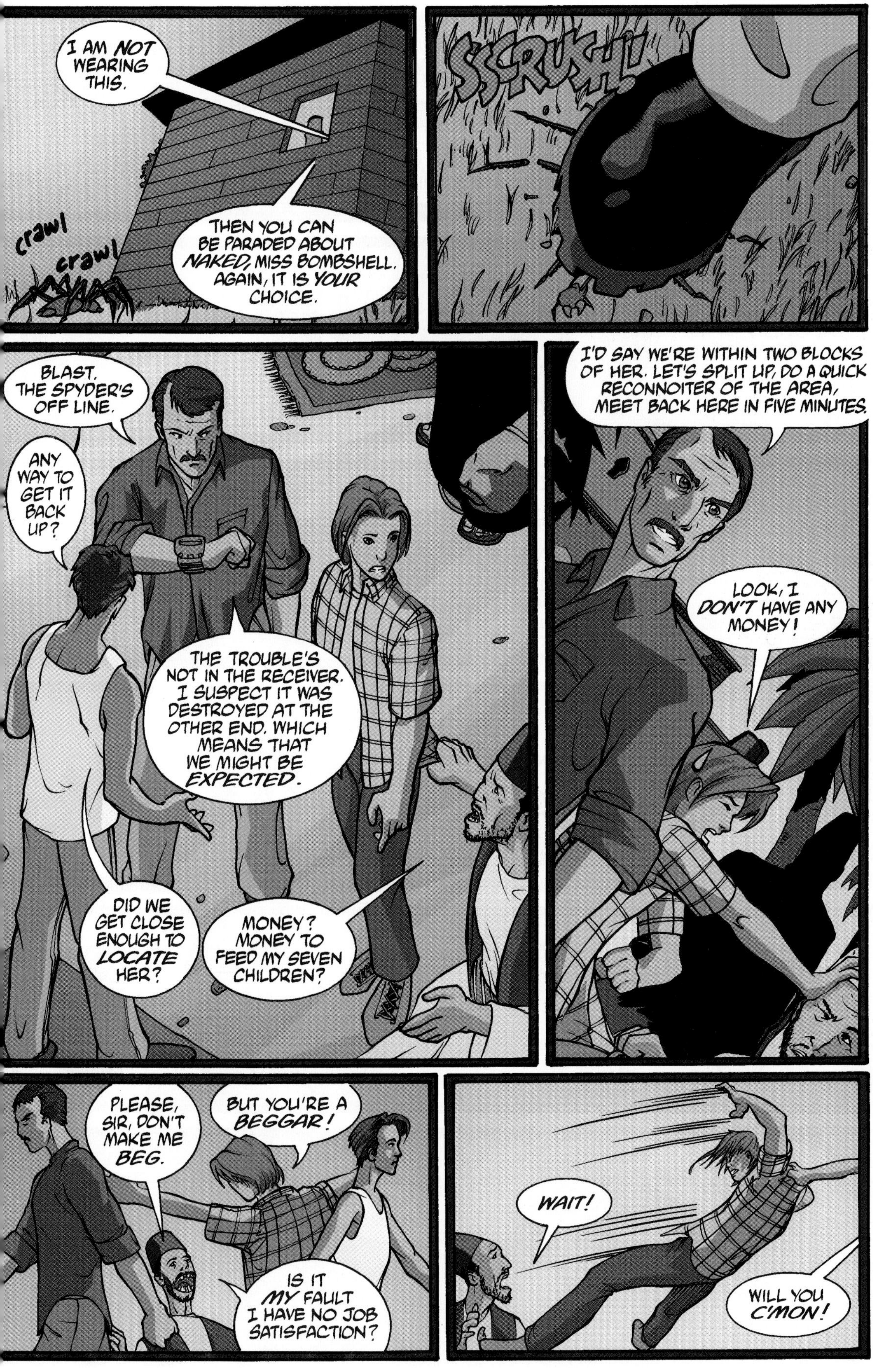
I AM NOT WEARING THIS.
THEN YOU CAN BE PARADED ABOUT NAKED, MISS BOMBSHELL. AGAIN, IT IS YOUR CHOICE.
crawl
crawl
SSCRUSH!
BLAST. THE SPYDER'S OFF LINE.
ANY WAY TO GET IT BACK UP?
THE TROUBLE'S NOT IN THE RECEIVER. I SUSPECT IT WAS DESTROYED AT THE OTHER END. WHICH MEANS THAT WE MIGHT BE EXPECTED.
DID WE GET CLOSE ENOUGH TO LOCATE HER?
MONEY? MONEY TO FEED MY SEVEN CHILDREN?
I'D SAY WE'RE WITHIN TWO BLOCKS OF HER. LET'S SPLIT UP, DO A QUICK RECONNOITER OF THE AREA, MEET BACK HERE IN FIVE MINUTES.
LOOK, I DON'T HAVE ANY MONEY!
PLEASE, SIR, DON'T MAKE ME BEG.
BUT YOU'RE A BEGGAR!
IS IT MY FAULT I HAVE NO JOB SATISFACTION?
WAIT!
WILL YOU C'MON!

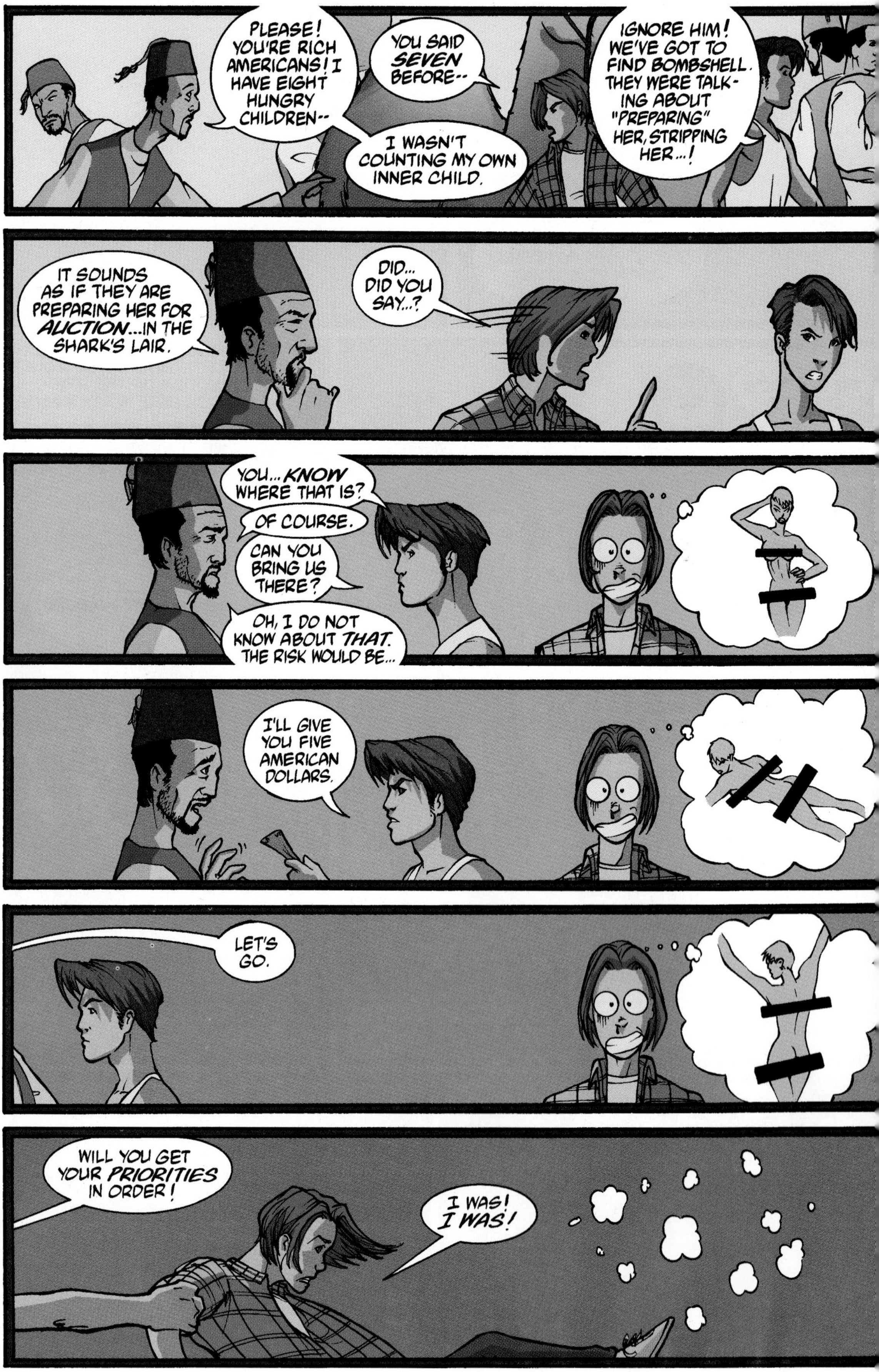
PLEASE! YOU'RE RICH AMERICANS! I HAVE EIGHT HUNGRY CHILDREN--
YOU SAID SEVEN BEFORE--
I WASN'T COUNTING MY OWN INNER CHILD.
IGNORE HIM! WE'VE GOT TO FIND BOMBSHELL. THEY WERE TALKING ABOUT "PREPARING" HER, STRIPPING HER...!
IT SOUNDS AS IF THEY ARE PREPARING HER FOR AUCTION...IN THE SHARK'S LAIR.
DID... DID YOU SAY...?
YOU...KNOW WHERE THAT IS?
OF COURSE.
CAN YOU BRING US THERE?
OH, I DO NOT KNOW ABOUT THAT. THE RISK WOULD BE...
I'LL GIVE YOU FIVE AMERICAN DOLLARS.
LET'S GO.
WILL YOU GET YOUR PRIORITIES IN ORDER!
I WAS! I WAS!

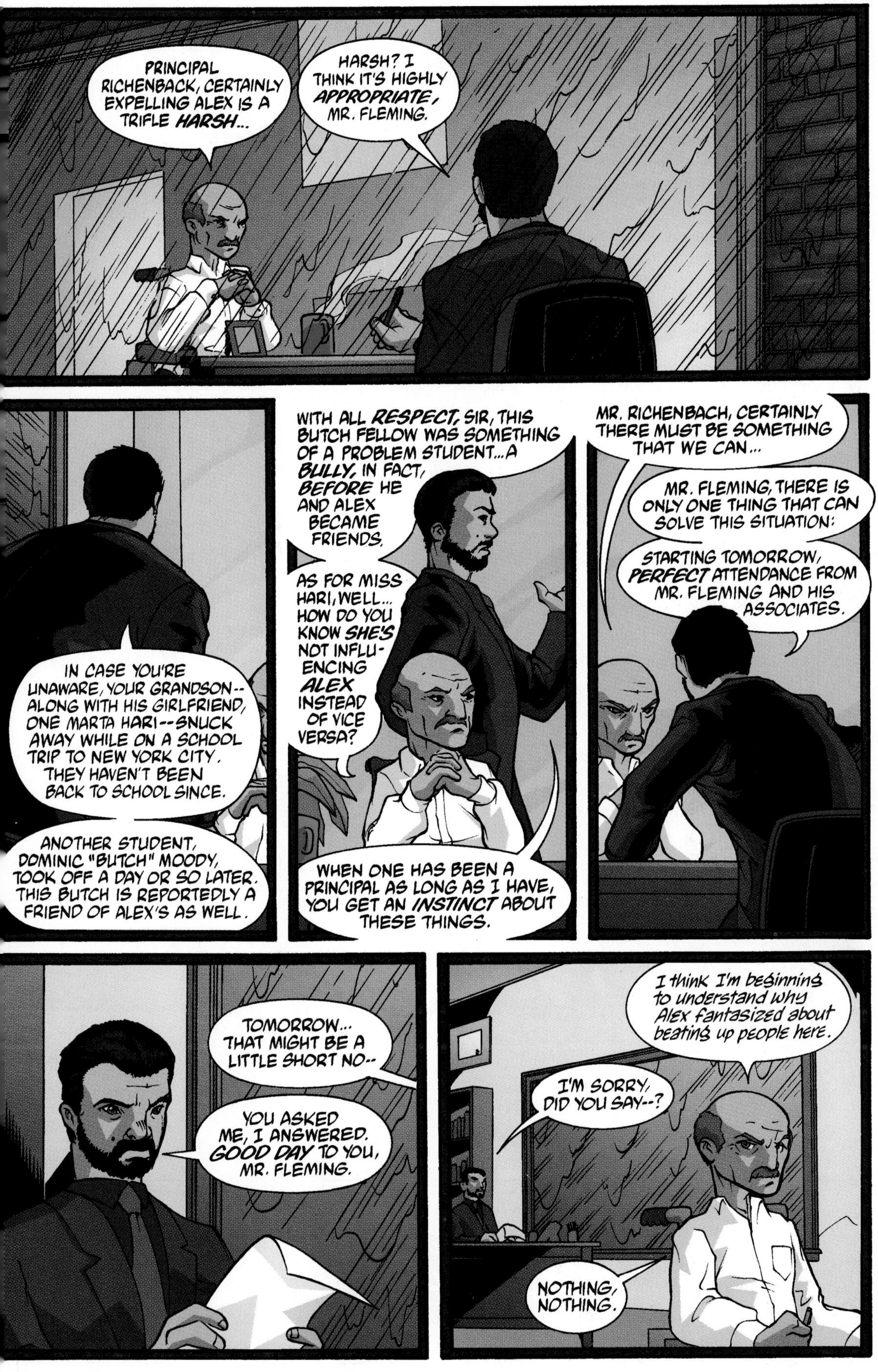
PRINCIPAL RICHENBACK, CERTAINLY EXPELLING ALEX IS A TRIFLE HARSH...
HARSH? I THINK IT'S HIGHLY APPROPRIATE, MR. FLEMING.
IN CASE YOU'RE UNAWARE, YOUR GRANDSON--ALONG WITH HIS GIRLFRIEND, ONE MARTA HARI--SNUCK AWAY WHILE ON A SCHOOL TRIP TO NEW YORK CITY. THEY HAVEN'T BEEN BACK TO SCHOOL SINCE.
ANOTHER STUDENT, DOMINIC "BUTCH" MOODY, TOOK OFF A DAY OR SO LATER. THIS BUTCH IS REPORTEDLY A FRIEND OF ALEX'S AS WELL.
WITH ALL RESPECT, SIR, THIS BUTCH FELLOW WAS SOMETHING OF A PROBLEM STUDENT...A BULLY, IN FACT, BEFORE HE AND ALEX BECAME FRIENDS.
AS FOR MISS HARI, WELL... HOW DO YOU KNOW SHE'S NOT INFLU-ENCING ALEX INSTEAD OF VICE VERSA?
WHEN ONE HAS BEEN A PRINCIPAL AS LONG AS I HAVE, YOU GET AN INSTINCT ABOUT THESE THINGS.
MR. RICHENBACH, CERTAINLY THERE MUST BE SOMETHING THAT WE CAN...
MR. FLEMING, THERE IS ONLY ONE THING THAT CAN SOLVE THIS SITUATION:
STARTING TOMORROW, PERFECT ATTENDANCE FROM MR. FLEMING AND HIS ASSOCIATES.
TOMORROW... THAT MIGHT BE A LITTLE SHORT NO--
YOU ASKED ME, I ANSWERED. GOOD DAY TO YOU, MR. FLEMING.
I think I'm beginning to understand why Alex fantasized about beating up people here.
I'M SORRY, DID YOU SAY--?
NOTHING, NOTHING.

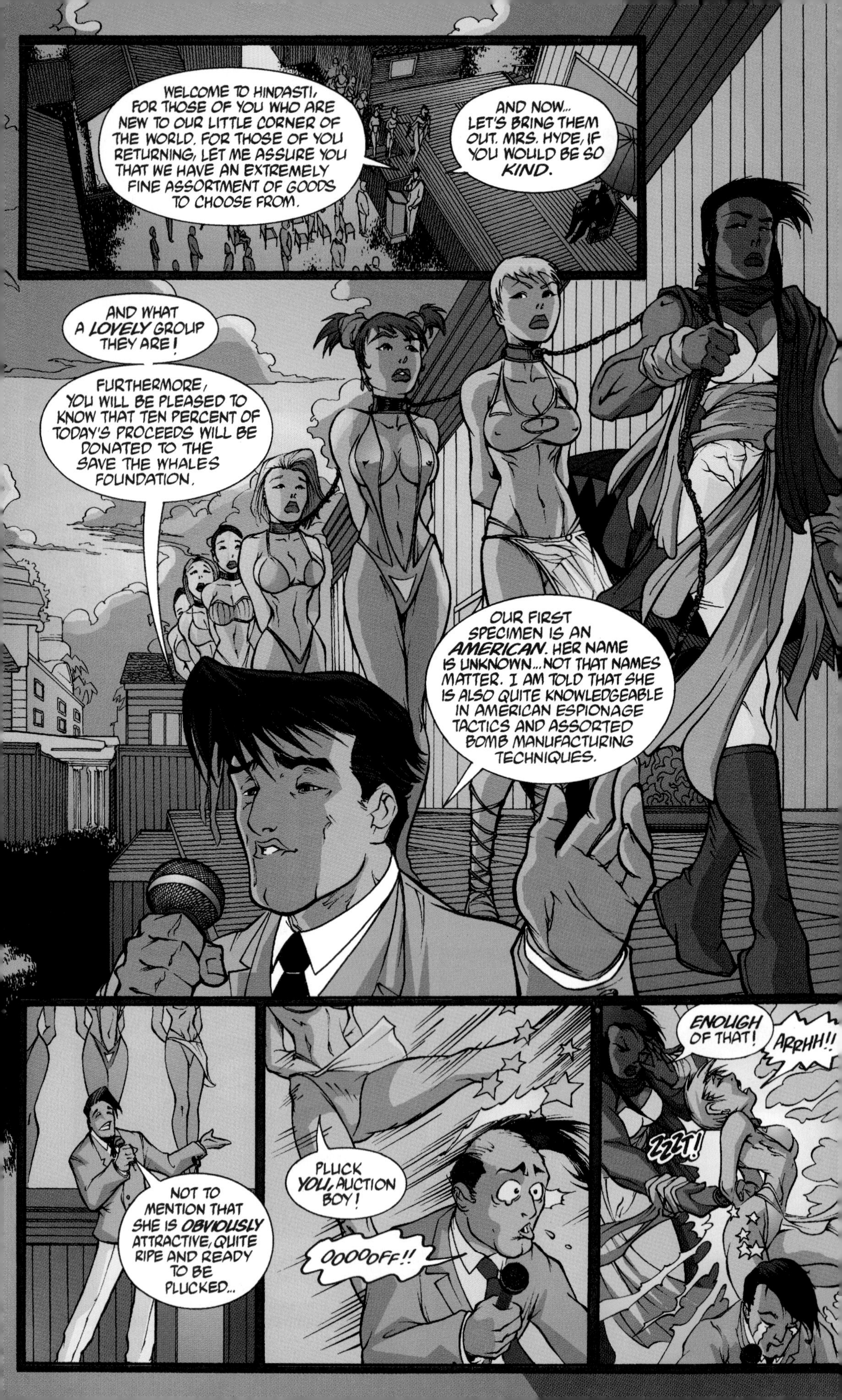
WELCOME TO HINDASTI, FOR THOSE OF YOU WHO ARE NEW TO OUR LITTLE CORNER OF THE WORLD. FOR THOSE OF YOU RETURNING, LET ME ASSURE YOU THAT WE HAVE AN EXTREMELY FINE ASSORTMENT OF GOODS TO CHOOSE FROM.
AND NOW... LET'S BRING THEM OUT. MRS. HYDE, IF YOU WOULD BE SO KIND.
AND WHAT A LOVELY GROUP THEY ARE!
FURTHERMORE, YOU WILL BE PLEASED TO KNOW THAT TEN PERCENT OF TODAY'S PROCEEDS WILL BE DONATED TO THE SAVE THE WHALES FOUNDATION.
OUR FIRST SPECIMEN IS AN AMERICAN. HER NAME IS UNKNOWN...NOT THAT NAMES MATTER. I AM TOLD THAT SHE IS ALSO QUITE KNOWLEDGEABLE IN AMERICAN ESPIONAGE TACTICS AND ASSORTED BOMB MANUFACTURING TECHNIQUES.
NOT TO MENTION THAT SHE IS OBVIOUSLY ATTRACTIVE, QUITE RIPE AND READY TO BE PLUCKED...
PLUCK YOU, AUCTION BOY!
OOOOOFF!!
ENOUGH OF THAT!
ARRHH!!
ZZZT!

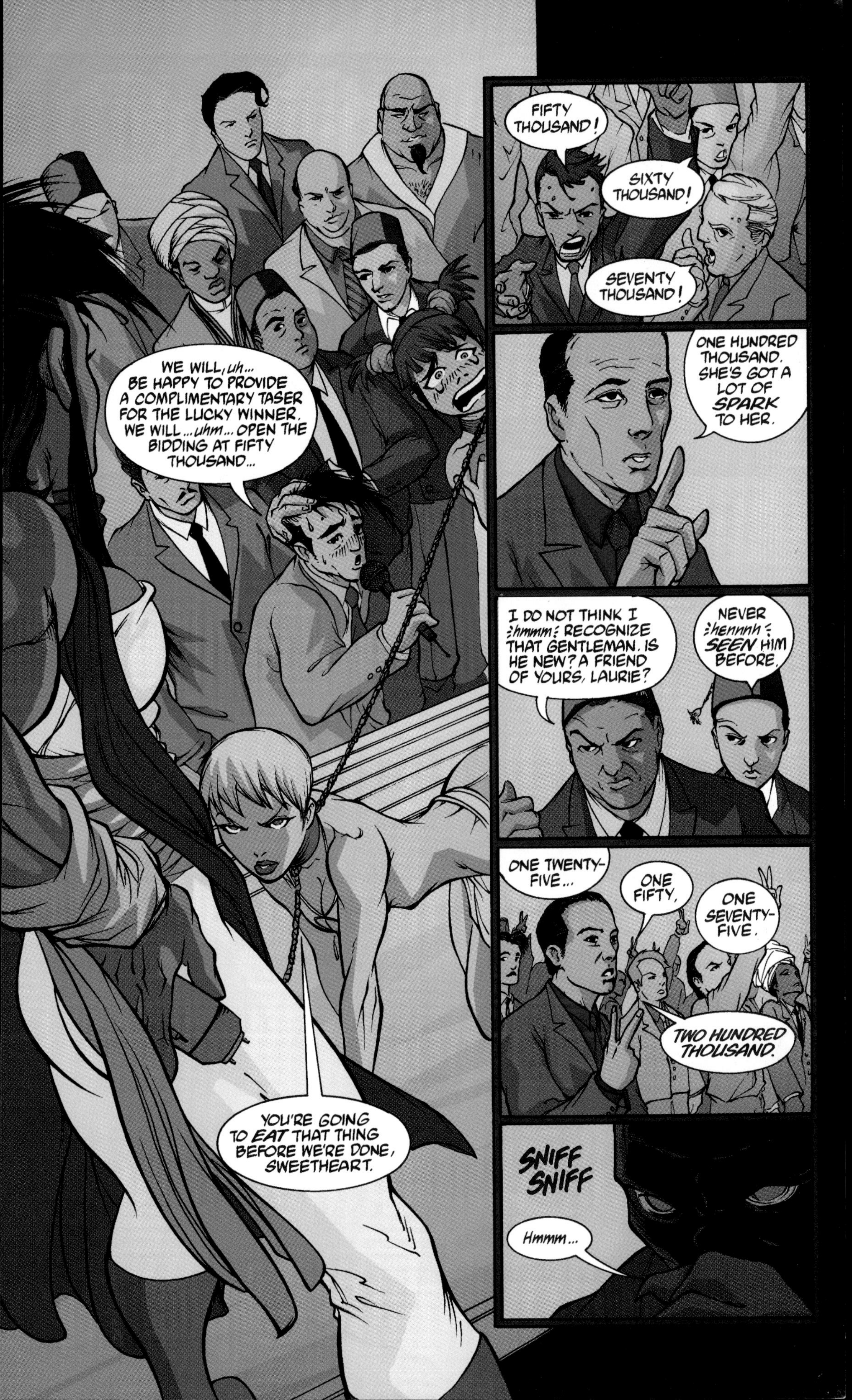
WE WILL, uh... BE HAPPY TO PROVIDE A COMPLIMENTARY TASER FOR THE LUCKY WINNER. WE WILL ...uhm... OPEN THE BIDDING AT FIFTY THOUSAND...
YOU'RE GOING TO EAT THAT THING BEFORE WE'RE DONE, SWEETHEART.
FIFTY THOUSAND!
SIXTY THOUSAND!
SEVENTY THOUSAND!
ONE HUNDRED THOUSAND. SHE'S GOT A LOT OF SPARK TO HER.
I DO NOT THINK I hmmm RECOGNIZE THAT GENTLEMAN. IS HE NEW? A FRIEND OF YOURS, LAURIE?
NEVER hennnh SEEN HIM BEFORE.
ONE TWENTY-FIVE...
ONE FIFTY,
ONE SEVENTY-FIVE.
TWO HUNDRED THOUSAND.
SNIFF SNIFF
Hmmm...

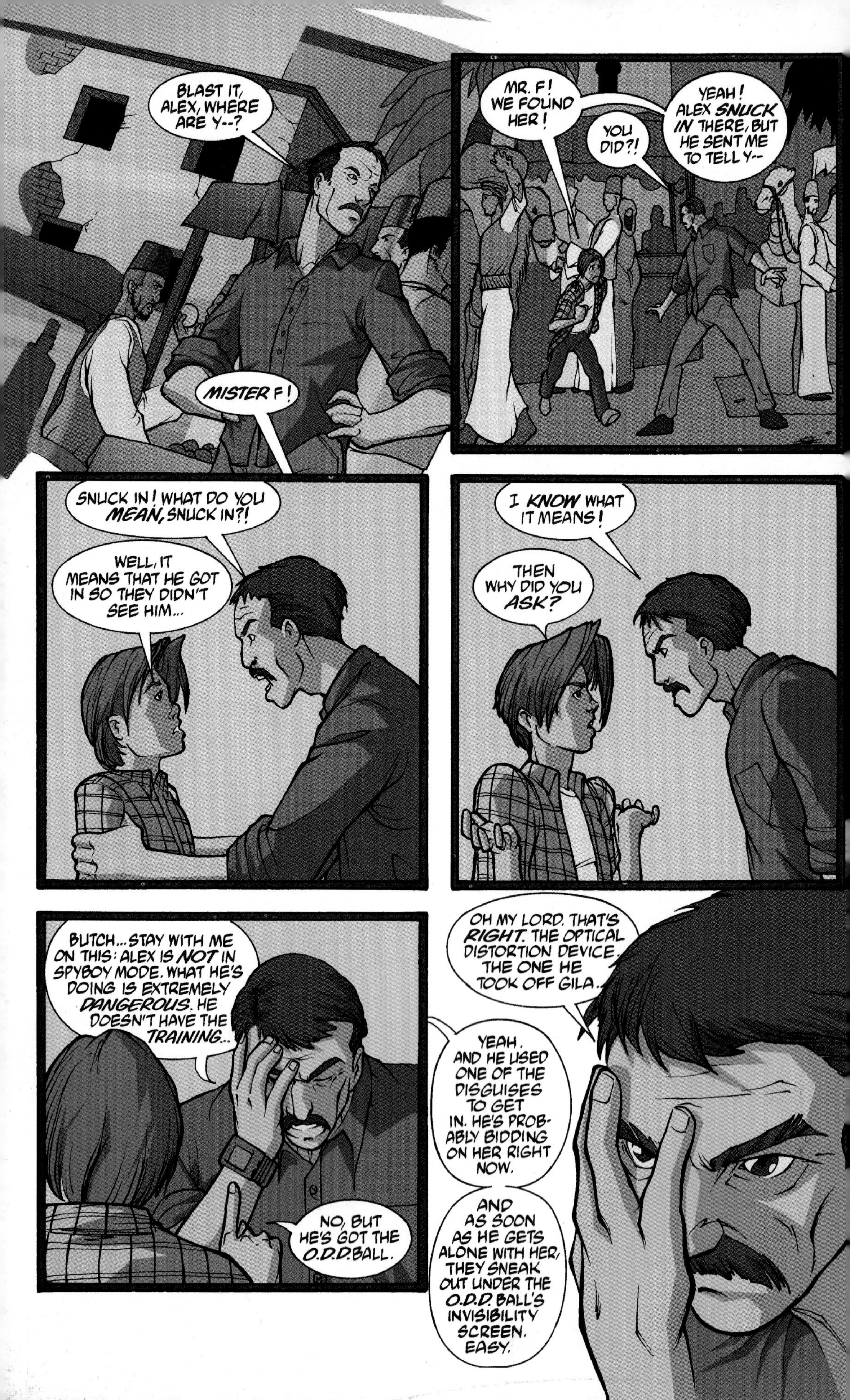

BLAST IT, ALEX, WHERE ARE Y--?
MISTER F!
MR. F! WE FOUND HER!
YOU DID?!
YEAH! ALEX SNUCK IN THERE, BUT HE SENT ME TO TELL Y--
SNUCK IN! WHAT DO YOU MEAN, SNUCK IN?!
WELL, IT MEANS THAT HE GOT IN SO THEY DIDN'T SEE HIM...
I KNOW WHAT IT MEANS!
THEN WHY DID YOU ASK?
BUTCH... STAY WITH ME ON THIS: ALEX IS NOT IN SPYBOY MODE. WHAT HE'S DOING IS EXTREMELY DANGEROUS. HE DOESN'T HAVE THE TRAINING...
NO, BUT HE'S GOT THE O.D.D. BALL.
OH MY LORD. THAT'S RIGHT. THE OPTICAL DISTORTION DEVICE. THE ONE HE TOOK OFF GILA...
YEAH. AND HE USED ONE OF THE DISGUISES TO GET IN. HE'S PROBABLY BIDDING ON HER RIGHT NOW.
AND AS SOON AS HE GETS ALONE WITH HER, THEY SNEAK OUT UNDER THE O.D.D. BALL'S INVISIBILITY SCREEN. EASY.

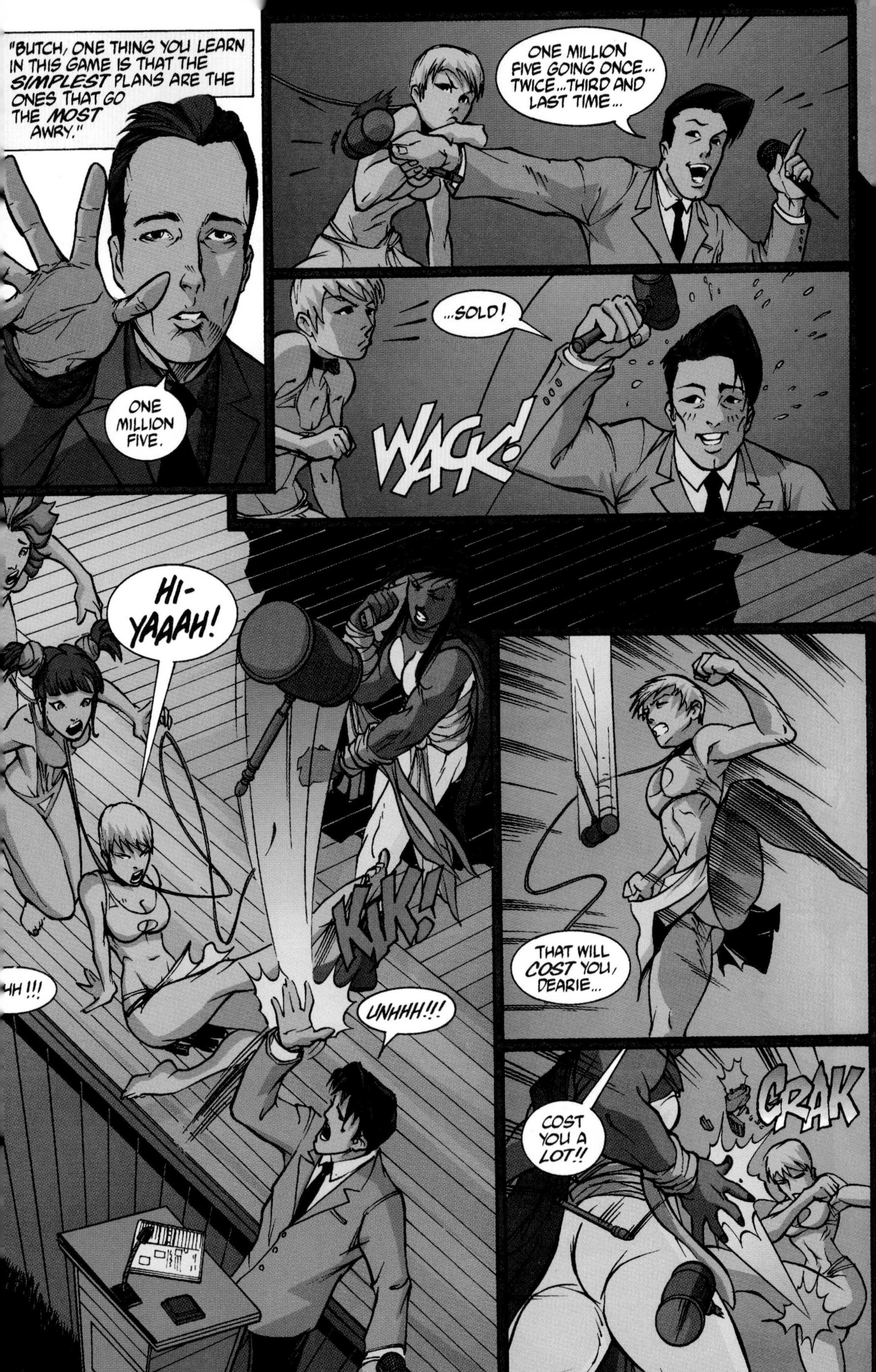

"BUTCH, ONE THING YOU LEARN IN THIS GAME IS THAT THE SIMPLEST PLANS ARE THE ONES THAT GO THE MOST AWRY."
ONE MILLION FIVE.
ONE MILLION FIVE GOING ONCE... TWICE...THIRD AND LAST TIME...
...SOLD!
WACK!
HI-YAAAH!
KIK!
UNHHH!!!
THAT WILL COST YOU, DEARIE...
COST YOU A LOT!!
CRAK

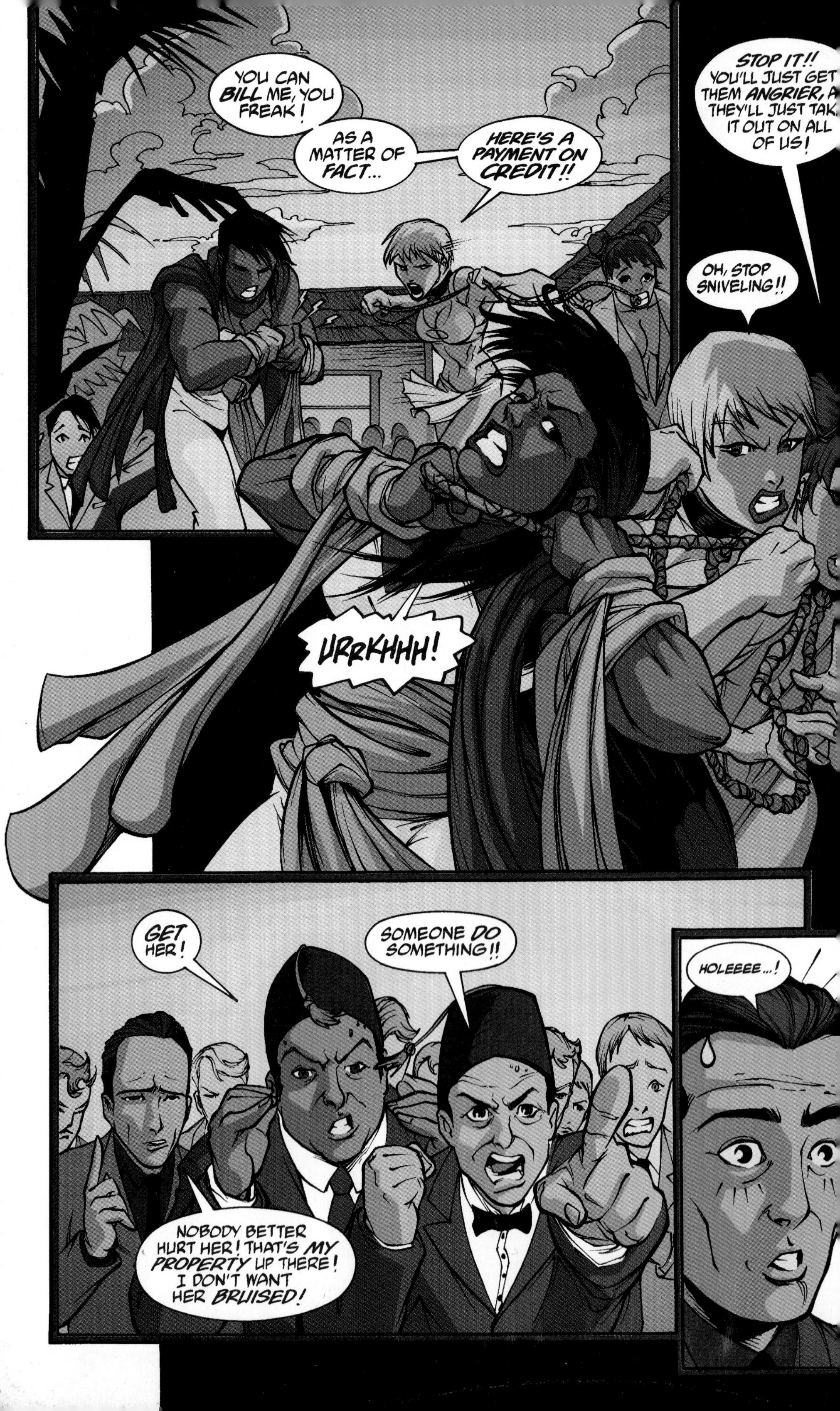
YOU CAN BILL ME, YOU FREAK!
AS A MATTER OF FACT...
HERE'S A PAYMENT ON CREDIT!!
STOP IT!! YOU'LL JUST GET THEM ANGRIER, A THEY'LL JUST TAK IT OUT ON ALL OF US!
OH, STOP SNIVELING!!
URRKHHH!
GET HER!
SOMEONE DO SOMETHING!!
NOBODY BETTER HURT HER! THAT'S MY PROPERTY UP THERE! I DON'T WANT HER BRUISED!
HOLEEEE...!

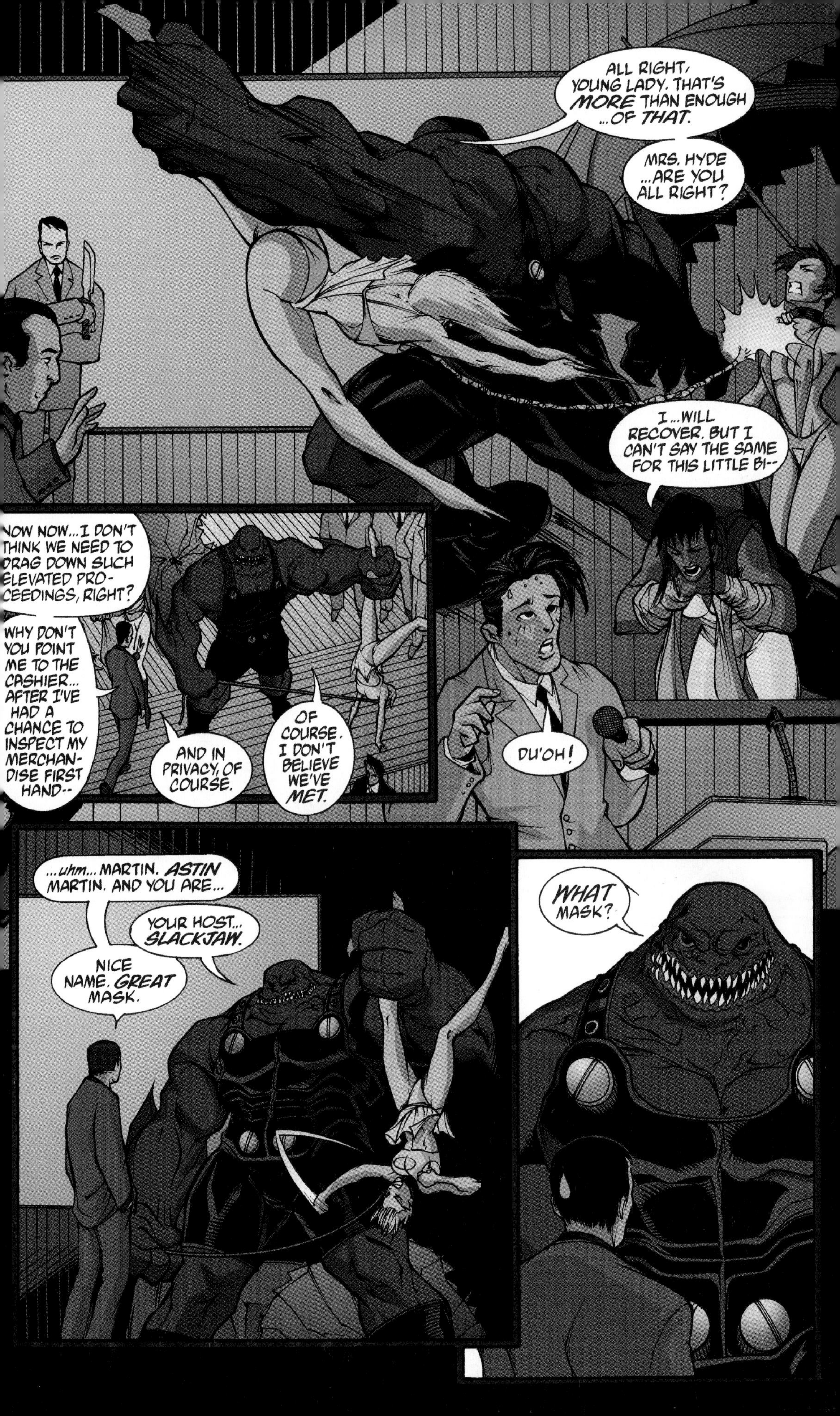
ALL RIGHT, YOUNG LADY. THAT'S MORE THAN ENOUGH ...OF THAT.
MRS. HYDE ...ARE YOU ALL RIGHT?
I...WILL RECOVER. BUT I CAN'T SAY THE SAME FOR THIS LITTLE BI--
NOW NOW...I DON'T THINK WE NEED TO DRAG DOWN SUCH ELEVATED PRO-CEEDINGS, RIGHT?
WHY DON'T YOU POINT ME TO THE CASHIER... AFTER I'VE HAD A CHANCE TO INSPECT MY MERCHAN-DISE FIRST HAND--
AND IN PRIVACY, OF COURSE.
OF COURSE. I DON'T BELIEVE WE'VE MET.
DU'OH!
...uhm... MARTIN. ASTIN MARTIN. AND YOU ARE...
YOUR HOST... SLACKJAW.
NICE NAME. GREAT MASK.
WHAT MASK?

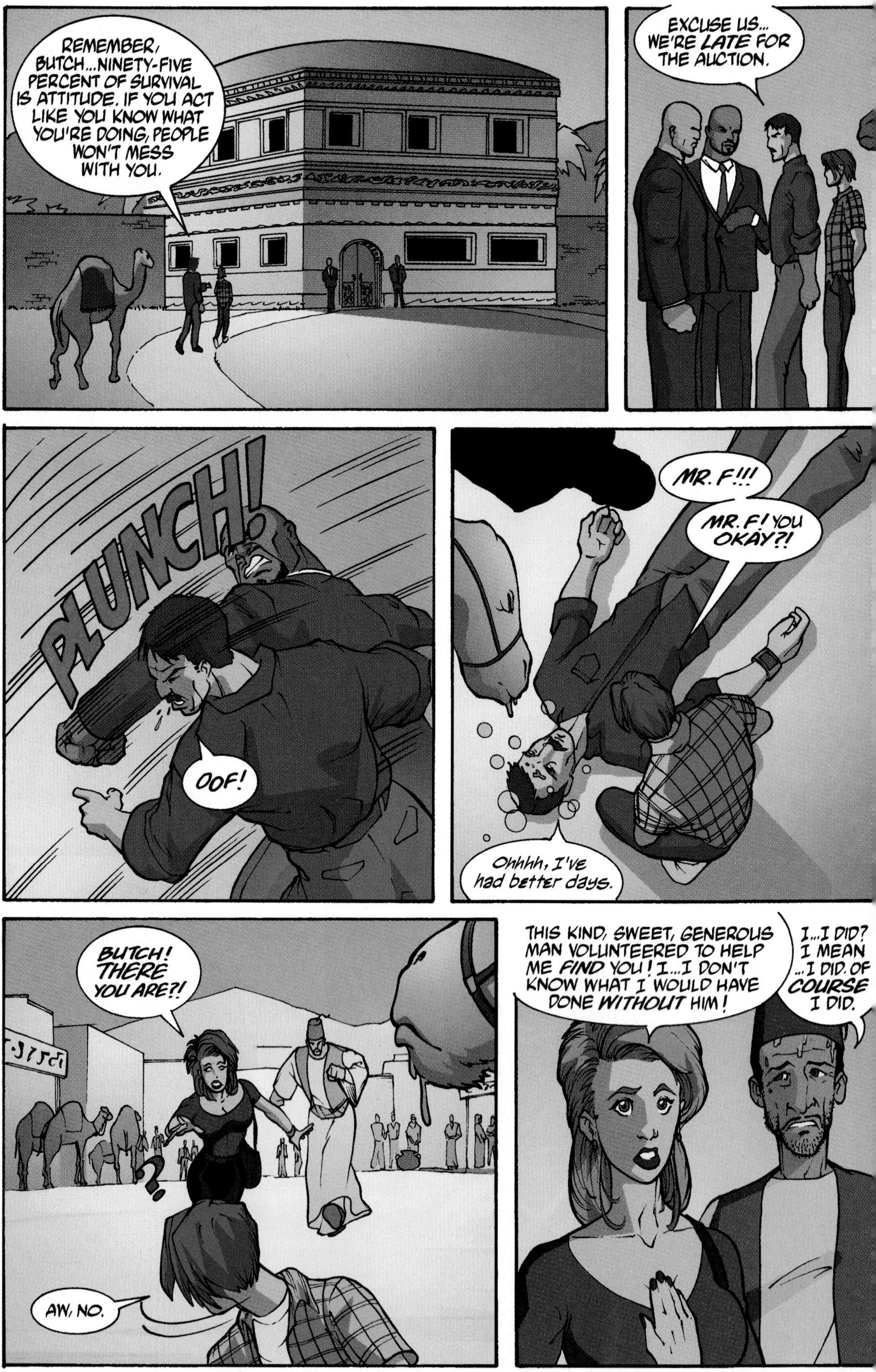
REMEMBER, BUTCH...NINETY-FIVE PERCENT OF SURVIVAL IS ATTITUDE. IF YOU ACT LIKE YOU KNOW WHAT YOU'RE DOING, PEOPLE WON'T MESS WITH YOU.
EXCUSE US... WE'RE LATE FOR THE AUCTION.
PLUNCH!
OOF!
MR. F!!!
MR. F! YOU OKAY?!
Ohhhh, I've had better days.
BUTCH! THERE YOU ARE?!
AW, NO.
THIS KIND, SWEET, GENEROUS MAN VOLUNTEERED TO HELP ME FIND YOU! I...I DON'T KNOW WHAT I WOULD HAVE DONE WITHOUT HIM!
I...I DID? I MEAN ...I DID. OF COURSE I DID.

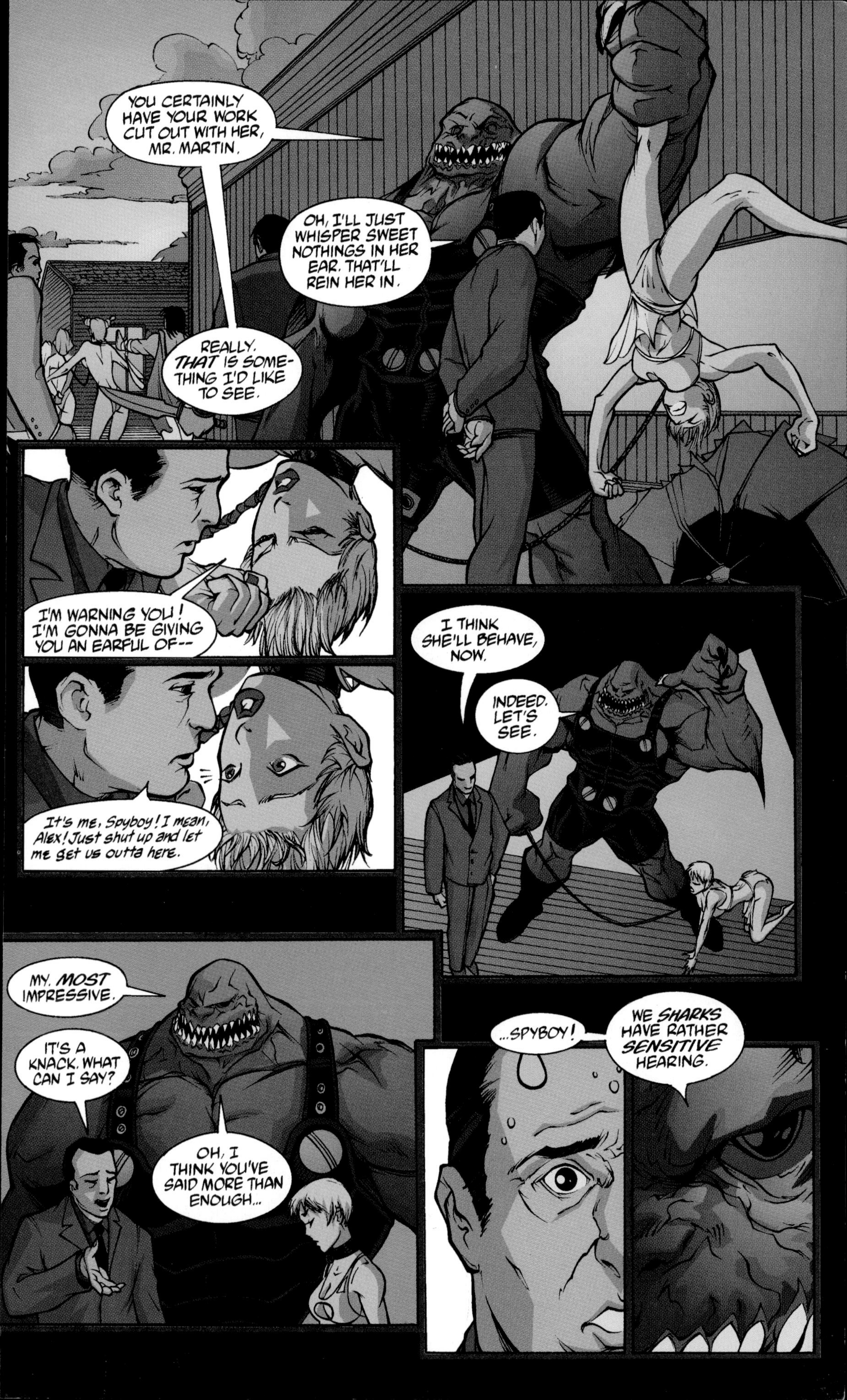
YOU CERTAINLY HAVE YOUR WORK CUT OUT WITH HER, MR. MARTIN.
OH, I'LL JUST WHISPER SWEET NOTHINGS IN HER EAR. THAT'LL REIN HER IN.
REALLY. THAT IS SOMETHING I'D LIKE TO SEE.
I'M WARNING YOU! I'M GONNA BE GIVING YOU AN EARFUL OF--
It's me, Spyboy! I mean, Alex! Just shut up and let me get us outta here.
I THINK SHE'LL BEHAVE, NOW.
INDEED. LET'S SEE.
MY. MOST IMPRESSIVE.
IT'S A KNACK. WHAT CAN I SAY?
OH, I THINK YOU'VE SAID MORE THAN ENOUGH...
...SPYBOY!
WE SHARKS HAVE RATHER SENSITIVE HEARING.

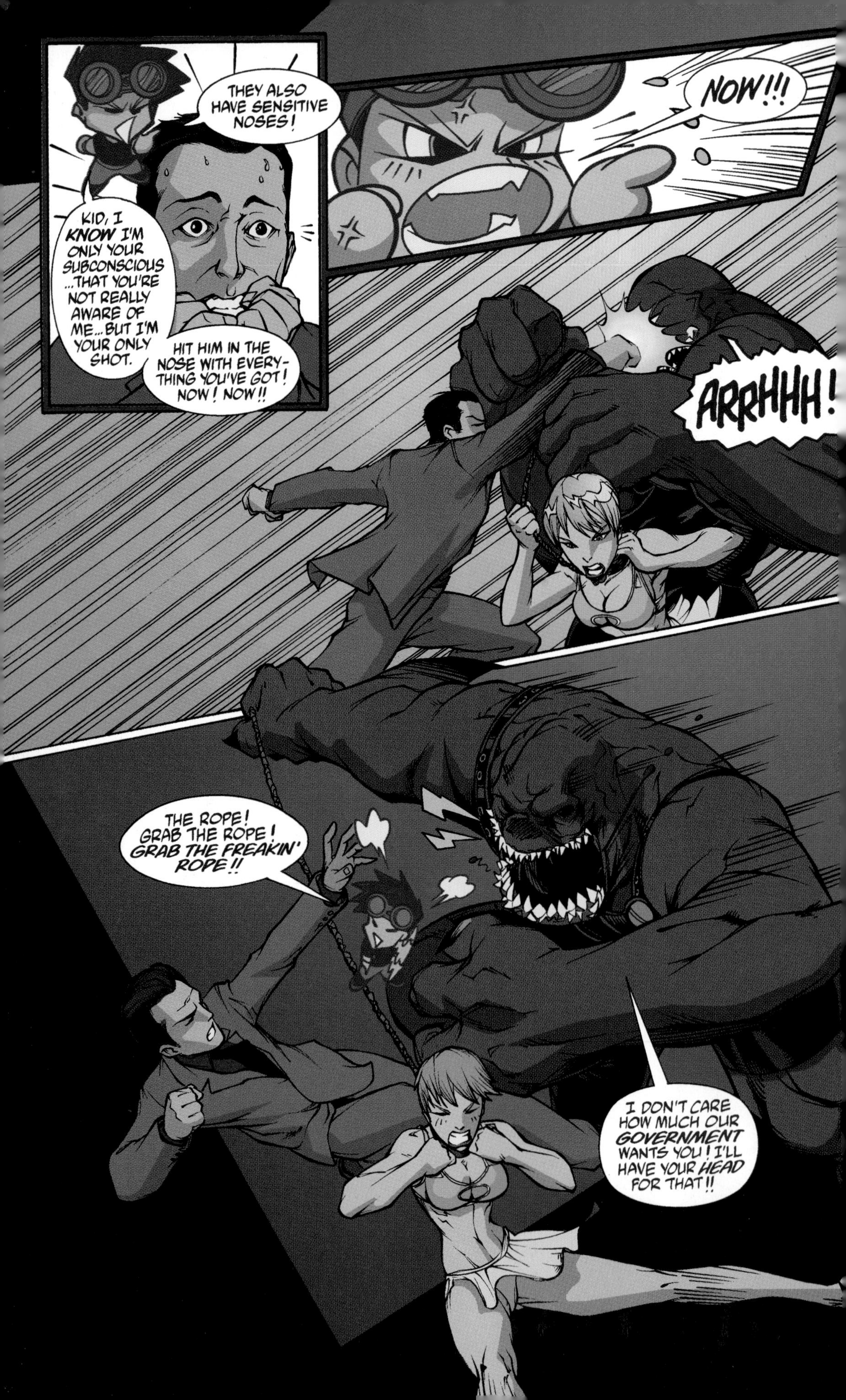
THEY ALSO HAVE SENSITIVE NOSES!
KID, I **KNOW** I'M ONLY YOUR SUBCONSCIOUS ...THAT YOU'RE NOT REALLY AWARE OF ME... BUT I'M YOUR ONLY SHOT.
HIT HIM IN THE NOSE WITH EVERYTHING YOU'VE GOT! NOW! NOW!!
NOW!!!
ARRHHH!
THE ROPE! GRAB THE ROPE! **GRAB THE FREAKIN' ROPE!!**
I DON'T CARE HOW MUCH OUR **GOVERNMENT** WANTS YOU! I'LL HAVE YOUR **HEAD** FOR THAT!!

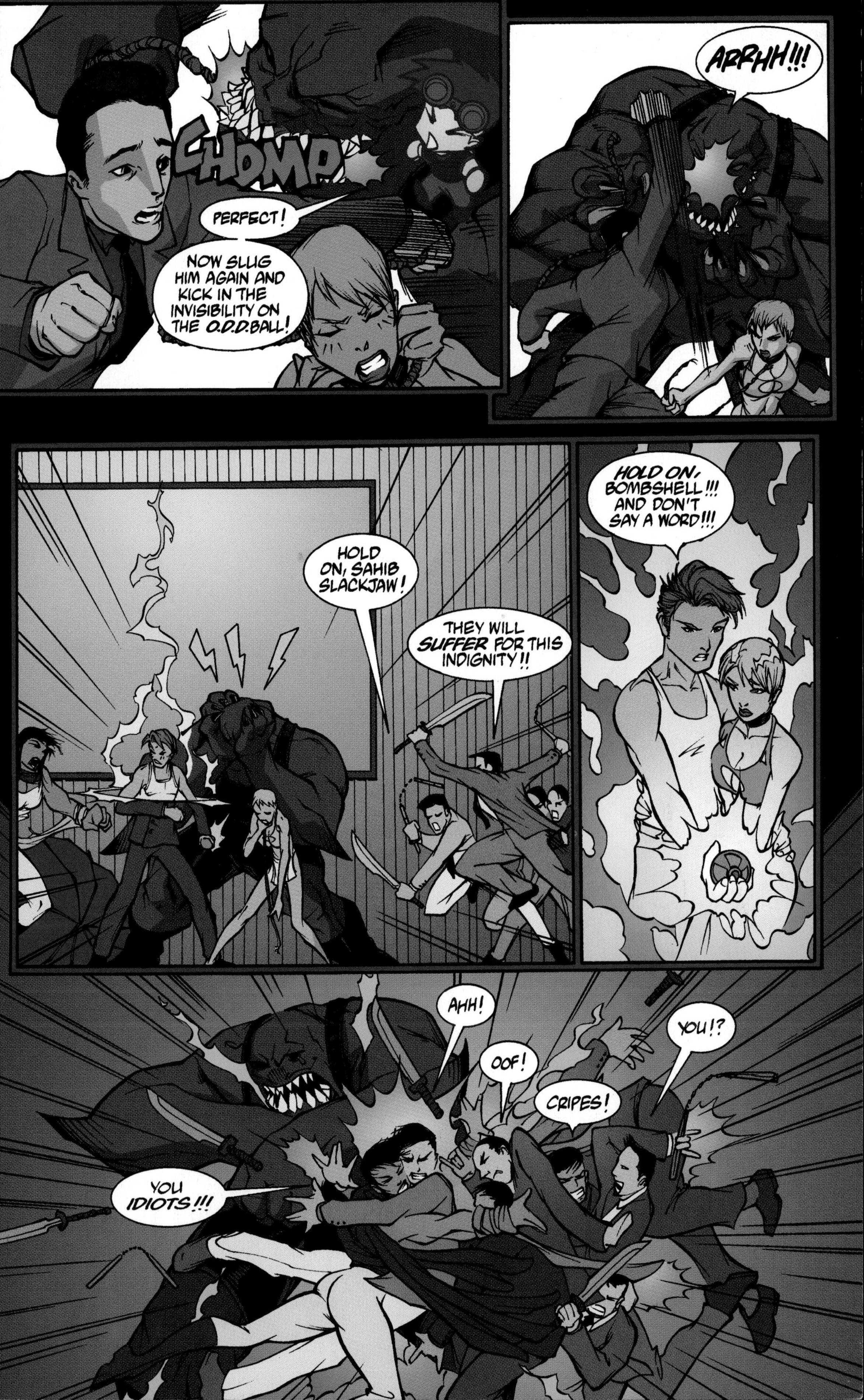
CHOMP
PERFECT!
NOW SLUG HIM AGAIN AND KICK IN THE INVISIBILITY ON THE O.D.D.BALL!
ARRHH!!!
HOLD ON, SAHIB SLACKJAW!
THEY WILL SUFFER FOR THIS INDIGNITY!!
HOLD ON, BOMBSHELL!!! AND DON'T SAY A WORD!!!
AHH!
OOF!
YOU!?
CRIPES!
YOU IDIOTS!!!

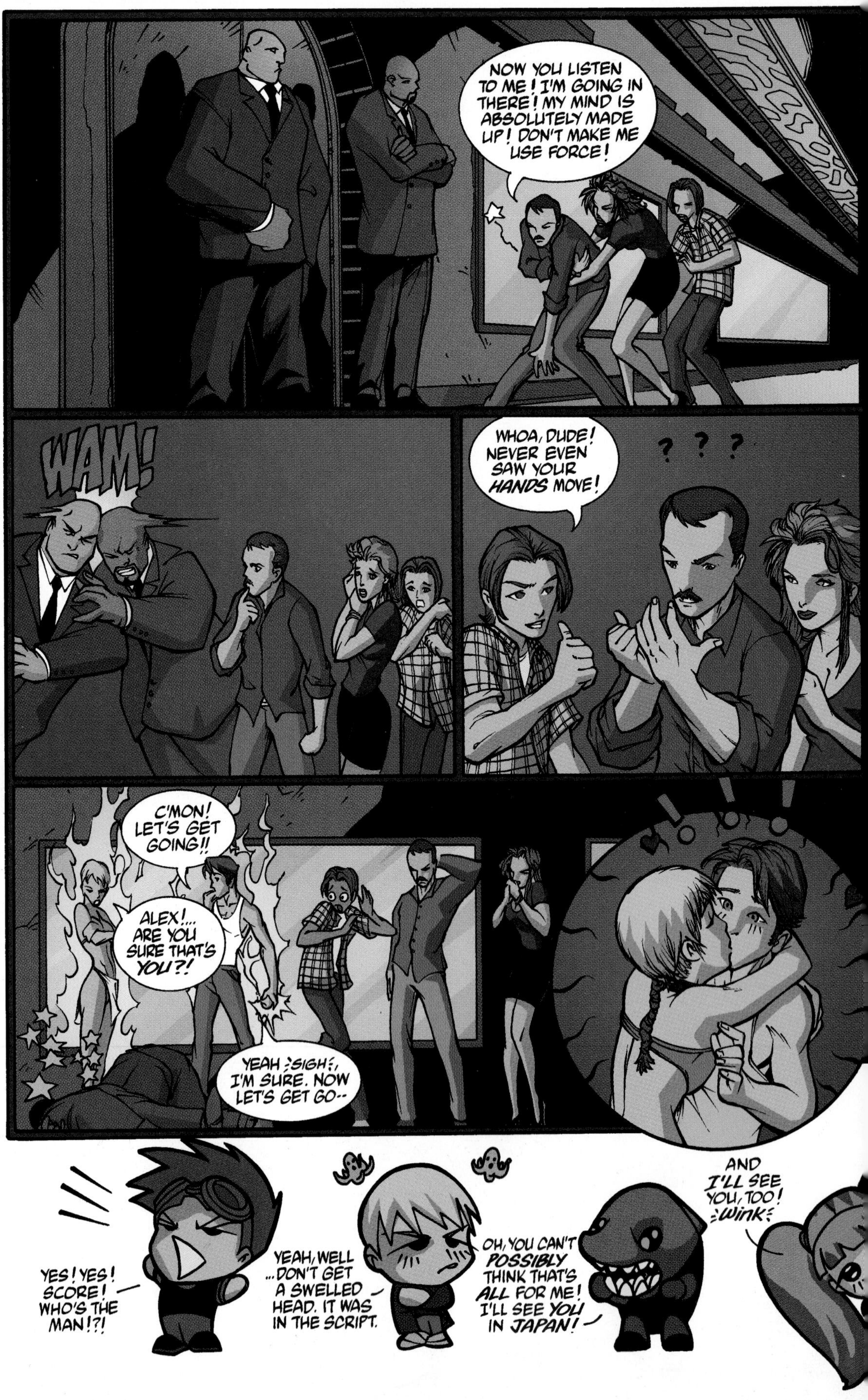

NOW YOU LISTEN TO ME! I'M GOING IN THERE! MY MIND IS ABSOLUTELY MADE UP! DON'T MAKE ME USE FORCE!
WAM!
WHOA, DUDE! NEVER EVEN SAW YOUR HANDS MOVE!
? ? ?
C'MON! LET'S GET GOING!!
ALEX!... ARE YOU SURE THAT'S YOU?!
YEAH :SIGH:, I'M SURE. NOW LET'S GET GO--
YES! YES! SCORE! WHO'S THE MAN!?!
YEAH, WELL ...DON'T GET A SWELLED HEAD. IT WAS IN THE SCRIPT.
OH, YOU CAN'T POSSIBLY THINK THAT'S ALL FOR ME! I'LL SEE YOU IN JAPAN!
AND I'LL SEE YOU, TOO! :Wink:

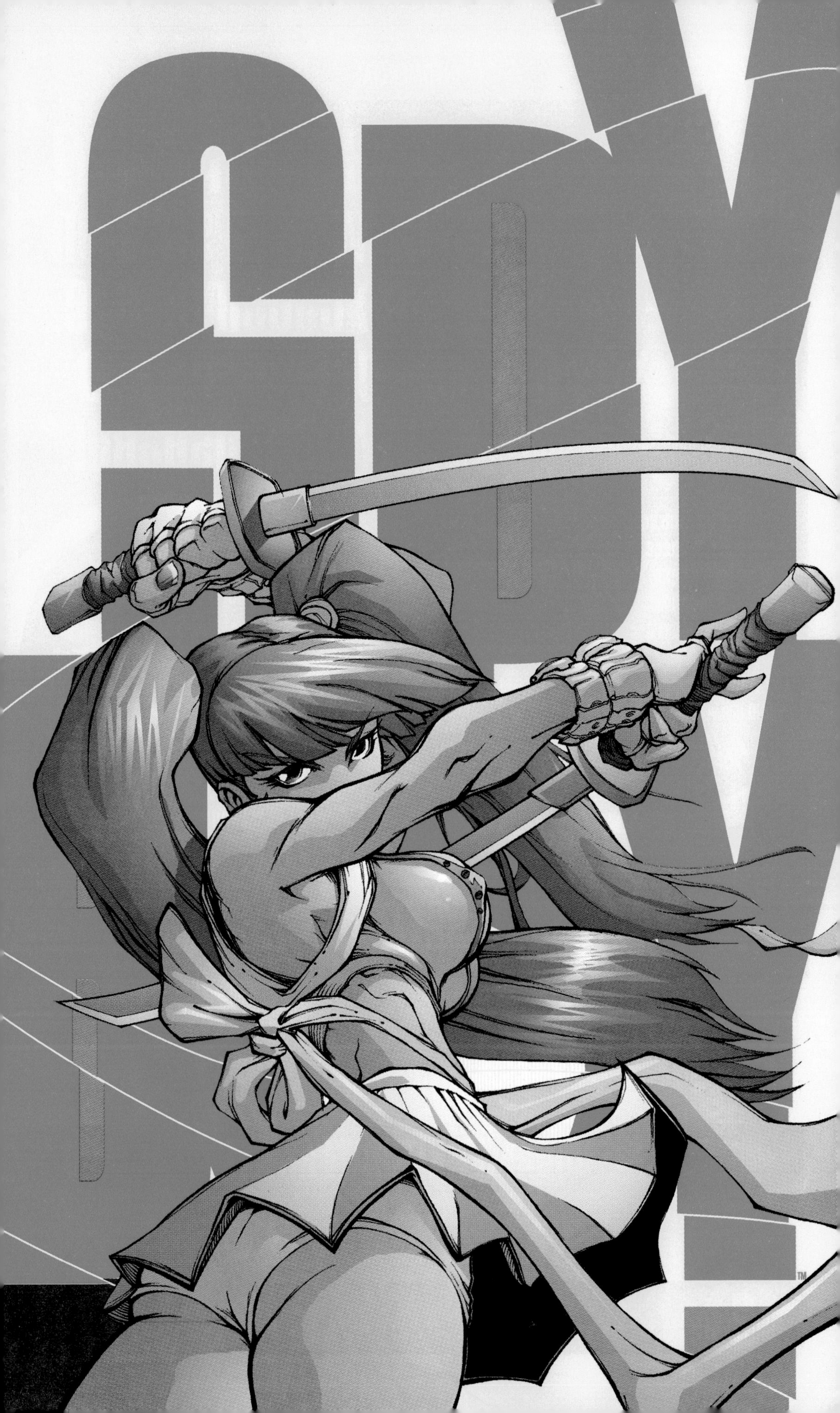

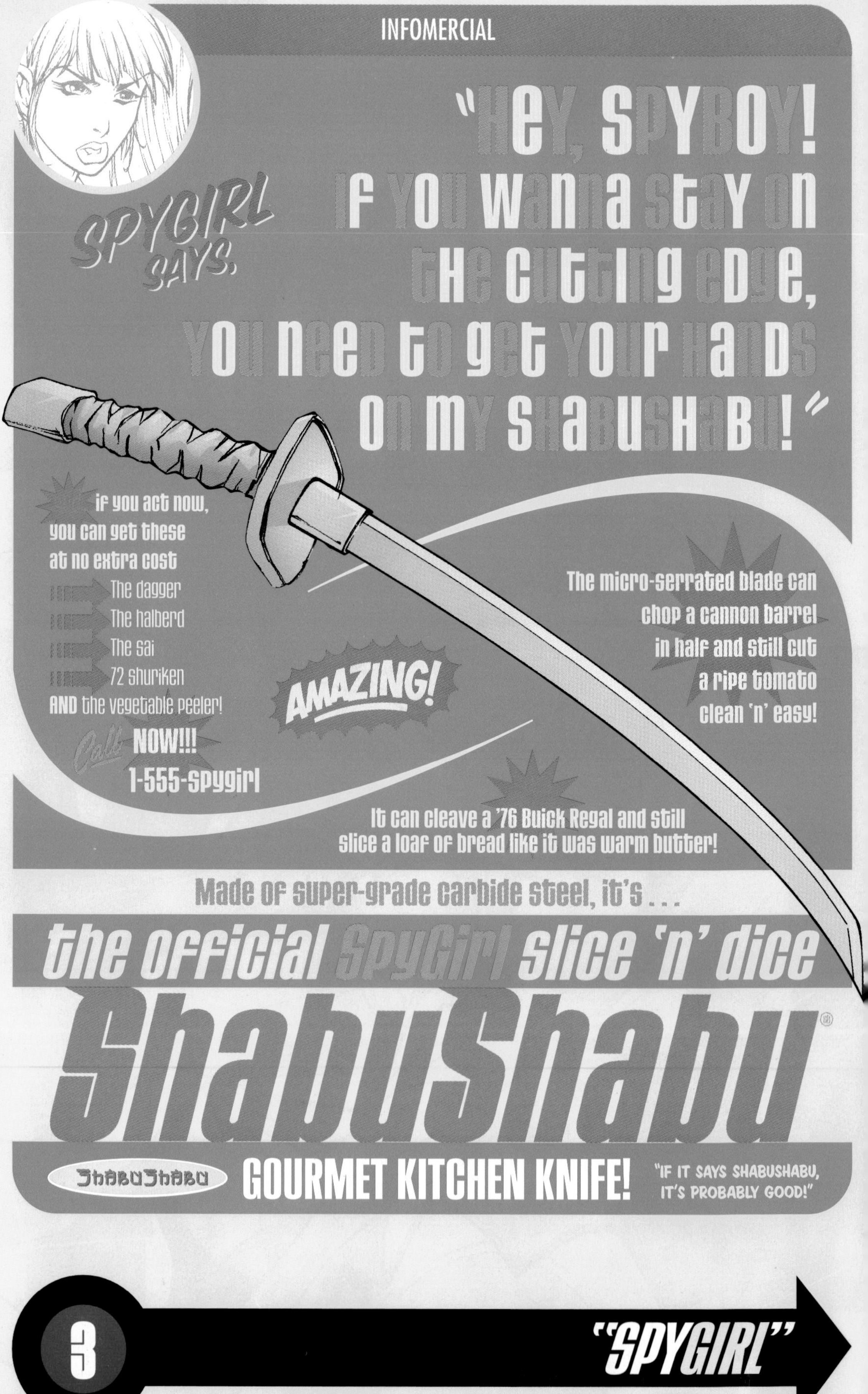
INFOMERCIAL
SPYGIRL SAYS,
"HEY, SPYBOY! IF YOU WANNA STAY ON THE CUTTING EDGE, YOU NEED TO GET YOUR HANDS ON MY SHABUSHABU!"
if you act now, you can get these at no extra cost
The dagger
The halberd
The sai
72 shuriken
AND the vegetable peeler!
Call NOW!!! 1-555-spygirl
AMAZING!
The micro-serrated blade can chop a cannon barrel in half and still cut a ripe tomato clean 'n' easy!
It can cleave a '76 Buick Regal and still slice a loaf of bread like it was warm butter!
Made of super-grade carbide steel, it's . . .
the official SpyGirl slice 'n' dice
ShabuShabu®
SHABUSHABU
GOURMET KITCHEN KNIFE!
"IF IT SAYS SHABUSHABU, IT'S PROBABLY GOOD!"
3
"SPYGIRL"

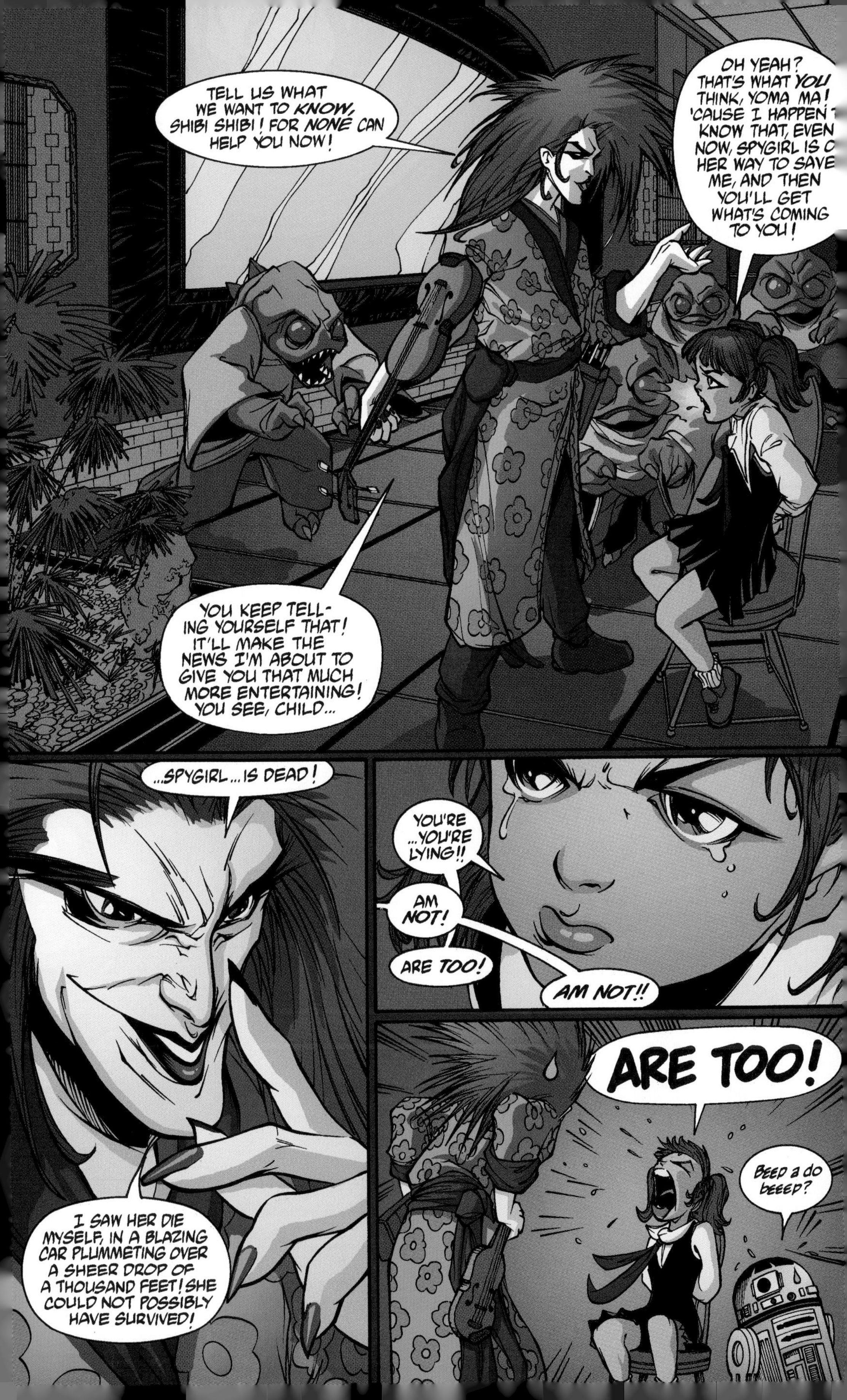
TELL US WHAT WE WANT TO KNOW, SHIBI SHIBI! FOR NONE CAN HELP YOU NOW!
OH YEAH? THAT'S WHAT YOU THINK, YOMA MA! 'CAUSE I HAPPEN TO KNOW THAT, EVEN NOW, SPYGIRL IS ON HER WAY TO SAVE ME, AND THEN YOU'LL GET WHAT'S COMING TO YOU!
YOU KEEP TELL-ING YOURSELF THAT! IT'LL MAKE THE NEWS I'M ABOUT TO GIVE YOU THAT MUCH MORE ENTERTAINING! YOU SEE, CHILD...
...SPYGIRL...IS DEAD!
I SAW HER DIE MYSELF, IN A BLAZING CAR PLUMMETING OVER A SHEER DROP OF A THOUSAND FEET! SHE COULD NOT POSSIBLY HAVE SURVIVED!
YOU'RE ...YOU'RE LYING!!
AM NOT!
ARE TOO!
AM NOT!!
ARE TOO!
Beep a do beeep?

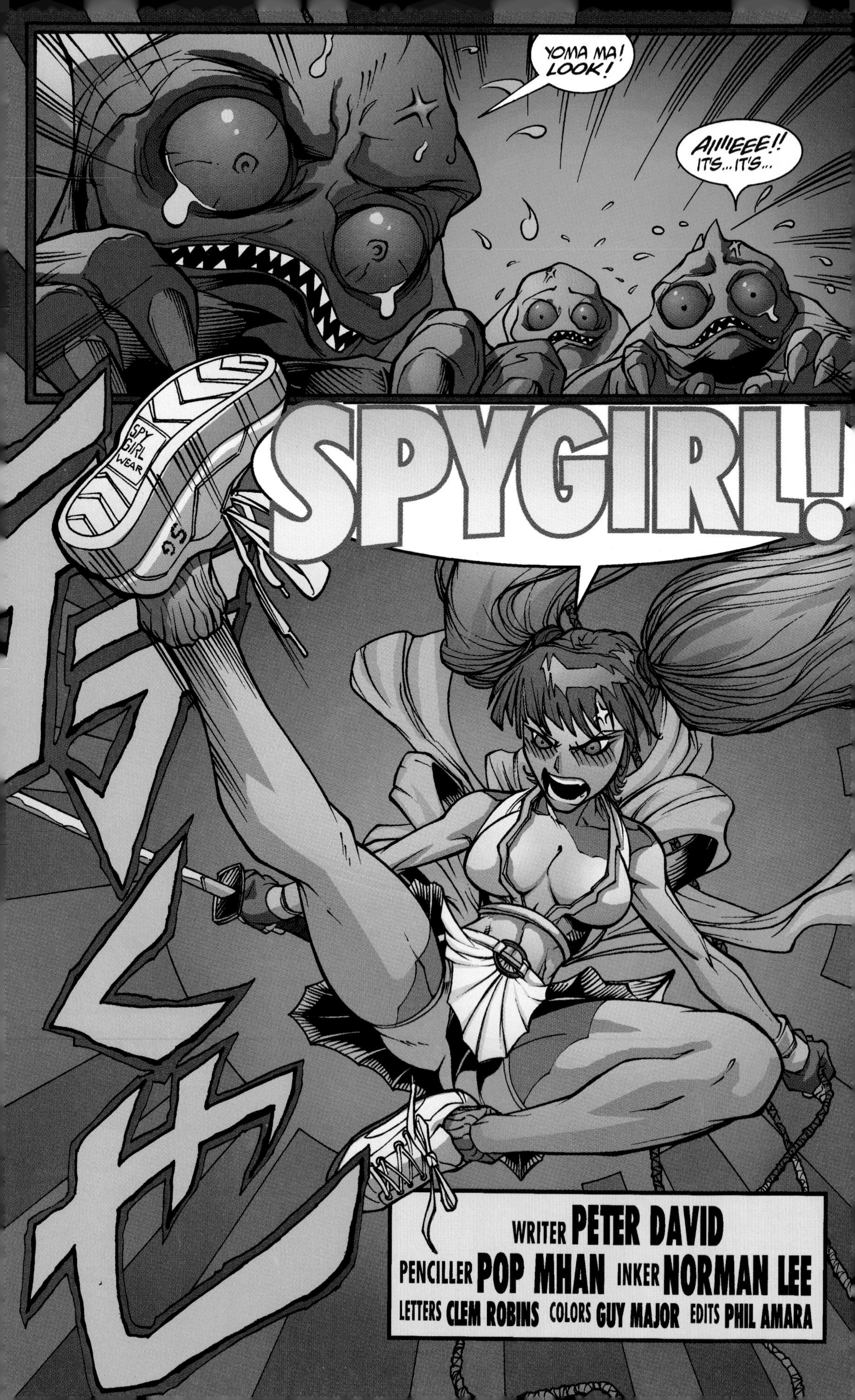
YOMA MA! LOOK!
AIIIEEE!! IT'S... IT'S...
SPYGIRL!
SPY GIRL WEAR
SG
WRITER PETER DAVID
PENCILLER POP MHAN INKER NORMAN LEE
LETTERS CLEM ROBINS COLORS GUY MAJOR EDITS PHIL AMARA

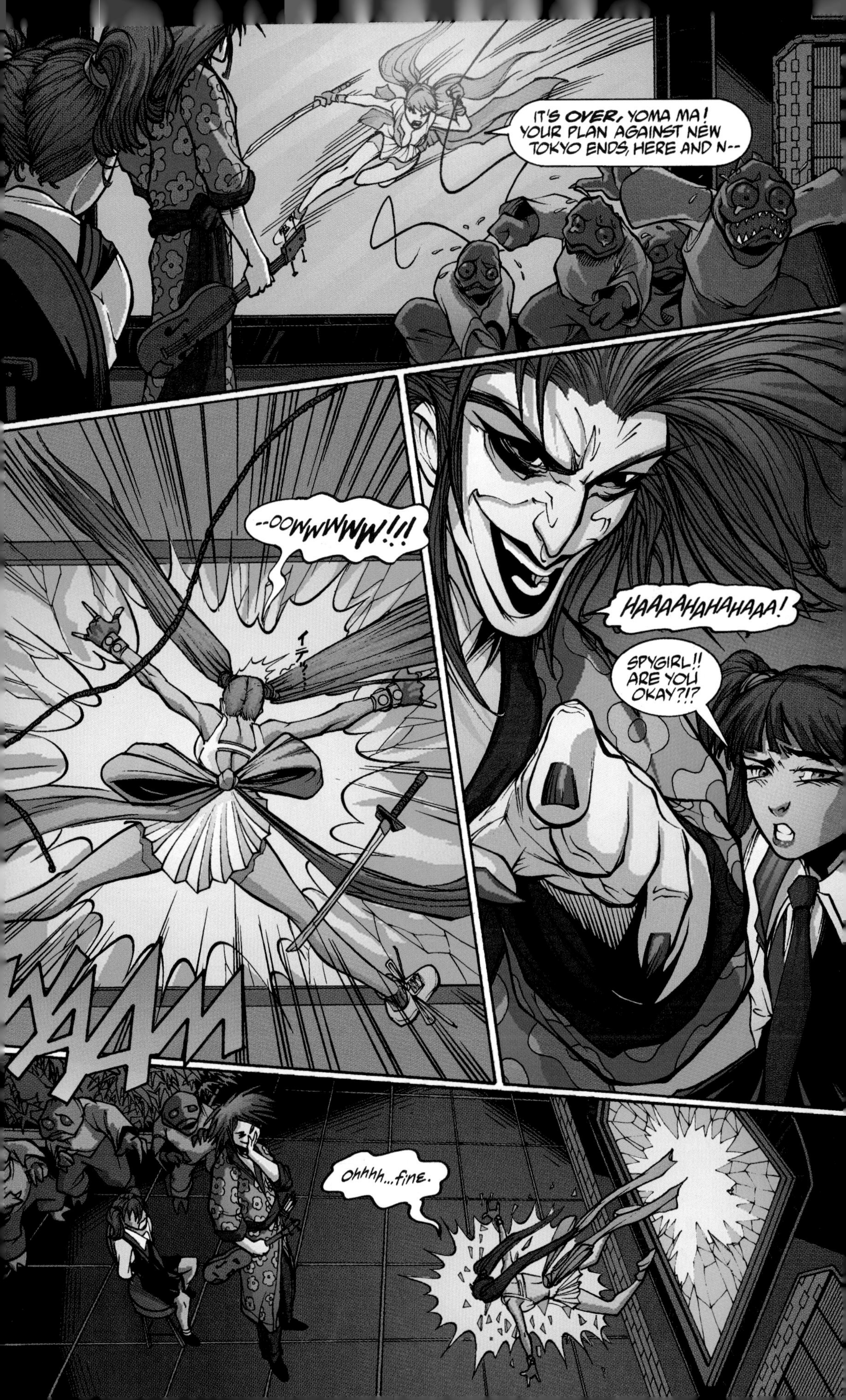
IT'S OVER, YOMA MA! YOUR PLAN AGAINST NEW TOKYO ENDS, HERE AND N--
--OOWWWWW!!!
イテッ...
WHAM
HAAAAHAHAHAAA!
SPYGIRL!! ARE YOU OKAY?!!?
Ohhhh...fine.

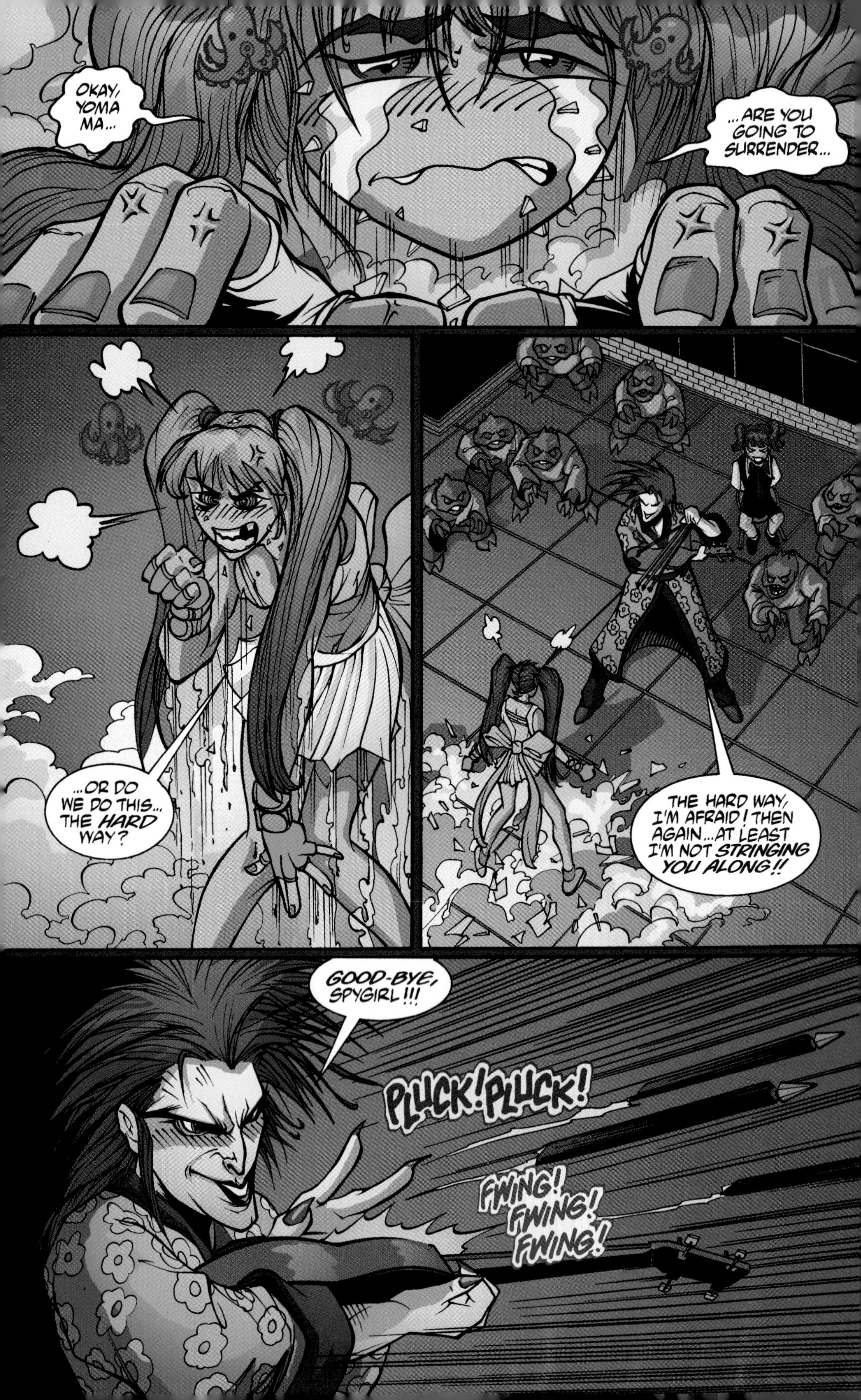
OKAY, YOMA MA...
...ARE YOU GOING TO SURRENDER...
...OR DO WE DO THIS... THE HARD WAY?
THE HARD WAY, I'M AFRAID! THEN AGAIN...AT LEAST I'M NOT STRINGING YOU ALONG!!
GOOD-BYE, SPYGIRL!!!
PLUCK! PLUCK!
FWING! FWING! FWING!

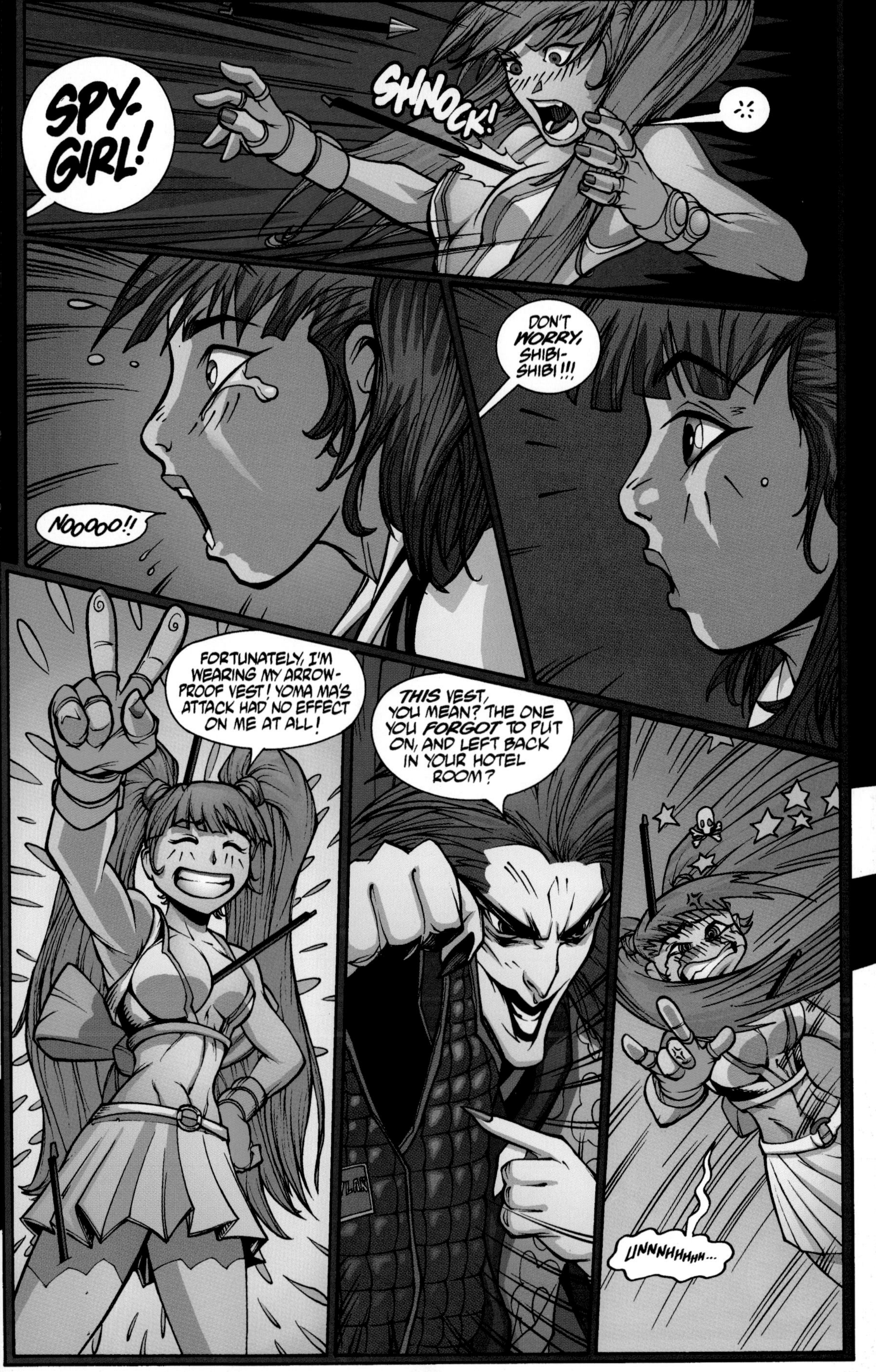
SPY-GIRL!
SHNOCK!
NOOOOO!!
DON'T WORRY, SHIBI-SHIBI!!!
FORTUNATELY, I'M WEARING MY ARROW-PROOF VEST! YOMA MA'S ATTACK HAD NO EFFECT ON ME AT ALL!
THIS VEST, YOU MEAN? THE ONE YOU FORGOT TO PUT ON, AND LEFT BACK IN YOUR HOTEL ROOM?
UNNNHHHHH...

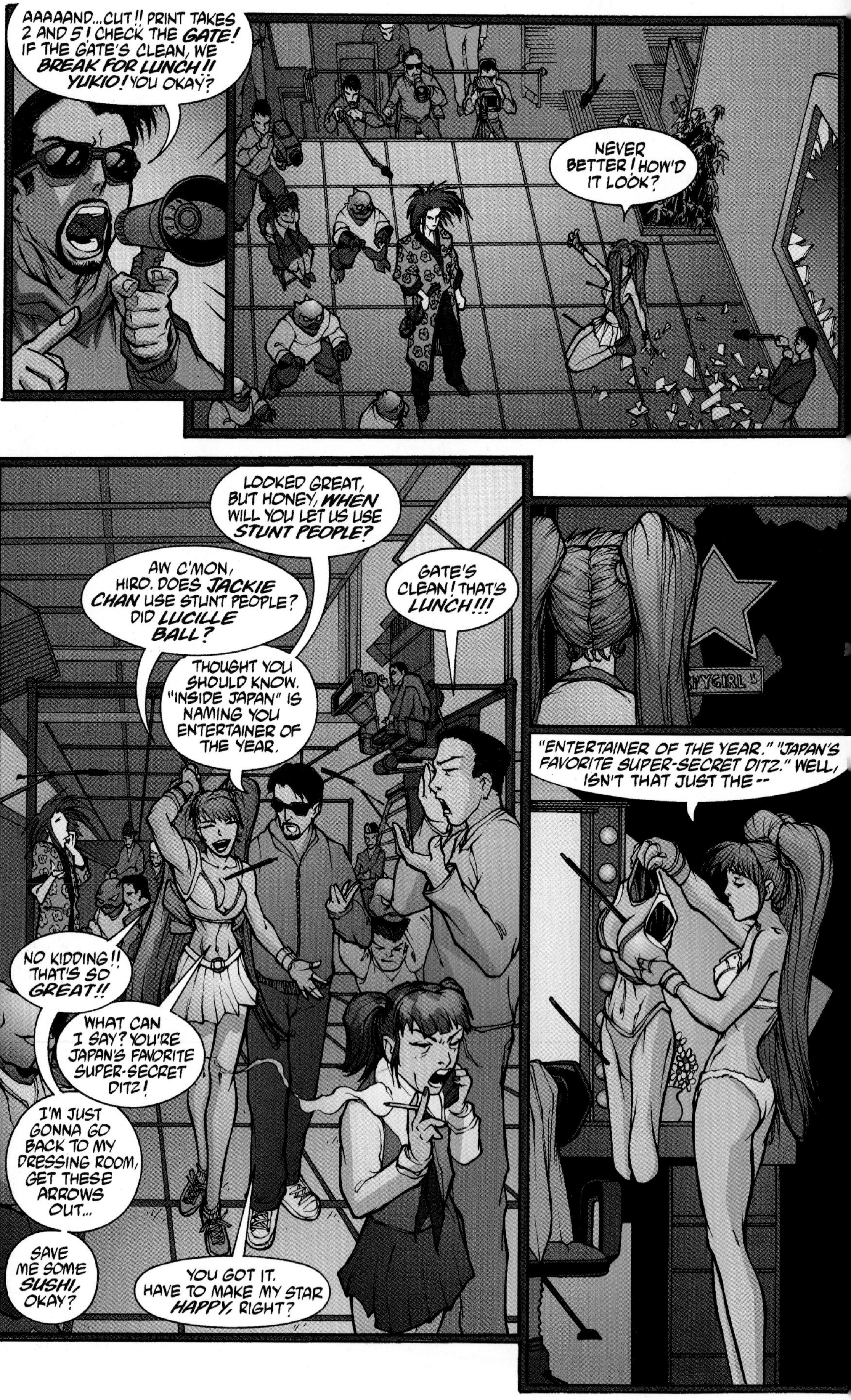
AAAAAND...CUT!! PRINT TAKES 2 AND 5! CHECK THE GATE! IF THE GATE'S CLEAN, WE BREAK FOR LUNCH!! YUKIO! YOU OKAY?
NEVER BETTER! HOW'D IT LOOK?
LOOKED GREAT, BUT HONEY, WHEN WILL YOU LET US USE STUNT PEOPLE?
AW C'MON, HIRO. DOES JACKIE CHAN USE STUNT PEOPLE? DID LUCILLE BALL?
GATE'S CLEAN! THAT'S LUNCH!!!
THOUGHT YOU SHOULD KNOW. "INSIDE JAPAN" IS NAMING YOU ENTERTAINER OF THE YEAR.
NO KIDDING!! THAT'S SO GREAT!!
WHAT CAN I SAY? YOU'RE JAPAN'S FAVORITE SUPER-SECRET DITZ!
I'M JUST GONNA GO BACK TO MY DRESSING ROOM, GET THESE ARROWS OUT...
SAVE ME SOME SUSHI, OKAY?
YOU GOT IT. HAVE TO MAKE MY STAR HAPPY, RIGHT?
"ENTERTAINER OF THE YEAR." "JAPAN'S FAVORITE SUPER-SECRET DITZ." WELL, ISN'T THAT JUST THE --

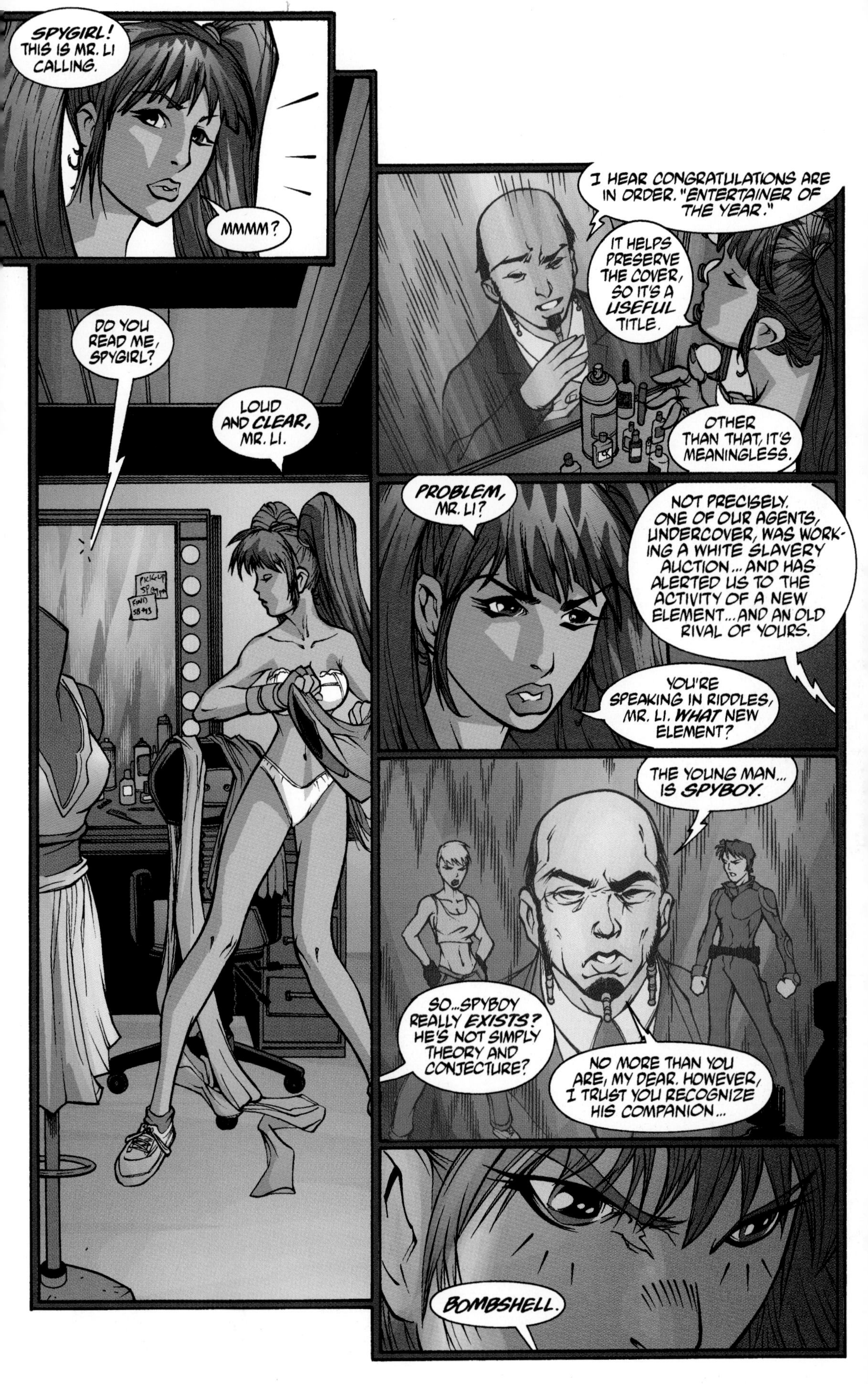

SPYGIRL! THIS IS MR. LI CALLING.
MMMM?
DO YOU READ ME, SPYGIRL?
LOUD AND CLEAR, MR. LI.
I HEAR CONGRATULATIONS ARE IN ORDER. "ENTERTAINER OF THE YEAR."
IT HELPS PRESERVE THE COVER, SO IT'S A USEFUL TITLE.
OTHER THAN THAT, IT'S MEANINGLESS.
PROBLEM, MR. LI?
NOT PRECISELY. ONE OF OUR AGENTS, UNDERCOVER, WAS WORKING A WHITE SLAVERY AUCTION...AND HAS ALERTED US TO THE ACTIVITY OF A NEW ELEMENT...AND AN OLD RIVAL OF YOURS.
YOU'RE SPEAKING IN RIDDLES, MR. LI. WHAT NEW ELEMENT?
THE YOUNG MAN... IS SPYBOY.
SO...SPYBOY REALLY EXISTS? HE'S NOT SIMPLY THEORY AND CONJECTURE?
NO MORE THAN YOU ARE, MY DEAR. HOWEVER, I TRUST YOU RECOGNIZE HIS COMPANION...
BOMBSHELL.

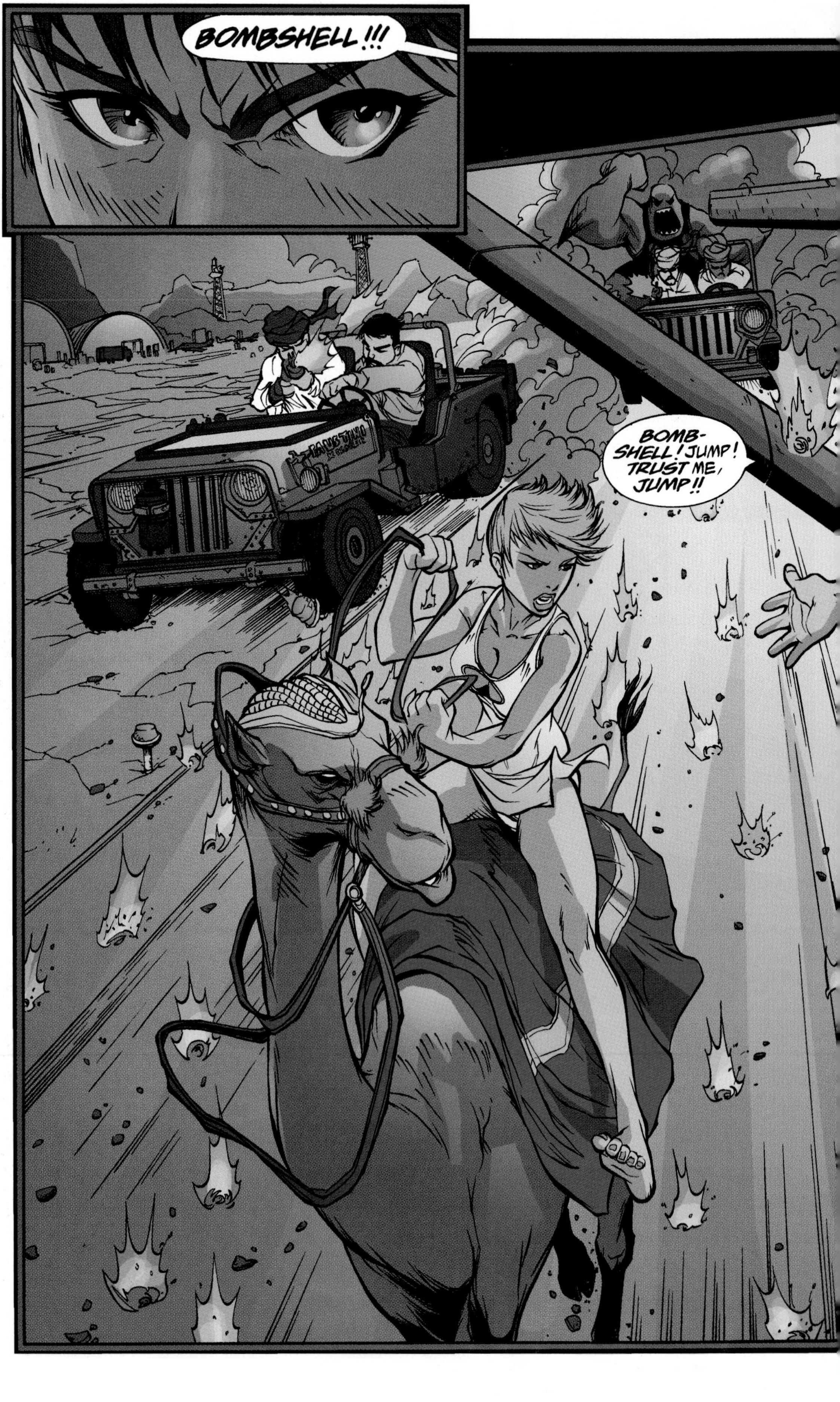
BOMBSHELL!!!
BOMB-SHELL! JUMP! TRUST ME, JUMP!!

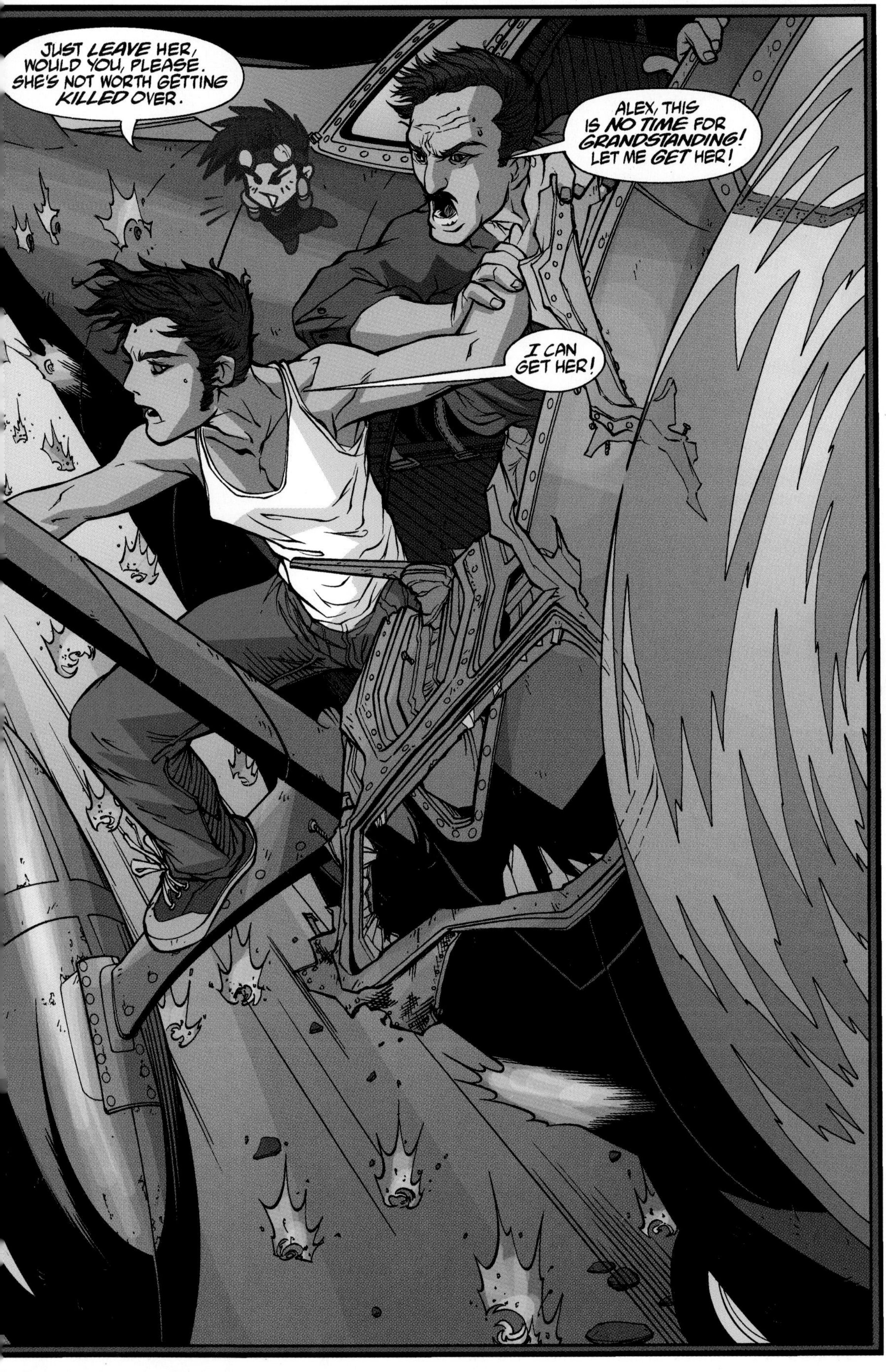
JUST LEAVE HER, WOULD YOU, PLEASE. SHE'S NOT WORTH GETTING KILLED OVER.
ALEX, THIS IS NO TIME FOR GRANDSTANDING! LET ME GET HER!
I CAN GET HER!

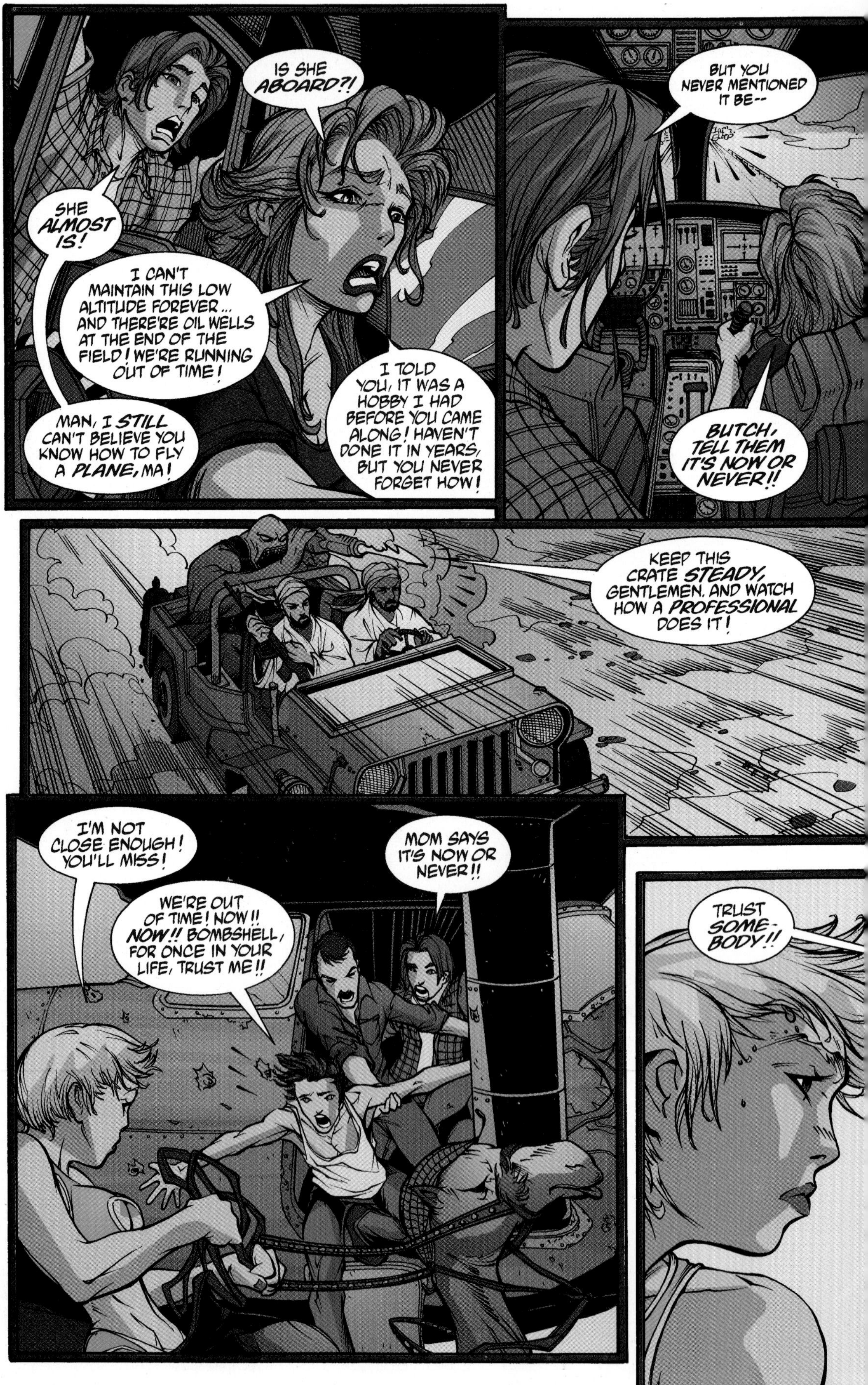
IS SHE ABOARD?!
SHE ALMOST IS!
I CAN'T MAINTAIN THIS LOW ALTITUDE FOREVER... AND THERE'RE OIL WELLS AT THE END OF THE FIELD! WE'RE RUNNING OUT OF TIME!
MAN, I STILL CAN'T BELIEVE YOU KNOW HOW TO FLY A PLANE, MA!
I TOLD YOU, IT WAS A HOBBY I HAD BEFORE YOU CAME ALONG! HAVEN'T DONE IT IN YEARS, BUT YOU NEVER FORGET HOW!
BUT YOU NEVER MENTIONED IT BE--
BUTCH, TELL THEM IT'S NOW OR NEVER!!
KEEP THIS CRATE STEADY, GENTLEMEN, AND WATCH HOW A PROFESSIONAL DOES IT!
I'M NOT CLOSE ENOUGH! YOU'LL MISS!
MOM SAYS IT'S NOW OR NEVER!!
WE'RE OUT OF TIME! NOW!! NOW!! BOMBSHELL, FOR ONCE IN YOUR LIFE, TRUST ME!!
TRUST SOME-BODY!!

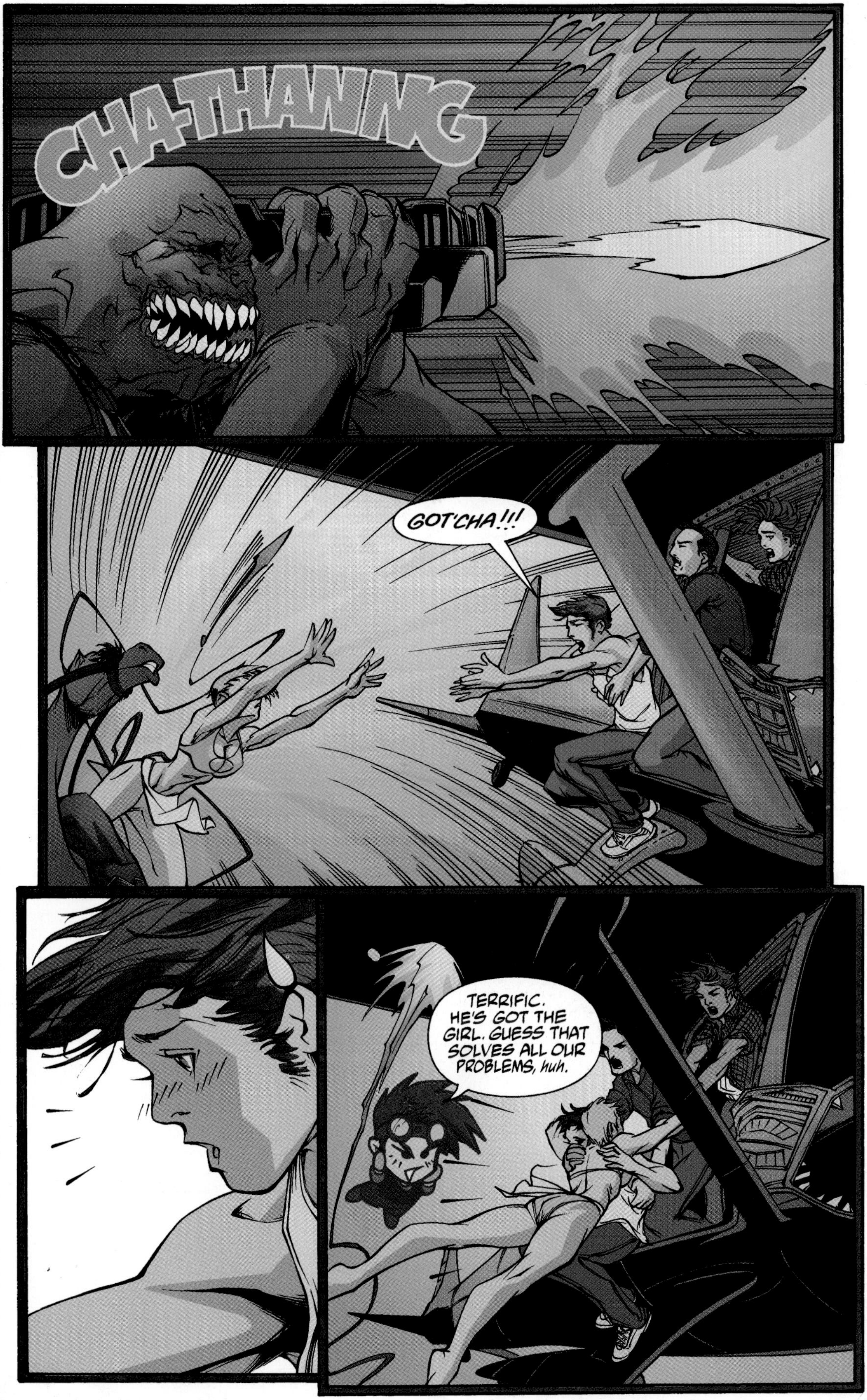
CHATHANNG
GOT'CHA!!!
TERRIFIC. HE'S GOT THE GIRL. GUESS THAT SOLVES ALL OUR PROBLEMS, huh.

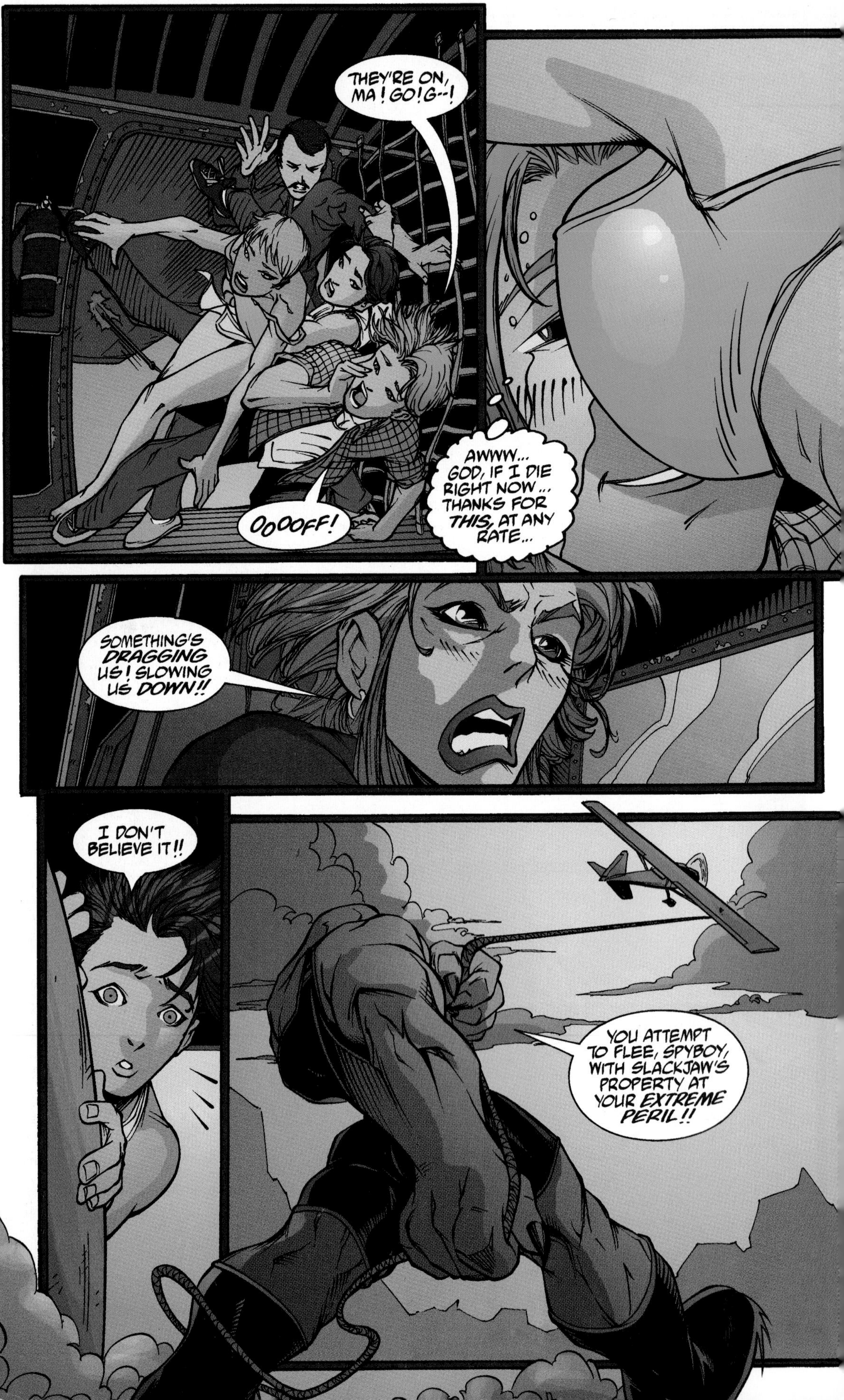
THEY'RE ON, MA! GO! G--!
OOOOFF!
AWWW... GOD, IF I DIE RIGHT NOW... THANKS FOR *THIS*, AT ANY RATE...
SOMETHING'S *DRAGGING* US! SLOWING US *DOWN*!!
I DON'T BELIEVE IT!!
YOU ATTEMPT TO FLEE, SPYBOY, WITH SLACKJAW'S PROPERTY AT YOUR *EXTREME PERIL*!!

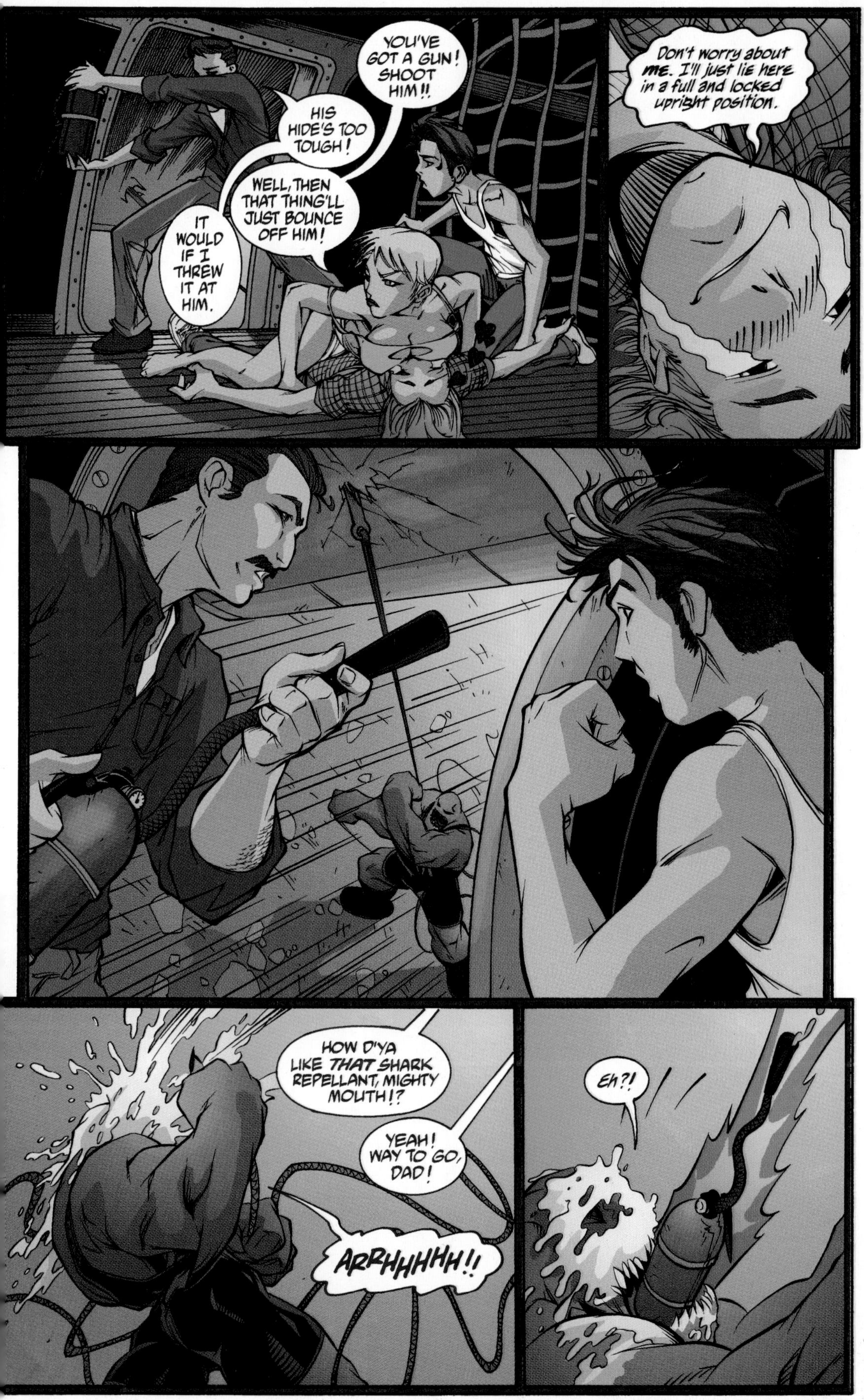
YOU'VE GOT A GUN! SHOOT HIM!!
HIS HIDE'S TOO TOUGH!
WELL, THEN THAT THING'LL JUST BOUNCE OFF HIM!
IT WOULD IF I THREW IT AT HIM.
Don't worry about me. I'll just lie here in a full and locked upright position.
HOW D'YA LIKE THAT SHARK REPELLANT, MIGHTY MOUTH!?
YEAH! WAY TO GO, DAD!
ARRHHHHH!!
Eh?!

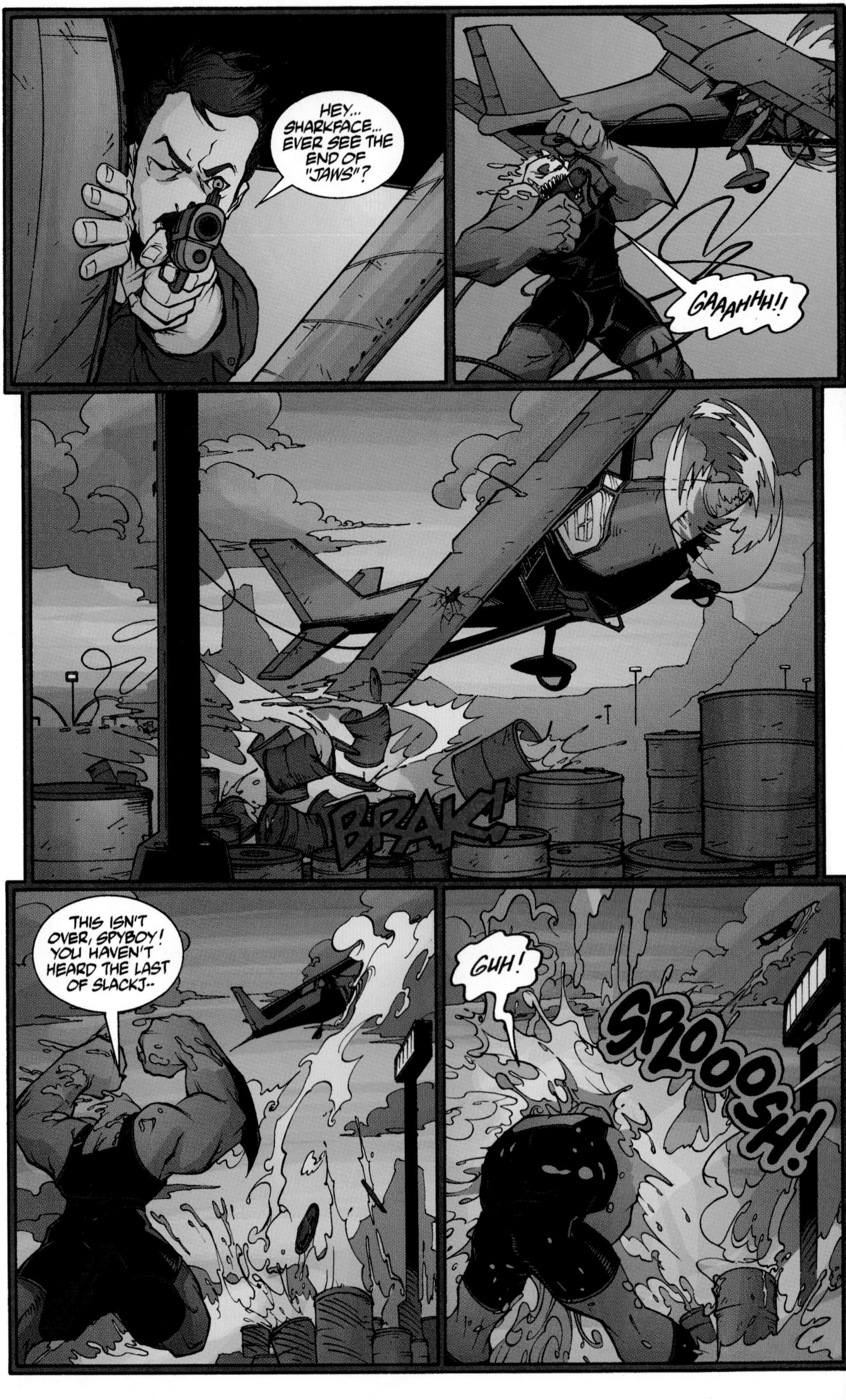
HEY... SHARKFACE... EVER SEE THE END OF "JAWS"?
GAAAHHH!!
BRAK!
THIS ISN'T OVER, SPYBOY! YOU HAVEN'T HEARD THE LAST OF SLACKJ--
GUH!
SPLOOOSH!

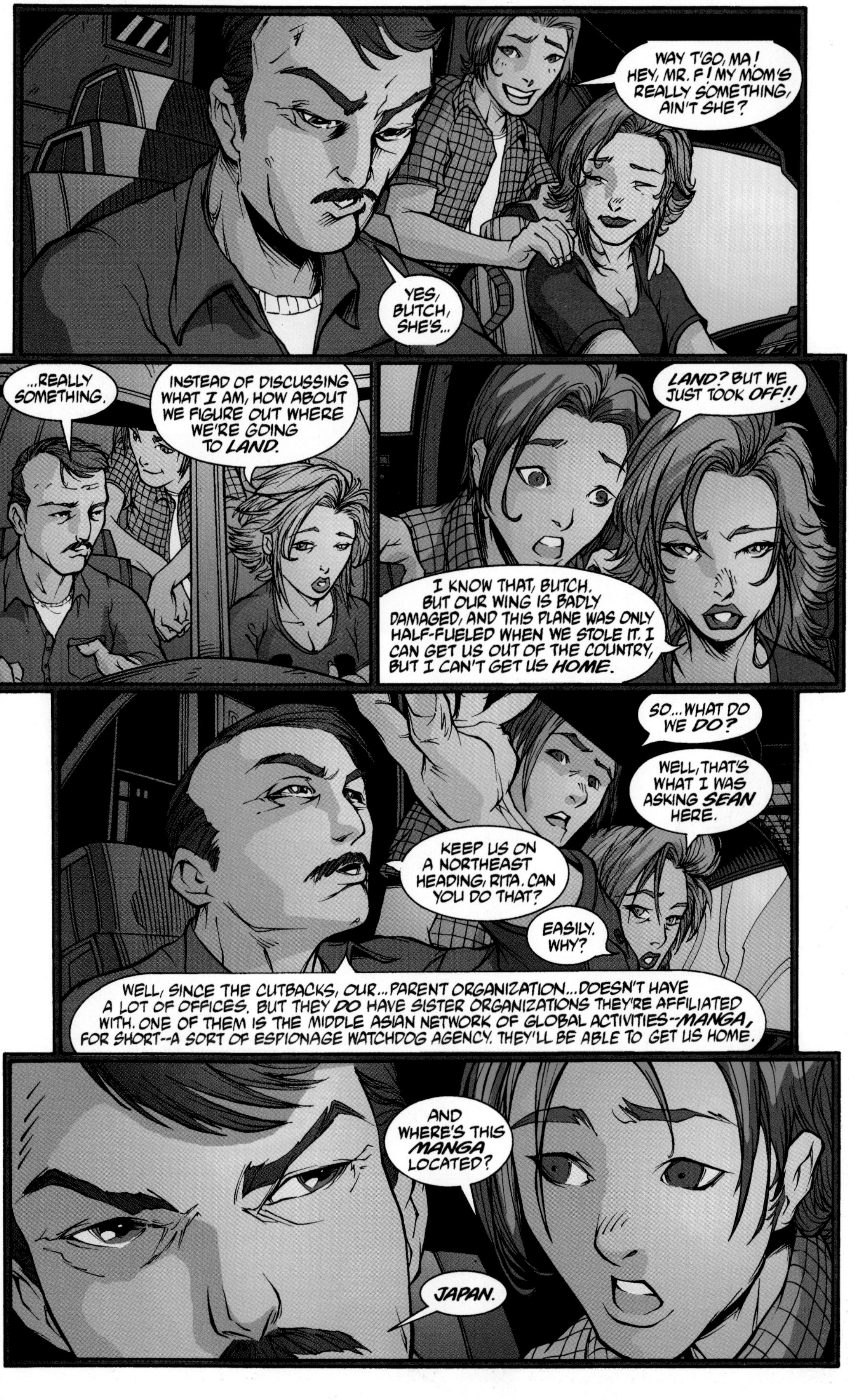
WAY T'GO, MA! HEY, MR. F! MY MOM'S REALLY SOMETHING, AIN'T SHE?
YES, BUTCH, SHE'S...
...REALLY SOMETHING.
INSTEAD OF DISCUSSING WHAT I AM, HOW ABOUT WE FIGURE OUT WHERE WE'RE GOING TO LAND.
LAND? BUT WE JUST TOOK OFF!!
I KNOW THAT, BUTCH, BUT OUR WING IS BADLY DAMAGED, AND THIS PLANE WAS ONLY HALF-FUELED WHEN WE STOLE IT. I CAN GET US OUT OF THE COUNTRY, BUT I CAN'T GET US HOME.
SO...WHAT DO WE DO?
WELL, THAT'S WHAT I WAS ASKING SEAN HERE.
KEEP US ON A NORTHEAST HEADING, RITA. CAN YOU DO THAT?
EASILY. WHY?
WELL, SINCE THE CUTBACKS, OUR...PARENT ORGANIZATION...DOESN'T HAVE A LOT OF OFFICES. BUT THEY DO HAVE SISTER ORGANIZATIONS THEY'RE AFFILIATED WITH. ONE OF THEM IS THE MIDDLE ASIAN NETWORK OF GLOBAL ACTIVITIES--MANGA, FOR SHORT--A SORT OF ESPIONAGE WATCHDOG AGENCY. THEY'LL BE ABLE TO GET US HOME.
AND WHERE'S THIS MANGA LOCATED?
JAPAN.

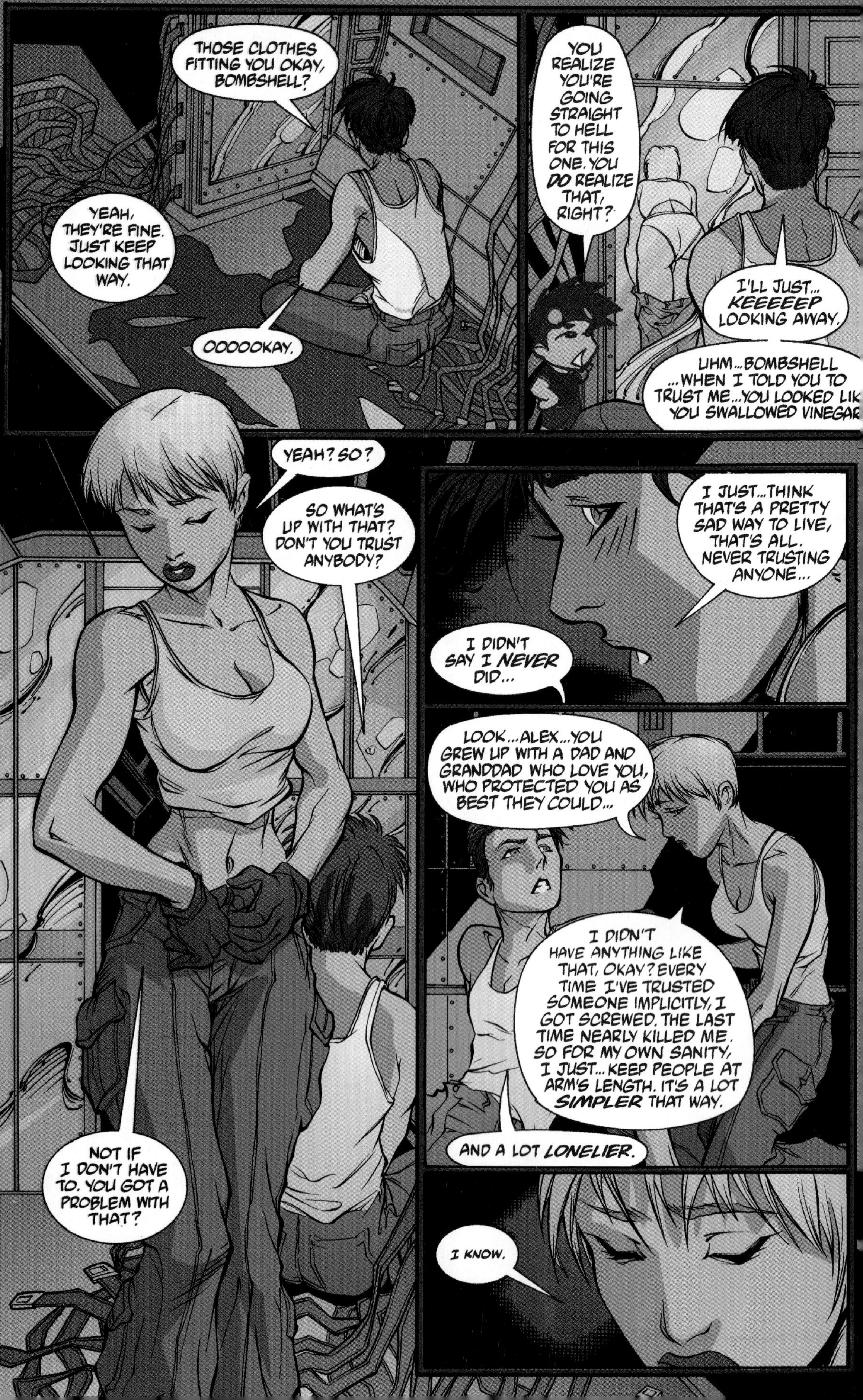
THOSE CLOTHES FITTING YOU OKAY, BOMBSHELL?
YEAH, THEY'RE FINE. JUST KEEP LOOKING THAT WAY.
OOOOOKAY.
YOU REALIZE YOU'RE GOING STRAIGHT TO HELL FOR THIS ONE. YOU DO REALIZE THAT, RIGHT?
I'LL JUST... KEEEEEP LOOKING AWAY.
UHM...BOMBSHELL ...WHEN I TOLD YOU TO TRUST ME...YOU LOOKED LIK YOU SWALLOWED VINEGAR
YEAH? SO?
SO WHAT'S UP WITH THAT? DON'T YOU TRUST ANYBODY?
NOT IF I DON'T HAVE TO. YOU GOT A PROBLEM WITH THAT?
I JUST...THINK THAT'S A PRETTY SAD WAY TO LIVE, THAT'S ALL. NEVER TRUSTING ANYONE...
I DIDN'T SAY I NEVER DID...
LOOK...ALEX...YOU GREW UP WITH A DAD AND GRANDDAD WHO LOVE YOU, WHO PROTECTED YOU AS BEST THEY COULD...
I DIDN'T HAVE ANYTHING LIKE THAT, OKAY? EVERY TIME I'VE TRUSTED SOMEONE IMPLICITLY, I GOT SCREWED. THE LAST TIME NEARLY KILLED ME. SO FOR MY OWN SANITY, I JUST... KEEP PEOPLE AT ARM'S LENGTH. IT'S A LOT SIMPLER THAT WAY.
AND A LOT LONELIER.
I KNOW.

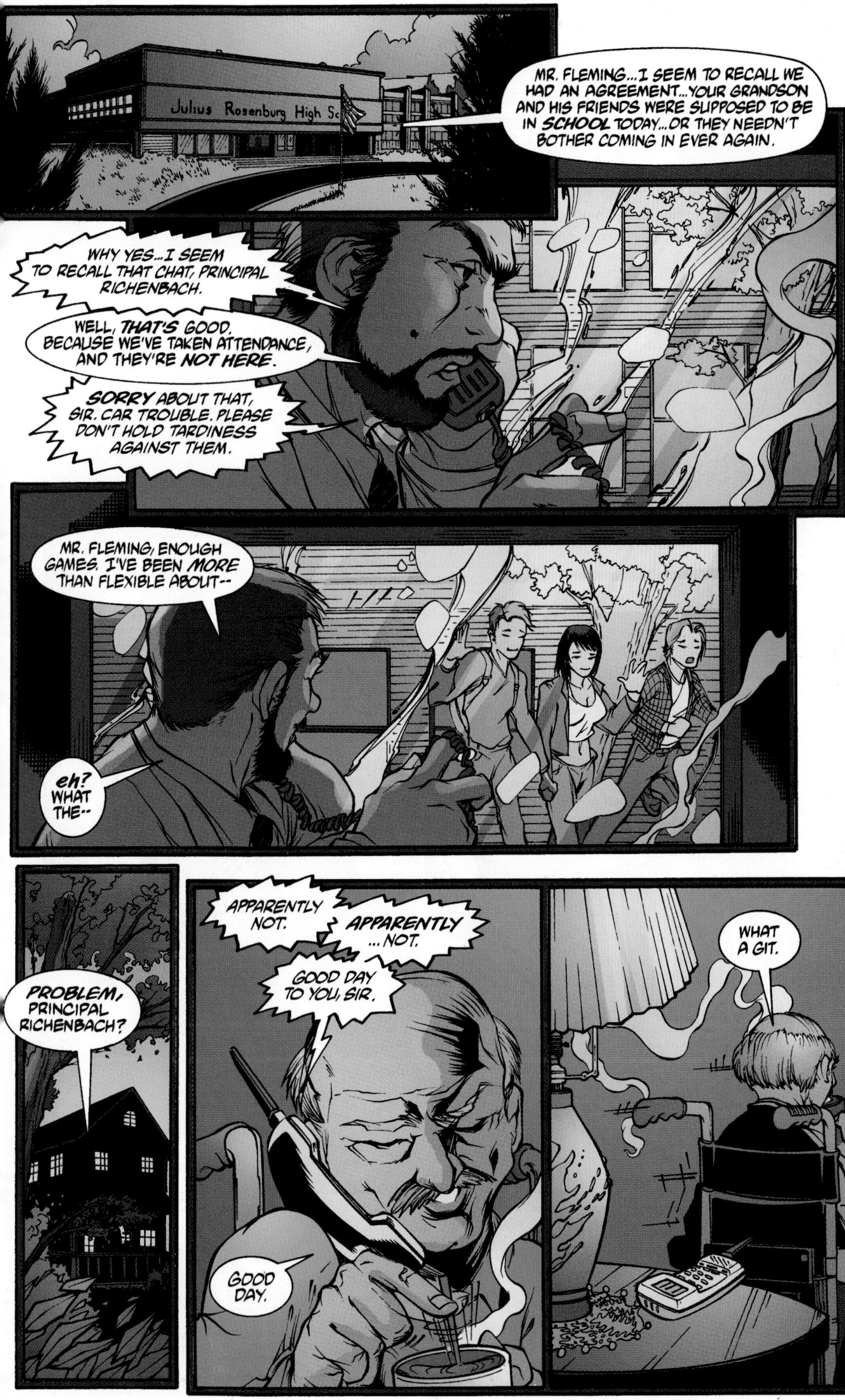
Julius Rosenburg High Sc
MR. FLEMING...I SEEM TO RECALL WE HAD AN AGREEMENT...YOUR GRANDSON AND HIS FRIENDS WERE SUPPOSED TO BE IN SCHOOL TODAY...OR THEY NEEDN'T BOTHER COMING IN EVER AGAIN.
WHY YES...I SEEM TO RECALL THAT CHAT, PRINCIPAL RICHENBACH.
WELL, THAT'S GOOD. BECAUSE WE'VE TAKEN ATTENDANCE, AND THEY'RE NOT HERE.
SORRY ABOUT THAT, SIR. CAR TROUBLE. PLEASE DON'T HOLD TARDINESS AGAINST THEM.
MR. FLEMING, ENOUGH GAMES. I'VE BEEN MORE THAN FLEXIBLE ABOUT--
eh? WHAT THE--
PROBLEM, PRINCIPAL RICHENBACH?
APPARENTLY NOT.
APPARENTLY ...NOT.
GOOD DAY TO YOU, SIR.
GOOD DAY.
WHAT A GIT.

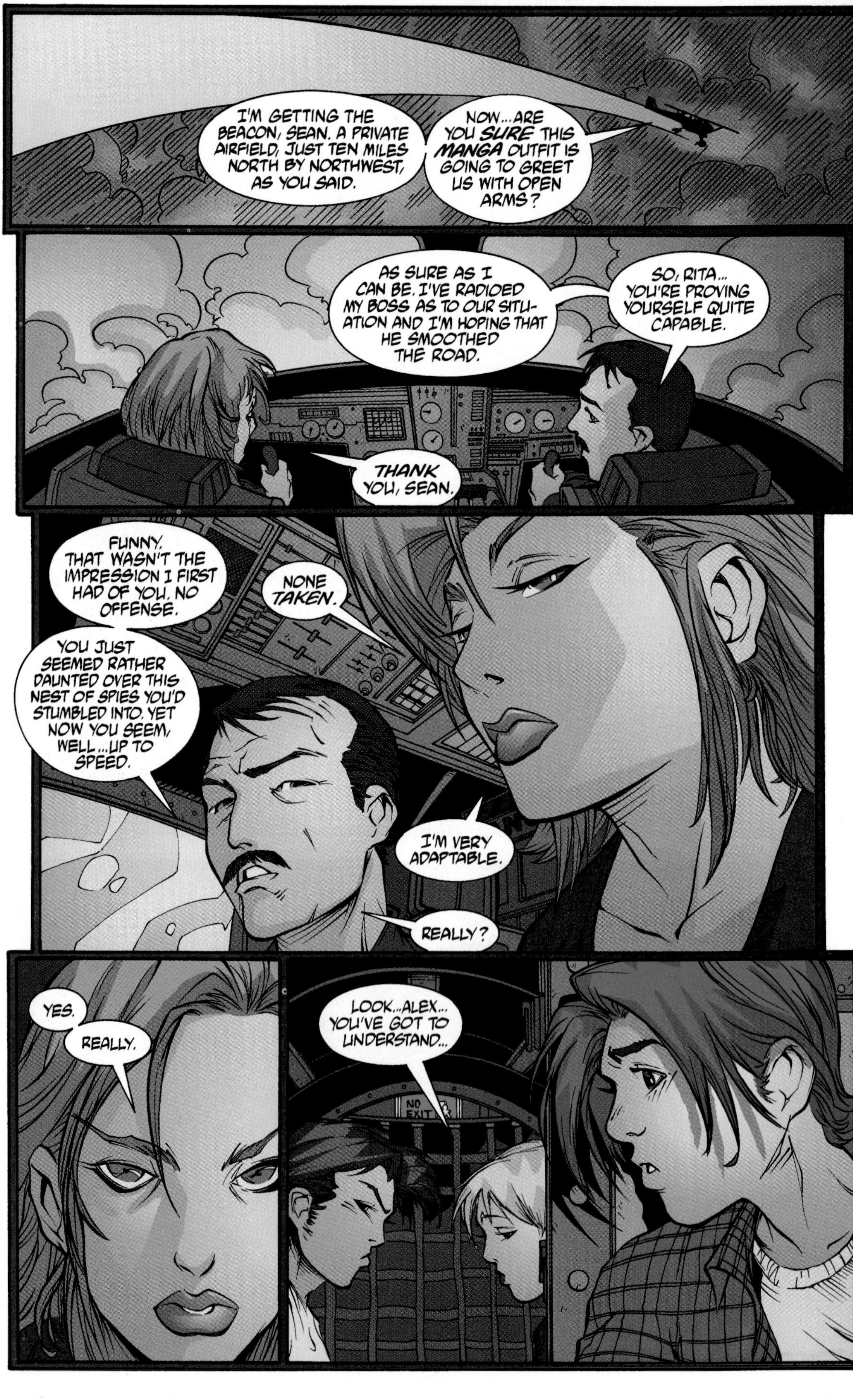
I'M GETTING THE BEACON, SEAN. A PRIVATE AIRFIELD, JUST TEN MILES NORTH BY NORTHWEST, AS YOU SAID.
NOW...ARE YOU SURE THIS MANGA OUTFIT IS GOING TO GREET US WITH OPEN ARMS?
AS SURE AS I CAN BE. I'VE RADIOED MY BOSS AS TO OUR SITU-ATION AND I'M HOPING THAT HE SMOOTHED THE ROAD.
SO, RITA... YOU'RE PROVING YOURSELF QUITE CAPABLE.
THANK YOU, SEAN.
FUNNY. THAT WASN'T THE IMPRESSION I FIRST HAD OF YOU. NO OFFENSE.
NONE TAKEN.
YOU JUST SEEMED RATHER DAUNTED OVER THIS NEST OF SPIES YOU'D STUMBLED INTO. YET NOW YOU SEEM, WELL...UP TO SPEED.
I'M VERY ADAPTABLE.
REALLY?
YES.
REALLY.
LOOK...ALEX... YOU'VE GOT TO UNDERSTAND...
NO EXIT

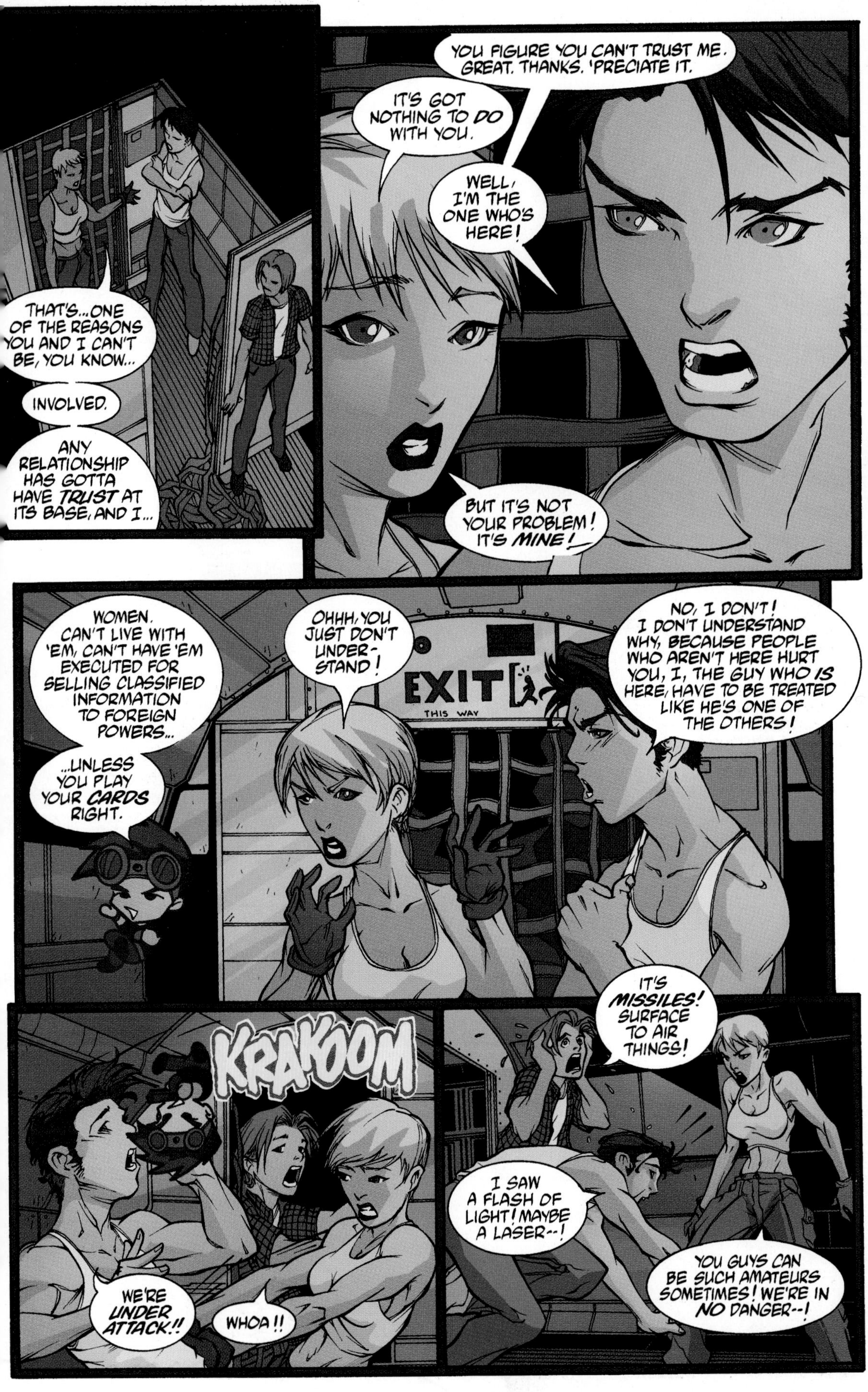

THAT'S...ONE OF THE REASONS YOU AND I CAN'T BE, YOU KNOW...
INVOLVED.
ANY RELATIONSHIP HAS GOTTA HAVE TRUST AT ITS BASE, AND I...
YOU FIGURE YOU CAN'T TRUST ME. GREAT. THANKS. 'PRECIATE IT.
IT'S GOT NOTHING TO DO WITH YOU.
WELL, I'M THE ONE WHO'S HERE!
BUT IT'S NOT YOUR PROBLEM! IT'S MINE!
WOMEN. CAN'T LIVE WITH 'EM, CAN'T HAVE 'EM EXECUTED FOR SELLING CLASSIFIED INFORMATION TO FOREIGN POWERS...
...UNLESS YOU PLAY YOUR CARDS RIGHT.
OHHH, YOU JUST DON'T UNDER-STAND!
EXIT
THIS WAY
NO, I DON'T! I DON'T UNDERSTAND WHY, BECAUSE PEOPLE WHO AREN'T HERE HURT YOU, I, THE GUY WHO IS HERE, HAVE TO BE TREATED LIKE HE'S ONE OF THE OTHERS!
KRAKOOM
WE'RE UNDER ATTACK!!
WHOA!!
IT'S MISSILES! SURFACE TO AIR THINGS!
I SAW A FLASH OF LIGHT! MAYBE A LASER--!
YOU GUYS CAN BE SUCH AMATEURS SOMETIMES! WE'RE IN NO DANGER--!

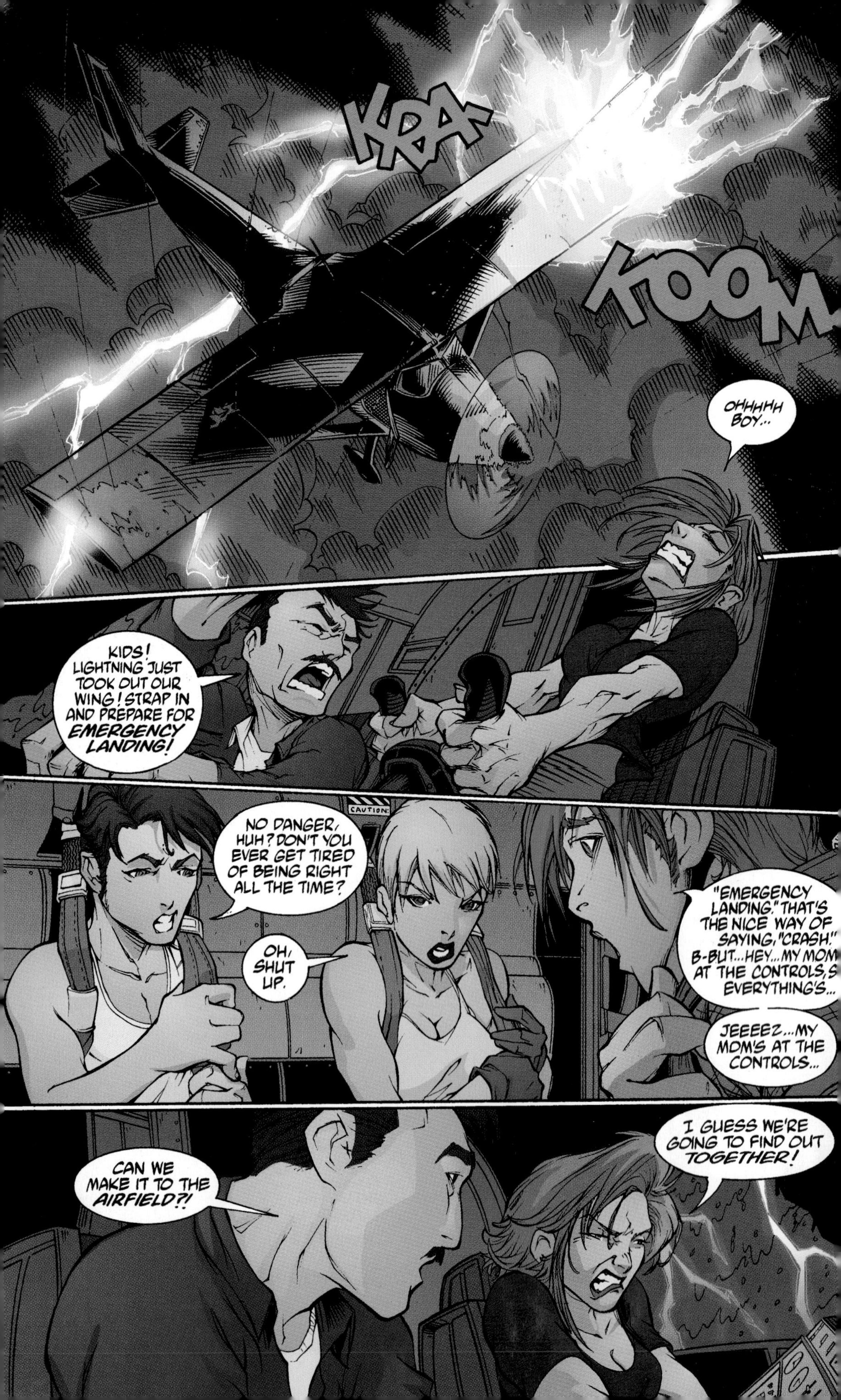
KRA-
KOOM
OHHHHH BOY...
KIDS! LIGHTNING JUST TOOK OUT OUR WING! STRAP IN AND PREPARE FOR EMERGENCY LANDING!
CAUTION
NO DANGER, HUH? DON'T YOU EVER GET TIRED OF BEING RIGHT ALL THE TIME?
OH, SHUT UP.
"EMERGENCY LANDING." THAT'S THE NICE WAY OF SAYING, "CRASH." B-BUT...HEY...MY MOM AT THE CONTROLS, S EVERYTHING'S...
JEEEEZ...MY MOM'S AT THE CONTROLS...
CAN WE MAKE IT TO THE AIRFIELD?!
I GUESS WE'RE GOING TO FIND OUT TOGETHER!

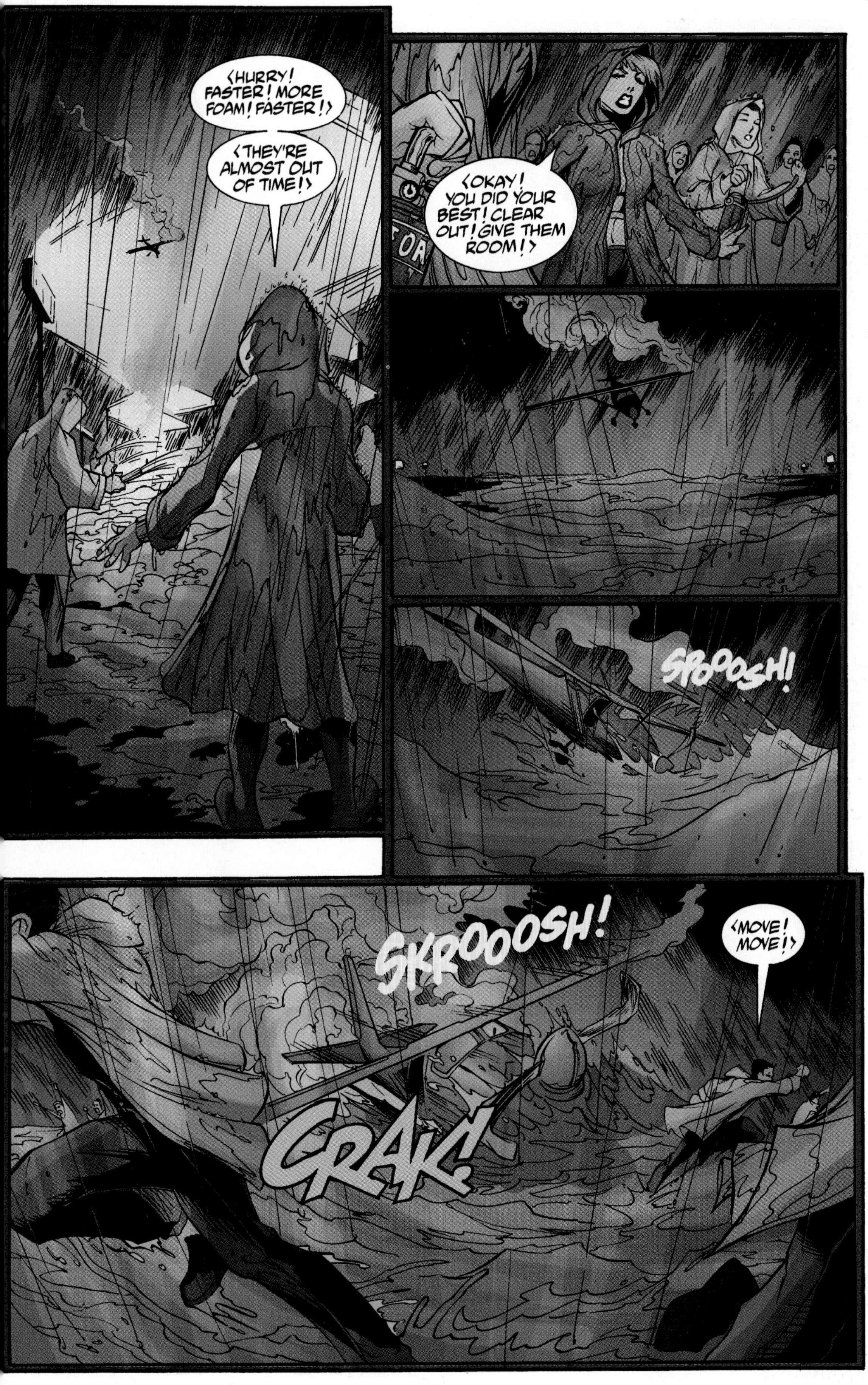

‹HURRY! FASTER! MORE FOAM! FASTER!›
‹THEY'RE ALMOST OUT OF TIME!›
‹OKAY! YOU DID YOUR BEST! CLEAR OUT! GIVE THEM ROOM!›
SPOOOSH!
SKROOOSH!
‹MOVE! MOVE!›
CRAK!

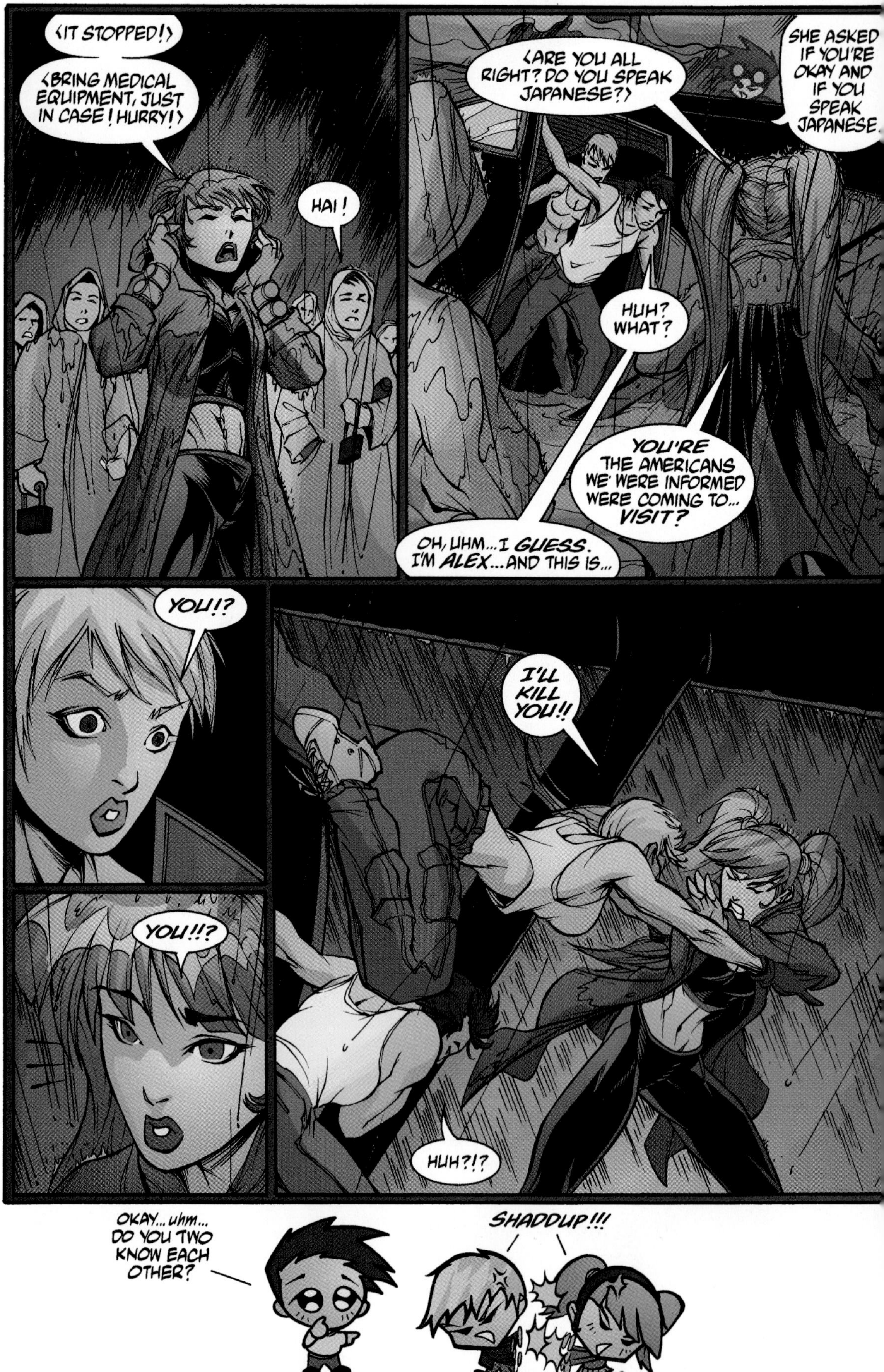
<IT STOPPED!>
<BRING MEDICAL EQUIPMENT, JUST IN CASE! HURRY!>
HAI!
<ARE YOU ALL RIGHT? DO YOU SPEAK JAPANESE?>
SHE ASKED IF YOU'RE OKAY AND IF YOU SPEAK JAPANESE.
HUH? WHAT?
YOU'RE THE AMERICANS WE WERE INFORMED WERE COMING TO... VISIT?
OH, UHM... I GUESS. I'M ALEX... AND THIS IS...
YOU!?
YOU!!?
I'LL KILL YOU!!
HUH?!?
OKAY... uhm... DO YOU TWO KNOW EACH OTHER?
SHADDUP!!!

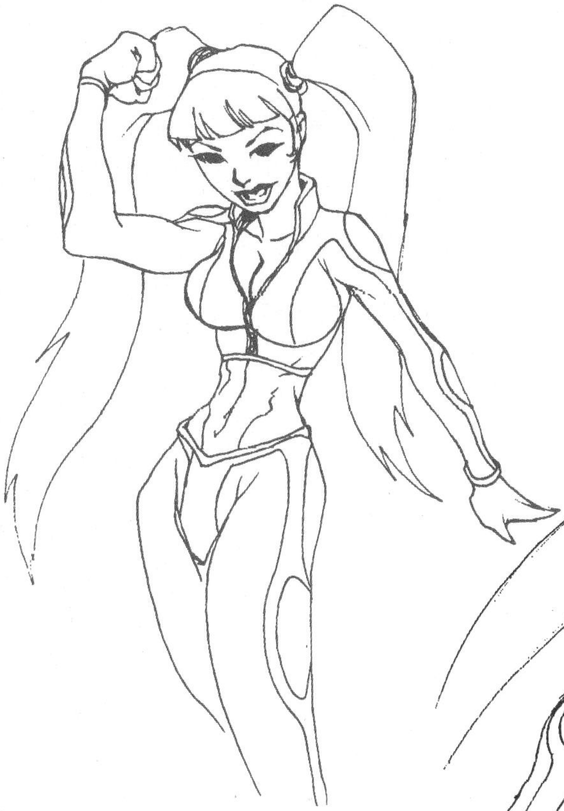

Sketch Gallery!

This page and following: Rare Pop Mhan sketches, including prototype designs for SpyGirl!

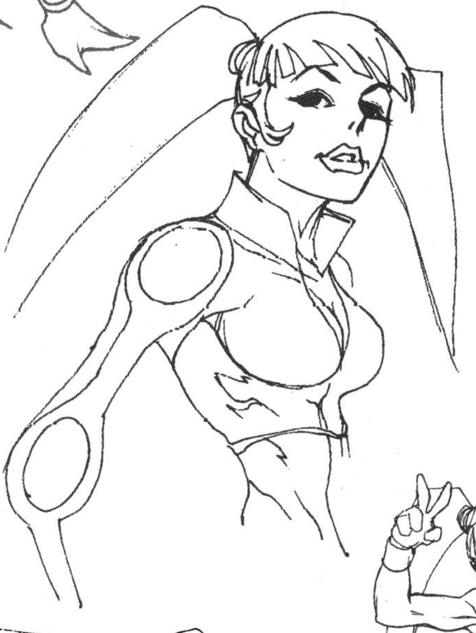

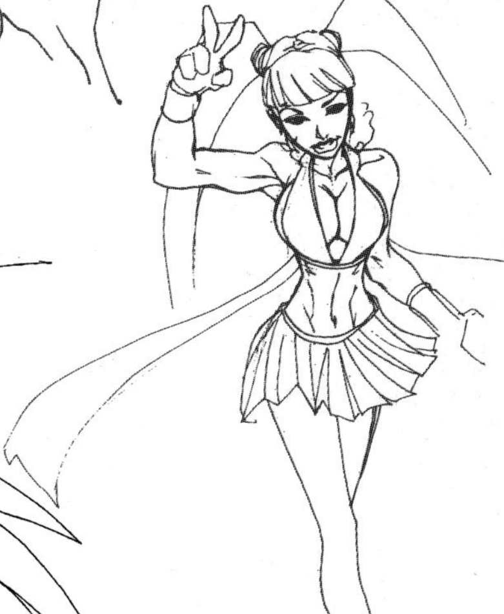

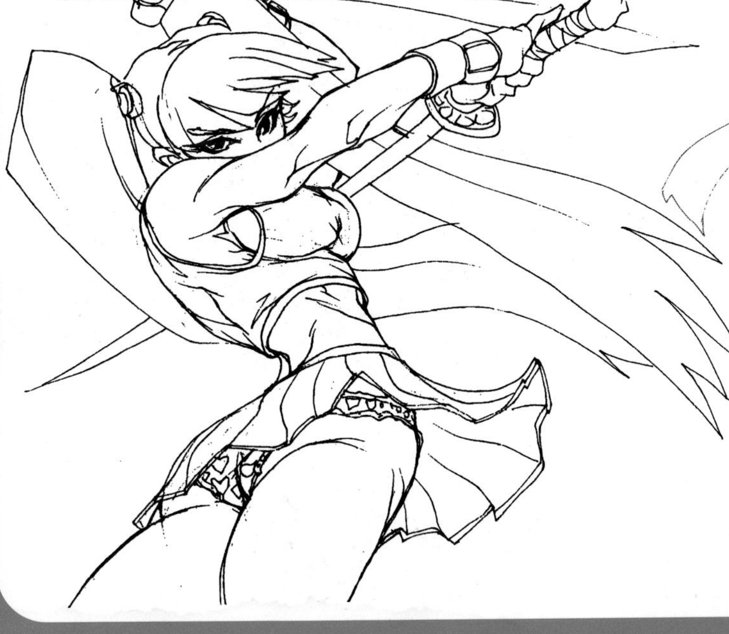

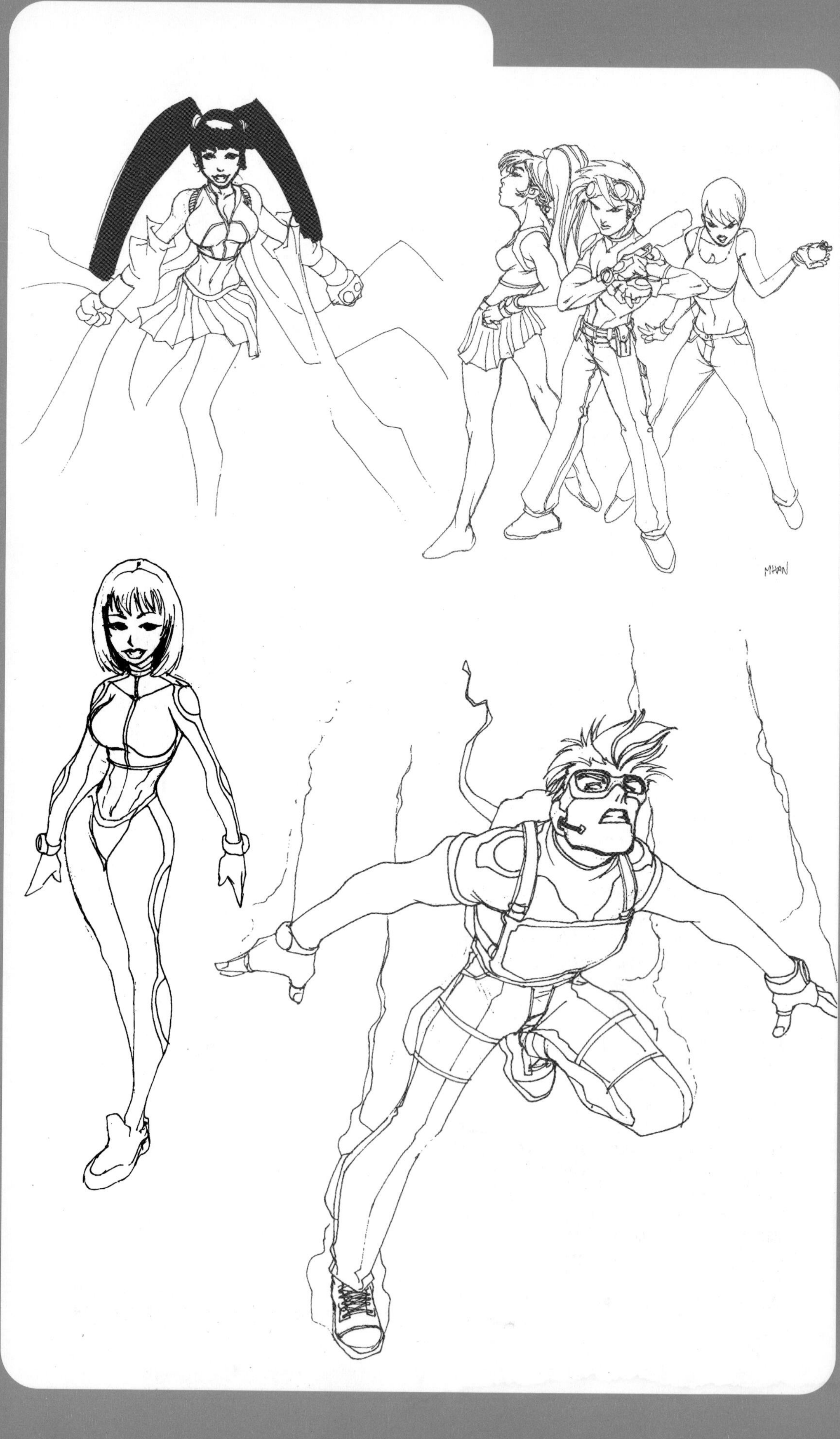
MHAN

When does **Peter David** find time to sleep? Lined up page to page, the comics he's written, including legendary stints on *The Incredible Hulk*, *Spider-Man*, *Aquaman*, *Wolverine*, and *Star Trek*, would circle the globe. Stacked one atop another, the novels he's written, including a series of best-selling *Star Trek* titles, would crash into the moon. His screenplays could block a superhighway, his teleplays could crush an M1A1 tank, and the total of his weekly *Comics Buyers' Guide* column, "But I Digress," could wallpaper the Pentagon to the depth of one meter and still line garbage cans from Miami to Missoula. He's won more awards than you can shake a stick at, including a Haxtur, which by itself is heavy enough to anchor a Carnival Cruise liner in rough seas.

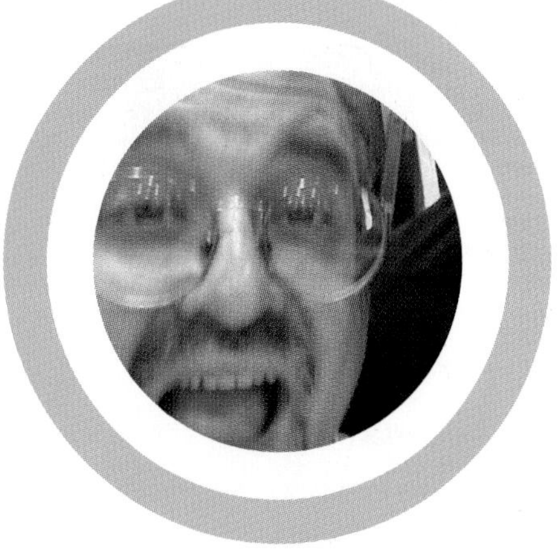

With a given mystery surname even he can't pronounce, penciller **Pop Mhan** has been drawing the admiration of fans and the heck out of comics since first breaking into the biz in 1994. Noted for their wild, fluid action and eye-straining detail, Pop's manga-influenced pencils have kicked out the jams on titles such as *Union*, *Stormwatch*, *GhostRider*, *Generation X*, *The Flash*, *Impulse*, *Magic: The Gathering*, and *Oni* #0. Pop is an unrepentant techno-gearhead, with email and everything. Try *www.popmhan.com*, if you've got the guts.

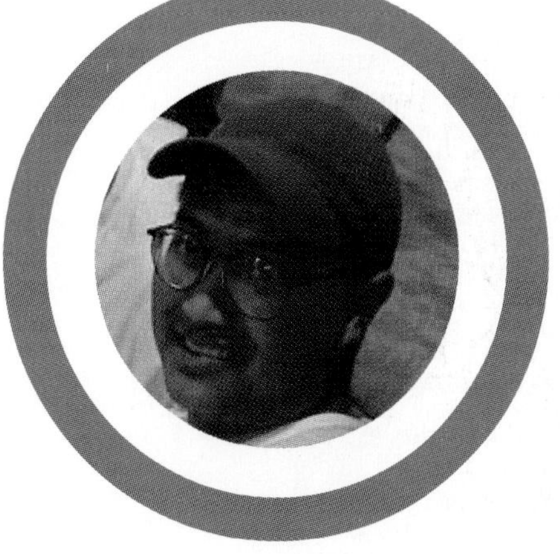

Norman Lee can kick your butt. Don't make him kick your butt. I know, I know, the guy has a degree in fashion illustration, but that won't stop him from kicking your butt. Norman has left a long list of terrific ink jobs and terrified editors in his mighty wake, including gigs on *Wolverine*, *Cable*, *X-Force*, *Starman*, *Rise of Apocalypse*, *Deadpool*, and *Oni*, not to mention *Magic: The Gathering* and *Oni* #0 with old friend and punching bag Pop Mhan. Norman is also a personal trainer who will personally train you not to crack too wise about that fashion illustration thing.

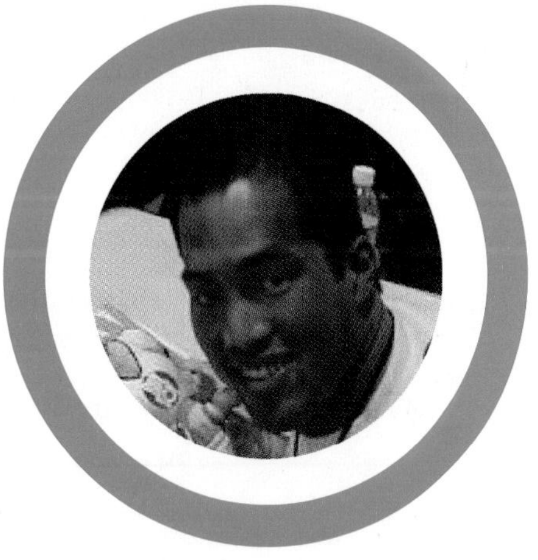

Sunny Lee (not pictured) is a relative newcomer to comics. He's worked for DC, and helps out with the art chores on *SpyBoy* from time to time. He's perhaps best known for his amazing work on the *Oni* comic series, based on the incredible Rock Star video game, and written by cookbook author/Amish pro wrestler, Dave Land. When not drawing comics, Sunny spends his time racing his dragster, and tending to his line of homemade sodas, Sunny-Pop!, which he and friend Pop Mhan started as a Home Ec. project in high school.

Photos: Phil Amara

SpyBoy will return!

OTHER GREAT TITLES FROM DARK HORSE COMICS!